THE CHARM FROM DELHI

Jack Eadon

ELOQUENCE PRESS
Tustin, California

This is a work of fiction Any similarity between
the characters appearing herein and any real persons,
living or dead, is purely coincidental.

FIRST EDITION

Published by Eloquence Press
2092 Burnt Mill Road
Tustin, CA 92782

Manufactured in the United States of America
ISBN: 0-975-33002-0

NOTE TO READER

In this book, reference is made to the infamous explosion at Sterling Hall on the Madison, Wisconsin campus of the University of Wisconsin in 1970. It was a violent crime committed by a gang of student antiwar protesters and parallels the Oklahoma City bombing decades later. One person, who happened to be in the building, died at the hands of the perpetrators and a number of buildings were damaged by the enormity of the blast.

Besides my use of the name Sterling Hall, the target of the blast, the representation of such an event, including the participation of my character Jeremy Lucas, is a fictitious rendering.

Throughout the book, references to Sterling Hall, the perpetrators of the 1970 blast, the University of Wisconsin(except for some locations on the Madison campus), and circumstances surrounding the Sterling Hall event are fictitious and are not intended to be an explicit or implicit representation of actual facts. Details are not meant to represent speculative renderings of that event—they are used for dramatic purposes only. Fictitious names of the perpetrators of the Sterling Hall explosion used herein are not meant to explicitly or implicitly represent the names of actual participants.

Acknowledgments

I want to thank Eloquence for their wonderful work on this, my fifth, book. The editing, handled initially by Esther Kelly, Lolette Kuby, and Tony Marco, was impeccable. Tony's challenge to "go over the top on this one" was sage advice which I hope I followed. I want to thank Bill Campbell, my lawyer/writer friend, for his indispensable counsel regarding the legal scenes. Bill helped CHARM ring with authenticity!

I also want to thank Raja, Jan H., Jan D., Nancy, and Penny for their endless stream of inspiration and "cheerleading" throughout the process. I appreciate Jan D.'s specific input regarding U of W and events surrounding the 1970 Sterling Hall blast so I could successfully incorporate a fictionalized version of the events, featuring my Jeremy character.

I want to thank particularly Tony Marco, my final editor, who always believed in CHARM—"this is the one," he said. I likewise thank Tony Wainwright, my mentor, friend, and also a writer, who said about CHARM: "What a rollercoaster!" and "Can you say movie?" With support like that from my Tonies I am thrilled to see the book, started years ago, at last become a reality. Finally, I thank Rita Markovics for her diligent proofing and editing of this second edition. Without her, CHARM wouldn't have turned out as clean! Finally, I dedicate THE CHARM FROM DELHI to the memory of my late father, John Ramsay Eadon. May his travels through the universe be peaceful.

Jack Eadon

THE CHARM FROM DELHI

"Man must create his own essence. It is throwing himself into the world, suffering there, struggling there that he gradually defines himself."

—Jean Paul Sartre

"Between stimulus and response, there is a space. In that space lies our freedom and power to choose our response. In our response lies our growth and freedom."

— Victor Frankl

Mortals cannot be delivered from the misfortunes of their fate.

—SOPHOCLES, *ANTIGONE*—
A New Translation by **D.W. Myatt**

Prologue *Delhi, India A. D. 1220*

Senji entered Delhi, wondering if his toil over the last three years would finally be worth it. His pack of coarsely spun cloth, tied together with several knots, dug into his lean, sunburnt shoulder. Unlike Senji's cool and breezy home near the mountains, miles to the North in Kashmir, Delhi was hot and dry because of its proximity to the great *Thar* desert. The sharp stones on the city's streets dug into Senji's feet, and dust hung in the air, for the rains of summer had not yet visited the city. Senji imagined wading in the Yamuna River as it flowed from the great Ganges, a holy place to bathe.

A moment later, Senji gasped. The *Qutub Minar* rose before him, as tall as twenty-five homes. *Surely it must touch the gods*, he thought.

Senji squinted up at the minaret, tall and thin and bright white in the sun. The tower was banded from top to bottom by rows of intricate Muslim inscriptions in the *Kufi* characters, interrupted four times by protruding balconies the size of a man or more. Sweat dripped into Senji's eyes as he studied the tower's height. He asked a nearby Buddhist monk just how tall it was. "Inside this fortress," the monk said, "four hundred steps lead to the top." As Senji approached the tower, he saw that Hindu inscriptions were mixed with Muslim, a small token permitted by the invaders who had built the structure.

Senji walked to the minaret and climbed a few steps up its sandy red base, to a large, weathered, wood door. Today was a special day for Senji, and timidity could not stop him from knocking on the door. He felt sure that he would only need to pull his charm from his pack to make anyone who opposed him stand back in awe. He prayed that the monk he had known several years ago would still be waiting there, as Senji had been told he would be. The large door rattled as Senji banged on it, and in a few moments, it opened.

"What do you want, boy?" a gangly old monk with sparkling eyes and a shaved head asked as he peeked out from the other side of the door. Then, he held up an index finger. "Wait. I think I remember you, son. Tell me your name."

"Senji, Teacher," he gasped. "Is it you?" He studied the monk.

"Ah, yes." The monk smiled and nodded. "Yes, my boy. I am me."

Senji sighed. "I have walked many miles. The short monk said I'd find you in this tower. I am surprised the Moslem invaders allowed a Buddhist monk to meditate here."

"It protects an old man from the sun." The monk scrunched the features of his leathery face. "Ah, I remember now. You moved your home to Kashmir. To walk here from there is quite a journey, my boy! You've grown since I last saw you. You must be twenty years by now."

"Nineteen years, Teacher. I have finished the charm you challenged me to make, casting it in bronze, silver, and copper, and inscribing it as you said. I have returned to Delhi to have you bless it."

The monk laughed affectionately. "I did not think you would take my challenge to heart. Such dedication for a young man!"

"I have worked on it for almost three years, Teacher," said Senji excitedly. "It has been a difficult feat to learn to melt the bronze, cast the charm, and inlay the other metals. My uncle helped me put the inscription in Sanskrit since he knows of these things. I have tried to preserve the essence of the Buddha's Second Noble Truth of causation so that it will never be forgotten—no matter how many times our land is invaded." He took a breath and looked at the monk for permission to continue his story.

The old man stood clad only in a loincloth of homespun *khadi*, and his thin ribs stretched his skin taut. His head and body glowed red, baked and blistered by the sun. His stomach caved inward and his knees wobbled. He was tall, spindly, and hunched, and his eyes protruded from their sockets. Wisps of white-gray hair sprung up randomly from his shiny baldness, like weeds on the desert. He had surely lived the life of a wandering holy man. His eyes sparkled. He rubbed his hands together. "Good, good. Let us see it, then."

The boy took the charm from its pack and held it above his bowed head.

"Oh, Senji!" The old monk drew back. "What a magnificent thing!"

"Teacher, you honor me!" Senji presented the bronze rectangle, the size of a large hand, and inlaid with copper and silver. On the front of it, in relief, *Prajnaparamita*, the Goddess of translucent wisdom, gleamed in the sun. She meditated in lotus position with four arms gracefully waving through the air, a content smile on her mouth and tranquility in her eyes.

"My-oh-my," the old monk said. "For this great feat, you will suffer few lifetimes in this world, my son. This I know."

"Look on the back, Teacher," Senji said. "That is where the inscriptions are."

"Oh, yes, let me see. But, why have you inscribed this in the Sanskrit, Senji?"

"My uncle is a very learned man and helped me. He said, since it is the classical language of *Bharat*, it will not soon disappear from our world. I do not understand these things."

The priest nodded. "Your charm will inspire many generations." He smiled as he read the Sanskrit words embedded in the metal. "Your uncle has accurately restated the Buddha's Second Noble Truth."

"What should I do with the charm now?" Senji asked.

The monk studied it. "Remember, I asked you to engrave on the charm . . . Wait, here it is. 'Discard this once you understand its message.' Perfect!"

"As you requested, Father." Senji bowed slightly.

"So, as it says, you must throw it away," the monk said peacefully. Confidence radiated from him as if a great truth had possessed him.

"That makes me sad to think that I have worked three years on this and walked so many miles—"

"Its message will be preserved for all time," the monk said. "Is that not right, Senji? You want this yourself?"

"Yes, but I do not understand how the message will be preserved if I throw the charm away."

The monk nodded knowingly. "You must follow its direction and throw it away."

Senji scratched his temple. "But, Teacher, I have worked so hard."

"Think, boy."

"But, Teacher—"

"You agree its power is its message?"

"Oh, yes."

"Well," the monk explained, "each time it is discarded, another person will find it and read it. Once they understand it, as the charm instructs, they will throw it away. So, the chain will continue, on and on, person to person. Your message will spread throughout *Bharat* and beyond its shores—on ships that sail to faraway lands."

"This is hard to believe," Senji said. "Won't the charm disappear?"

The monk laughed. "Never, Senji, because of its beauty. It will travel to many lands, I promise you."

"Now, I see, Teacher . . . I think." He hung his head. "But, how far could it travel?"

The monk smiled as he kissed the charm, then blessed it by holding it to the heavens and whispering. Then, he spoke: "No telling, my son. It will travel from land-to-land-to-land for all time, explaining the inevitability of karma, causation as determined by our choices. Just like it says. Most people will take it to heart so your charm will pass from person to person—forever. The charm will become a manifestation of the chain of causation, the power of karma—causation we each control. The Buddha's teachings will touch many. Don't you see?"

"But what if a person refuses to believe the truth of karma?" Senji asked. "Someone might mock or misinterpret it?"

The monk shook his head. "We can only pray for those poor souls," he said. He paused and studied the charm. "Ah, it is so beautiful." He gazed at the charm again, and read aloud more of the inscription: " *'Our choices determine what will become of us.'* So simple, but it is the truth in all human endeavor."

"What if those who find the charm are especially evil or even mock its truth? Will they ever understand it?"

"Senji, they will learn the power of karma—a great infinite power—when it becomes obvious that their corrupted lifestreams will never be put in balance in this or any lifetime. Then, they will experience the terrifying beauty of the universe. In front of their own eyes, their future essence will cease to exist . . . *for all time*."

"Is that possible?" Senji asked.

"Once they come face to face with their deeds, it is the worst an evil soul can experience. Imagine a soul being ripped apart, pulverized for all time. Becoming nothing."

Senji tried to imagine this event, but chilled when he realized how complete such a punishment would be. "I fear for those evil souls, Teacher." He frowned fearfully, then hung his head.

765 Years later

PART I - - **THE DEEDS**

1

Cascade, Wisconsin

Jeremy Lucas felt the blast of cold and spray of snowflakes as he slammed the townhouse door with a muffled thud. "Gosh," he said as he exhaled, his breath steaming. The chill gripped his exposed skin. To protect himself, he quickly buttoned his coat and stuffed his scarf around his neck. He glanced across the crowded parking lot, looking for his car, but the falling snow made visibility difficult.

What a bitch! he thought.

For the first time since he had begun his affair with Lana three years ago, he felt powerless. Tonight, she had threatened to reveal their relationship to his wife Rachel, and even pass a memo around the Archer Company office: *White trash slut!*

As Jeremy walked down the wooden stairs, he displaced fluffy flakes with every step. He glanced back at the peephole on Lana's door. She was probably watching him walk away.

"Fuck you, bitch!" he whispered. She can't see the reality of our situation.

Lana will show soon, he thought. He shuddered to think that, after five months or so, she could spout off about their affair, or maybe even try to accuse him of sexual harassment at work, or blackmail him.

For three years, Jeremy had given Rachel the “client dinner in Milwaukee” excuse on Wednesdays, and instead driven twenty-five miles from his home in Fond du Lac, Wisconsin to visit Lana in Cascade. But tonight she had made her announcement, and now expected him to upend his entire life for her. It wasn’t that he was being an asshole, he was just being realistic.

He should have expected this, though, the way she always talked about marriage. He’d always thought she was being facetious when she’d say that being his wife would improve her social standing, but she was dead serious—social climbing was her way.

Since Jeremy had always let his penis sway his decisions about relationships, he had refused to give up their cozy arrangement, despite Lana’s periodic bridal obsession. Now that their relationship was over, he’d have to keep his wits about him, and reconstruct a life without her.

He unlocked his Volvo, climbed in, and started the forty-five minute drive home. He knew the trip would take longer tonight due to the snow, but he figured that he could cut through the Kettle Moraine National Forest and shave a few minutes off his time—as long as the snow didn't get too bad. The trek would have been a cakewalk had he remembered to bring along chains. He pulled out of the complex parking lot and headed into Cascade.

As he drove down Parnell Street, he thought once again of his relationship with Lana, and began to feel more and more betrayed. After all, every Wednesday night, she had showered him with the kind of benefits he might have expected of a lover: great dinners, sexy outfits, smooth wine, sultry dance steps, whiffs of lilac—all the hot buttons. While she had brought up the "leaving Rachel" business frequently, she had never spoken quite as emphatically about it as she had tonight, punctuating the issue by making her announcement.

Jeremy turned right onto Scenic Drive. *Snow looks really bad,* he thought.

Earlier that evening, Lana had been picking at the sides of her perfectly manicured fingernails, creating tiny bits of hanging skin.

"What is it?" he asked. "Something bugging you?"

"Jer, I have an announcement."

Oh, shit. The way she had said those words sounded ominous. She stood, clasped her hands together, and hung her head. She looked silly, standing there in a teddy and wobbly heels, slouched like a sad, out-of-work clown.

Jeremy took a sip of wine and sat back on the couch, thinking Lana was just pouting again. "Are you going to explain the lack of nooky tonight? You owe me that, girl."

"I'm feeling a little sick, Jer," she barked. "That okay?"

"You don't have to get hostile!" Jeremy said. "What are you," he asked jokingly, "pregnant?"

She looked up suddenly. "Well, now that you mention it—"

"What?" He sat up, dripping wine on the carpet. "What about it?"

She folded her arms. "I am . . . *pregnant.*"

"You're kidding, right?"

"Actually, no," she mumbled and looked at the floor.

"What?! Man-oh-man."

"You're pissed," she said.

"What do you expect? A leap for joy?"

"Up yours, Jeremy. I thought now we could finally be together. You could leave Rachel like we've been talking about." Lana kicked off her heels and immediately lost four inches from her height.

"The midget cleaning lady appears," he snickered. "You mean like *you've* been saying, don't you?"

"Jer, we've both talked about it," she whined. "Come on . . . "

"What? Do you expect me to drop everything and run to Lana because she blew it with the birth control? No, wait, you probably planned this, is that it?"

"Up yours, Jeremy." She paced back and forth with fists clenched. "I knew you'd wimp out on me if this ever happened. You think 'cause you're the big corporate honcho with the studly face, superior intelligence, great sense of humor, and smooth talk, you can get away with anything!"

"Well—" He pushed back his neck-length brown hair. "At least you appreciate me for the guy I am. You can't prove the kid's mine anyway."

She stopped and glared at him. "I can prove it, all right! Who else? Just think who I could tell!"

Jeremy slammed his glass down on the table. "You wouldn't have the nerve."

"It's not like I have all these lovers. It has to be yours!"

Jeremy stood. "Yeah, right. Say, sorry about the wine spill. I'm gonna head out." He looked at his watch. "Getting late anyway and with the goddamned snow . . ."

"Jeremy," Lana moaned, "is that the end of us, then? Am I on my own here?" She tossed back her ash-blonde hair.

"Don't I help you with the apartment? Buy you things? I've done the best I can. This kid bit is over the top. It had to come to an end sometime—this has to be it. I'm sorry."

"You always make it about money," she said. "Jeez!"

"Impresses the hell out of you, too." He laughed. "Just get an abortion? It's the only thing that makes sense."

"Jeremy!" Her eyes filled with tears. "You don't give a damn, do you? We're talking about my real baby here. Now you're talking about killing it!"

He walked to the door. "Well, you really think I'm going to drop everything and destroy my life?"

"Your perfect yuppie life with ass-kisser, Rachel, who'll do anything for you?" She wiped her nose. "That's all you care about! Jeremy Lucas, you better not walk out that door!"

He turned. “What are you gonna do, chubby, sue me? That’d be one way to get your mitts on my inheritance.”

“Fuck you, Jeremy! It’s over between us. Is that what you wanted to hear? It’s over! I hate you!”

“Whatever.” He shrugged and shook his head.

“Now you’re going home to get it from the hag like nothing ever happened. And she’ll deliver, no doubt.”

“At least she doesn’t scream like a banshee when I screw her. She lies perfectly still.”

“You asshole!” Lana shouted. “Maybe I’ll call her tomorrow. Would you like that?”

Jeremy turned around. “Lana, you bitch. You wouldn’t dare.”

“Try me,” she said. “Maybe I’ll pass a note around at Archer, too. Start with big-mouthed Mary—she’ll tell everyone how you’re a dominance freak and Rachel’s just your slave.”

“Right.” He laughed. “I’ll just say you’re lying. Who are they going to believe? A vice president or his trashy, pregnant assistant whose biggest dream in life is to win the lottery?”

“Jeremy, you truly are a bastard!” She threw a plastic tumbler of soda at him. He dodged it, but got splattered with

Coke and ice as the cup bounced off the wall.

"Hey, watch it," he said. "You're just flustered about being pregnant. I know you'll work it out; you're inventive." He winked.

"It's over," she cried and then said slowly, "I knew it."

"Well, whiz kid, what did *you* think I would do? Suddenly give you a ring?" Jeremy laughed as he threw two hundred dollar bills on the coffee table. "Here, you'll need this. I creamed Bob at racquetball today." Jeremy casually put on his coat, opened the door, and walked out, vaguely kissing the air in Lana's direction as he left.

Lana Holub looked through the peephole on the door at the snow fluttering through the beam of the security light in the center of the parking lot.

She slumped into the bedroom. The life she'd always dreamt about was over. She had imagined flowery, soft focus images of a wedding day—the perfect white gown with a long train flowing down the aisle, a bouquet of miniature orchids and roses flying in slow motion to a hundred eager hands, and Jeremy gliding with her across an empty dance floor to joyous applause.

Now this—the dream had turned into a nightmare. In sparse light, she looked into the full-length mirror on the closet door. She tore off her teddy, ripping a spaghetti strap. She studied her figure, the vague impression of puffiness around her middle. She had never found it easy to keep her weight down, but always told herself she was pleasingly plump in all the right places. At least, that's what Jeremy had said, but tonight he had called her "a midget cleaning lady!"

She looked at her nails. Despite the fact that she had typed his boring memos for five years, she had kept her nails in great shape, except for the newly torn bits of cuticle around several of them.

The phone on the bedside table rang. She picked up the receiver. "Hello?" she said, sniffling.

"Hi, Baby," a stern female voice said. "Glad I didn't wake you."

"Oh, hi, Ma. Just got home from a date."

"You and your dates. It's a wonder you aren't married yet! Twenty-seven isn't so young, ya know. Why don't you settle down, get married, and give me a grandchild?"

Lana's mother always wanted her to be like her other daughter, Deborah, with two perfect kids from her first marriage, a Ford Aerostar, and new husband, Bryce, the most successful doctor in Topeka, Kansas.

Lana sighed.

"Something wrong, Sweetie?" Her mother coughed a ragged smokers' cough.

"Nothin'."

"Come on, Lana. There's something going on. A mother can always tell."

"Oh, Ma," Lana said, trying to control tears, "it's nothin' I can't handle."

"It's that guy, isn't it? Jerry somebody? Your boss?"

"The royal asshole," Lana cried, and stroked her tummy. "He just dumped me."

There was only silence. Then, her mother said, "Don't worry, honey. Just watch. He'll get what's coming to him. They always do."

2

Cascade, Wisconsin

Frazzled by Lana's surprise announcement, Jeremy turned the car radio on and off. He sniffed at her lingering lilac of her perfume and recalled the smooth feel of her skin. *Why did she blow it?* he thought. *It was so perfect.* Now, their three-year affair was over, and he had a baby to worry about. His stomach felt jittery as he imagined how she might retaliate. Maybe he had been too hard-ass with her. But, then again, she probably blew it with the birth control . . . and maybe on purpose.

In a way, though, Jeremy was relieved. He contemplated the solid security he had felt long before he started seeing Lana, right after school and beginning his job at Archer, before he started his affair with Sandy, his last assistant. In those days, he would arrive home each night to a waiting dinner and a happy Rachel who, since college, had demonstrated her love for him by catering to him unconditionally in every way—*every* way.

But, while her absolute submissiveness was nice, especially

sexually, Jeremy already felt the concomitant, claustrophobic feeling that resulted from a clinging spouse. He had achieved a truly monogamous state only periodically throughout ten years of marriage with Rachel.

For now, however, he could be guilt-free again, rather than continuing his wandering wolf ways—a role he had started in college, fooling around with Rachel's vulnerable girlfriend. There was a three-year affair with Sandy at Archer, before he became a VP and had to cut that off; then, he hired Lana and had a fling that evolved into a full-fledged affair. Now, the thought of *not* having a lover to balance a fulfilling, yet stifling relationship with Rachel was an odd one for Jeremy Lucas! He didn't have himself to blame . . . really. Because Rachel was the way she was, he was merely doing what any guy would do: being annoyed by her smothering ways and loving her irresistable submissiveness. *That's just normal!*

As he headed out of Cascade, Jeremy glimpsed the heavy snowfall through the rays of the last streetlight on Scenic Drive. The flakes persisted into the infinite darkness beyond the intersection. He easily made the choice to take the

Kettle Moraine shortcut. He turned slowly, barely stopping at the light.

He skidded slightly as he made a turn onto the forest road marked by the large sign that read, "Welcome to Kettle Moraine National Forest—a step back in time."

The more he thought about Lana, the more he hoped she could work something out—an abortion or lucky miscarriage. Then, she would show up at work like nothing had happened, and the two of them could resume the relationship. Otherwise, what would he do without his weekly visits to her, passionate buzzes ingrained in his normal routine that surely offset Rachel's clinging?

As small brown campground signs with white letters popped up on each side of the winding road, a yellow emergency truck appeared in Jeremy's headlights on the right shoulder. The truck was stopped, appearing to have completed its snow-plowing route. Jeremy slowly pulled around it, and, as he did, drove into snow four inches deep. He continued with no trouble. *I'll get through,* he thought. *I always get through.* He laughed at how things always seemed to work out for him.

He thought back to his college days at the University of Wisconsin at Madison.

As treasurer of the "Salesmen of the Future" club, he had found an inventive way to use new member dues. Five thousand bucks went into a private account to pay for a long weekend in Las Vegas for himself and his buddies, who helped him gamble it away. *I was in the right place at the right time!*

Then Ronny Schultz squealed. Jeremy almost got expelled from school, but smooth-talked his way out of the dilemma, negotiating a lesser punishment from Dean Winkel—expulsion for a term, repayment of the money, and a ban from joining any other university-sanctioned club. Not bad, considering the alternative could have been jail time and a record.

To return the money, Jeremy had ingeniously approached newly graduated Madison students who lived in the area and requested old tests they might have laying around the house, especially those given by instructors who were still teaching. He even paid the former students for their troubles. After putting together an extensive collection, he attracted a huge clientele of current students by visiting local bars to advertise his "underground test library." In just a few months, he managed to pay back the five thousand to the club and turn a nice profit for himself.

By spring of that next year, he convinced many of his clients to join him when he started the University's first chapter of SDS, the Students for a Democratic Society—not sanctioned by the university—primarily to disrupt the campus' administration of "pigs." By *starting* a new campus organization, he was also able to circumvent Dean Winkel's ban on his joining *existing* campus clubs—smart, as usual.

He named his personal cadre of friends, a handful of guys with nothing to do and with lots of energy and money, the Easter Gang. After they rented an airplane and dropped a bomb (that ended up being a dud) onto a campus building, they decided to regain their growing reputation as campus roustabouts by blowing up the MRC—the Department of Defense's Math Research Center.

Since the explosion, Jeremy experienced recurrent nightmares about the event. Back then, he had convinced the Jane County DA that his buddies were the actual culprits behind the blast; that he just went along for the ride and was unaware of their plans. *They should've paid anyway*, Jeremy thought. After all, they were the ones who really believed the crap the gang circulated around campus, about how the MRC was the headquarters for masterminding the genocide of countless thousands of innocent Vietnamese—*right*.

After graduating in 1972 and coasting through an entry-level job at a local company in Fond du Lac, Jeremy was hired as a marketing assistant at the Archer Toy Company, the town's largest employer. A year later, he became an assistant marketing manager. Then, in 1975, when he married Rachel, he implied to Archer president Bob Townsend that his boss had awarded contracts to suppliers in exchange for kickbacks, which Jeremy, in actual fact, had arranged for himself—just taking advantage of an obvious opportunity.

When his boss was let go and Jeremy was asked to be the new marketing manager for Archer, he tried to act surprised and appreciative. In his new position, he quickly terminated the suppliers to cover any traces of his own culpability in the scheme. *Burn bridges when you need to!*

He orchestrated his rise in the company by taking advantage of president Bob Townsend's apparent weakness in, and fear of, marketing-related issues—Jeremy's strength.

When Jeremy bragged that he would eventually inherit a significant sum from his widowed mother, his promotability seemed destined to flourish. Bob Townsend, a perpetual "climber" and son-in-law of Hadley Archer, the company's founder and CEO, put increasing stock in everything Jeremy said. Bob enjoyed being surrounded by wealth and groomed Jeremy for the VP spot as if it were his unalienable right. By 1978, Jeremy slid into his current position as VP of not only marketing, but also sales. Not bad for a young anti-war protester-turned-corporate riser.

As the snow fell more heavily, Jeremy realized that cutting through the Moraine might have been the wrong decision. As he made the next turn, he noticed that his tires were unable to maintain good traction. He slowed to a crawl.

There, I'll be okay, he thought. He remembered how recommending that the Archer Company introduce *Boomers* had been his decisive moment. *Talk about intuition!*

Targeting aging adults, *Boomers* was a board game which had sat in the Archer R&D department gathering dust until one day when Jeremy copied his insurance man's presentation of key demographics and used them in a staff meeting to support the *Boomers* proposition. Bob Townsend was dutifully impressed, and *Boomers* had a new life.

Voilà! The game took off the day it was introduced. Jeremy became Archer's new hero, and Bob bragged about the brilliance of his protégé. Bob described how he had made it clear to Hadley that Jeremy was indispensable to Archer Toys as its new VP. That obviously angered Carl Dietrich, Archer's long time Operations VP, because he began to respond defensively toward everyone—a real grump. His own hopes of eventually succeeding Bob Townsend as president were obviously fading.

Carl, the old warhorse! Jeremy reflected. Carl, the son of hard working, immigrant parents, clearly resented Jeremy's slick manner, precipitous rise, and moneyed destiny. He bristled every time Jeremy presumed to speak for him—"Bob, I'm sure Carl's in my camp. Right, Carl?" Jeremy hated Carl's obvious resistance to him, the angry old fart!

Splot! A wad of snow suddenly landed on Jeremy's windshield, startling him. He slammed on his brakes, throwing the Volvo into a forty-five degree skid across the little road. Then, he pumped his brakes, slowed to a near stop, and continued.

Considering his near scrape with a criminal record and slick rise in business, possessing both a wife and lover was a small-potatoes scheme.

During the past three years, Jeremy had developed rules of conduct so he knew when to favor Rachel or Lana, or when he should resent each of them. For instance, having family barbecues was clearly an activity in Rachel's arena. He would always tell jokes with her brother, Greg, embarrass Rachel by pinching and tickling her inappropriately, and making sarcastic comments about the relatives who hadn't attended. The ruder he got with his comments about those who hadn't attended, the more the other guests laughed. Being the jokester of the family gave him a sense of heritage—a definite improvement over his younger years when his mother became the wounded Lucas family matriarch after her husband, who had become wealthy after selling his burgeoning company, died unexpectedly.

Lana's territory would include things like sitting in the hot tub in Cascade with a bottle of Cabernet and cuddling until they went in to make wild love—she wriggled and screamed like a trapped lizard even though he constantly told her to be as still as she could just like he demanded of Rachel.

If a Lucas family event was scheduled on Lana's night, Jeremy would need to cut his visit short or he'd resent her. As he'd leave, she would tell him how she wanted to become a bigger part of his life and would cling to his arm unmercifully. At that point, he resented her intrusion into his "normal" family life.

Now, as he drove through the snow, he was in transition from his life of loving Lana to his life of controlling Rachel. Everything was changing—responsibilities, attitudes, vocabulary, even what was considered appropriate humor.

Earlier today, he had explained to Rachel that she'd have to eat alone because he had another weekly client dinner. He, in actuality, had blown off an afternoon of work at the office in favor of a trip to the field, an activity no one ever questioned. It was, after all, Jeremy's responsibility as VP of Marketing and Sales to study competitive ways of marketing toys—to see what young renegade Lego or old chief Parker Brothers were up to.

Tomorrow, over coffee, he would prepare his field report to Bob

Townsend—easy to fake after having made a quick visit to one or two toy stores on his way to Cascade. Bob always appreciated Jeremy's "on target" recommendations spawned from those reports. Jeremy had really learned to be an efficient upper manager!

The snow eased for several minutes. Then, despite a fleeting second thought, Jeremy drove farther into the rocky, woodsy area locals termed "the Moraine". As he entered the denser woods, *eskers* rose on his right. The cliffs had been formed eons ago, by streams that ran through retreating glaciers.

Out of the dark, a curving swirl of white fluffs burst into Jeremy's headlights like a volley of machine gun fire. He clutched the wheel tightly and slowed to fifteen miles per hour.

It was sort of funny, Jeremy recalled, that recently Rachel had become suspicious, teasing him about how incredibly clever she was. "You'll never be able to pull one over on me," she always said. "I know you too well."

Right. Jeremy's excursions to Lana's had become such a regular part of his life that the guilt he might have felt and the chances of discovery had vanished. He was too good at masquerading his relationship with Lana. In fact, it had gotten to the point that everything he saw wrong about Rachel was another justification to spend time with Lana—and vice versa—*perfect balance!*

Each of them served their purpose. While Lana had made him feel like a young stallion gliding across a field of tall green wind-swept grass, Rachel was the woman who dutifully washed the skid marks from his underwear and wore or didn't wear whatever he wanted—wherever. She'd been his rock ever since they'd married after six years of dating off and on. That was five years after the MRC bombing had punctuated Jeremy's increasingly wild college life. Since their first night together, Rachel cuddled him during his nightmares, but he had only vaguely described to Lana his commandoesque exploits that had taken place that night in 1970.

So, sharing the details of that SDS episode was absolutely reserved for Rachel. But now, long after he had shown up at Rachel's door that night, shaking and sweaty, looking for safe haven after the bombing, her warm blanket of security, coupled with her clinginess, had smothered him—something it did in spades every few years. After tonight, without Lana there to give him a regular breath of fresh air, he wondered how he would survive.

Jeremy wondered why sex with Rachel could no longer be as straightforward as his school years in Madison when, in a darkened movie theater where all the students went to neck, he had touched her everywhere, and on command she'd closed her eyes and moaned softly, if at all. Now, that kind of behavior had become a vague, unimaginable fantasy, which Lana tried to futilely emulate in the back row of the Cascade Theatre—but she had trouble *not* reacting to his fondling.

Now, every quarter mile was slower going than the one before it. The road became thinner and curvier. Jeremy's windshield wipers couldn't keep up with the barrage of fresh snow.

Man. He slid to a halt. A chill zipped up his spine. The thermometer on the bank building in Cascade had read zero. The wind-chill factor made the temperature at least twenty degrees below by now.

He thought about Rachel waiting at home. It was amazing to him that her ever-present radar hadn't detected the nature of his Cascade visits. He guessed she simply hadn't put the clues together—Lana's obvious lilac scent that always lingered on his clothes, the regularity of the Wednesday dinners, the hushed phone calls, the hang-ups when she answered. Maybe Rachel was oblivious to all of it because she adored him so unconditionally. He didn't know whether to respect her for blind loyalty or feel contempt for her stupidity. Maybe, though, she was just in a state of denial, and, underneath it all, really distrusted him—she certainly had been acting more and more jealous recently. Maybe she was feeling jealous because of her own behavior. Maybe she was having an affair! But, then, Jeremy laughed as he imagined her having a heart-to-heart with him, confessing her misdeeds. *Naw, she wouldn't cheat on me, she's not the type*.

Visibility was now close to zero. All Jeremy saw was a solid wall of car-lit flakes before him, eliminating all details on the road beyond. He slowed the car to a crawl. The snow, mixed with sleet, crunched underneath as his tires crept through it, barely audible above the whirring heater fan.

Jeremy became aware of his shallow, rapid breaths, which were fogging up the windshield. A light touch of the brakes sent his car slipping forward, cocked at an oblique angle. He slid to a stop and held his chest. The instant he did, snow enveloped his car from behind. He felt sudden fear. A fear of being stuck out there. Alone. These woods, normally so beautiful with their ravines and eskers, miles from any town, during a blizzard, looked dangerous tonight. So alone. He hadn't seen another vehicle since he passed the tow truck.

He revved the car and slowly raised the clutch. He barely had traction.

He saw a turn in the road ahead. He steered to the right in case another car suddenly approached from around the blind corner, which he almost hoped for, but as he turned, his car kept going right. Now his lights shined on the cliff that hugged the right side of the road. He stepped on his brakes, but kept sliding. He slid into the cliff wall. Loose pebbles pelted his hood from above as the car bounced into dead foliage. *Thank God, no serious damage!*

When he backed up, the car's wheels caught a little traction and he skidded backward across the road to the other side. He slid to a stop. He inched forward, then felt himself skidding on the ice—drifting to the left, as if the car were weightless.

His left rear wheel slumped back onto the soft shoulder. He revved the engine and eased out the clutch. With each acceleration, he felt himself dig a deeper rut with his rear tires. He tried rocking the car forward and back, but still couldn't get any traction.

"Fuck!" he screamed. Finally, angry and frightened, he jammed on the gas and popped the clutch while the car's gearshift was in reverse. The car lurched backward, out of the rut and off the shoulder.

Relief! He stepped on the brake.

The car kept sliding . . . down a six-foot embankment!

The car slammed to an abrupt halt on a ledge. Its front end pointed skyward, nearly perpendicular to the ledge and resting against the steep slope. A limb crashed through the rear window, spraying glass everywhere. The snow had cushioned the car's landing, so the gas tank apparently wasn't damaged. Jeremy picked pieces of glass off his coat. The Volvo creaked, its butt-end on the ledge six feet below road level. Its engine died and its heater fan whirred to a stop.

"Shit!" Jeremy shouted, pain shooting up and down his back.

He tried to wiggle his fingers and toes. Thank God he felt a response.

He purposefully breathed slowly and deeply, but he felt like screaming. Jeremy Lucas had used his shortcut through the middle of nowhere to avoid the snow and return safely to his life with Rachel. But now, he felt like he was being punished for having spent time with Lana.

"What the fuck am I going to do?" he mumbled.

He turned his key in the ignition. The engine cranked—slowly at first, then faster, then a zoom. His car phone beeped ON.

He dialed 911, then hit *SEND*.

"Thank God for my logical thinking," he said.

He felt the pulsing blood drain from his face and his muscles relax. *But, wait!* The phone didn't ring. The phone signal only beeped repeatedly amidst crackle. Being in the Moraine, a series of cliffs and gullies covered by dense forest might be splendid for camping and hiking, but it eliminated any possibility of good phone reception.

"Figures." He threw the receiver down on the car floor and turned off the engine. The car creaked.

3

Fond du Lac, Wisconsin

Miles away, Rachel Lucas leaned on the kitchen doorjamb, listening to her mother talk on the phone. She looked at her watch.

"But, Mum," she said, "I hate his meetings. They keep him out so late. And the snow tonight . . ."

"No worries, Rachel," her mother soothed. "He's doing important company business, he is. I always told you he was a winner. You have to be his support. Understand?"

"I guess."

They said their "good-byes" and hung up.

Rachel walked into the kitchen and studied the man crouched under the sink. "Aren't you finished yet, Paul?"

"Just about," the plumber mumbled.

"Do you think I worry about him too much?" she said louder, her Aussie accent showing.

"A-might," said Paul. "He is a big boy, after all. He won't do anything stupid."

Rachel looked out the window over the sink. "But the snow."

"Pretty bad, I'll say," Paul said. "Lucky I only have to go next door to get home." He maneuvered his large frame as he disengaged from his project. As he stood, only the back of his kinky, short-cropped, salt-and-pepper hair and bald spot faced Rachel. Then, he turned around and faced her, frowning his concern. "By the way, since I ran the new line in copper and your old one was galvi, I'm going to have to bring back a dialectic union to join the two. Sorry, you'll be out of commission for a day."

"That's okay," Rachel said. "What's the part called? Jeremy might want to know." She winced as she again peered out the kitchen window at the snow.

"A dialectic union. Never mind, Rach. You don't worry about that now . . . or Jeremy. He'll be fine. Oh, by the way, you might want this."

Paul held up a wedding band.

"Oh, thank you so much for finding it! That liquid soap made it come right off. Hasn't been off for ten years." Rachel held out her ring finger, and Paul slipped the gold band on.

She smiled.

"Now, you be careful in the future," he said.

Rachel breathed a deep sigh. "Thanks, Paul. You know, there was a time I didn't trust your work—back when we first moved in—when you were learning from your dad. But this is great."

Paul crawled under the sink again.

"Over the years," she said louder, "I don't think one of your jobs has ever gone bad. Ever." She smiled. "Maybe you can tell me: why don't you seem like the plumber type?"

Paul stretched out his thick, muscular body. "Four years of apprenticeship taught me something, I guess. Dad would be proud, I hope."

"Oh, he would, bless him." Rachel smiled, admiring Paul's form. "Your dad was something. But I trust you, I really do."

"What'd you say?" he echoed from under the sink.

"I said, I've come to—" Then she stopped, thinking. She *did* trust Paul. Not many people held that distinction. Her mum and dad; probably not Jeremy, if push came to shove. He was sharp, sure, but not necessarily trustworthy. But, definitely Paul—if he said he could do something, Rachel absolutely believed him. If he couldn't, he said so, and she trusted that, too. She believed anything he said without question.

She fiddled with her wedding band. "Boy, that's something."

"What?" Paul asked. He efficiently pulled out from under the sink. " . . . Claire's who I always trusted completely."

Rachel shook herself out of a daze.

"I mean, before she died," Paul said. "I swear, I'd let her throw knives at me if she said she could do it without killing me."

"Really?" Rachel said incredulously. "I couldn't imagine trusting Jeremy if he claimed he could do that. I'd figure he was bragging or showing off or just trying to kill me." She laughed. "I'd run."

Paul laughed as he stood. He sighed,and drew a picture in the air with his hands as he talked. "Claire had such graceful lines, fair skin, high cheekbones; steel blue eyes—like she came from privileged lineage or something. You know, I used to study her face with the TV glowing on it while she watched one of those old shows: *Upstairs, Downstairs*. She loved the PBS out of Milwaukee."

Rachel smiled.

"I always called her my goddess," he said.

"Paul, how beautiful."

"Well, I meant it. She was happy, too—all the time. You know, before the . . . illness, I don't think a day went by when she wasn't excited about the next birthday or holiday or family get together."

"Say, you never explained," Rachel said.

"About what?" Paul queried.

"About why you don't seem like the plumber type," she said.

"Maybe because the crack doesn't show."

"The crack?" she said. "Excuse me? What crack?"

He pointed to his butt.

"Oh!" She laughed with her hands over her mouth.

"You know, I really do have one. When Dad passed on the business, he made me show it. Part of the prerequisites."

Rachel giggled. "Paul! You're so silly. What did you do before the plumbing?"

"Dad never mentioned it?"

"Just something about Madison and cooking," she said.

"I studied psychology and anthropology over there off and on during my late twenties and early thirties," Paul answered. "Even got into the doctoral program and wrote the beginnings of my dissertation: 'Changing Cuisine — Its Effect on the Development of Civilization.' Then, I sold plumbing parts over at General until dad needed me."

"Ooh," Rachel said, "I never knew you were that serious about cooking. I thought you loved to cook because you used to be a chef in the service or something."

"Close. I was always a frustrated gourmet, even in high school."

"But where'd you get the hankering?"

"I don't know," Paul replied. "Army, I guess. Should've studied at the *Cordon Bleu*. When I got out, there was Claire, then Tommy right away, and then, I got a job at General Plumbing Supply. When Dad needed help making it with all those big, fancy plumbers coming into town, I decided to join him. "*Voilà!*" He threw his hand in the air. "Seemed like the decisions took care of themselves." His eyes glazed over. "Not much choice."

"I can tell you loved Claire a lot," Rachel said. "Whenever you talk about her, you sound like you're still crazy about her. I'm crazy about Jeremy, but really it's more devotion, you know? Or loyalty."

"When I look at Tommy, I still see her. He's like a male child version of her, the way he laughs—so careful and restrained." Paul sniffed a little and wiped his nose with a kerchief he pulled from his rear pocket. "What about Jer?"

Rachel put her index finger to her mouth and stroked her taut lower lip. “I honestly don’t think Jeremy loves me *that* deeply. More that he needs me—and I’m there. I don’t know, it’s confusing.”

He nodded. “Jeremy’s so serious and business-like all the time, he makes it clear he’s a different breed—no offense.”

“What do you mean, different breed?” she asked.

He looked at the floor. “I shouldn’t say.”

“No, really, Paul, go ahead. It’s okay. What about different breed?”

“You sure it’s okay?” He rubbed his chin. “Well, Jer’s always impressed me as the up and comer type, him being loaded and all that.”

“He doesn’t get that till his mum dies.”

“I guess.” Paul looked at Rachel and sighed. “If I can be honest, though, I never saw him as being much your type. I mean, on the surface, you know? He’s more like a boss.”

“What are you saying, Paul?” Rachel asked, backing away, putting her fists on her hips and furrowing her brow. “I sure hope he’s okay out there in that storm.”

“I knew I shouldn’t go mouthing off,” he said. “See, I get started talking and then I go mouthing off.”

"Paul, it's okay," Rachel said. "Tell me what you think my type is. Come on, I want to know."

"No, ma'am. I shouldn't say."

"Come on," she said. "Please?"

He turned back. "The truth? Only if you promise you won't hate me."

"Deal."

"Well, I always thought . . . with Claire gone and me spending more time around you . . . I've noticed that you seem like you're—"

"What, Paul, what?"

"Well, Jeremy seems so . . . well, different from you," he shrugged.

"So, why isn't Jer necessarily my type?" she asked.

"Well, you know, Tommy's always telling me how he thinks Jeremy sold out. Sorry if that offends."

"Why does he think Jeremy sold out?"

"Well," Paul said, "at Madison, that bombing happened at SDS fifteen years ago and they still talk about it. Jer was the main guy in that gang, right? That bombing?"

"He started the Easter Gang with his mates," Rachel said, "Ken and Harold Nordberg, and the rest of them."

"And now, Jeremy's a corporate type, right?" Paul said. "He was a protester and stood for something; now he's a player in the system. At least, that's how Tommy puts it—makes sense from his perspective—being a student at Madison."

"I guess," she said. "But 'selling out' is a little strong."

"Tom's always talking about that Ken Nordberg fellow, too," said Paul. "A few months ago, the people of Madison petitioned and got him and his brother out of prison five years early. Tommy says that now Ken hangs around campus on the State Street Mall across from the library. He sells smoothies and passes out fliers from a little cart. At least, he's still trying to live that idealistic life—world peace and all."

"Selling smoothies?" Rachel laughed.

"Being a proponent of peace. He's living real peace."

"Sounds flaky to me," she said. "But that may be Jeremy talking."

"Ken just believes in his dream."

"No worries." Rachel shrugged. "You have a right to your own point-of-view. Maybe I've just adopted Jeremy's over the years."

"Actually," Paul said, "it's Tommy's point of view. Anyway, the corporate riser doesn't seem like your type—cuddly, compassionate."

"Hmm, yeah. I guess." She smiled and cleared her throat. "You think I'm cuddly and compassionate?"

"Well, sure, you know. You're the type that's concerned about wildlife and the environment—causes. You're more the smoothie stand type I think," he said.

"Really?"

"Well, underneath this 'down-to-business' persona that you have."

"Hmm . . . I suppose," Rachel said shyly and fiddled with her fingers, "I didn't know you were so observant, Paul."

"Listen, Rachel, I'd better shut up. Don't want to over analyze it."

"Say, how's little Tommy liking school over at Madison?" she asked.

"He's not so little anymore," Paul said. "Wants me to call him Tom now. He sure does like Madison better than Fond du Lac."

"Who wouldn't? Madison's beautiful. The lake and all."

"He moved into a place on Mifflin," Paul said.

"That's the same street I lived on!"

"You did?" Paul said.

"That's where I met Jeremy. He saved me from a riot; carried me right out of there—police and sirens everywhere."

"Romantic," he said.

"I always was a sucker for that stuff. Jeremy was my knight all right; the up-and-comer, too. I saw him as my way out of a bleak existence."

"That's your Aussie inferiority bit flaring up," Paul grinned.

"Maybe." Rachel looked down. "Daughter of friggin' Harry Martin."

"Tom says there's still talk of Timothy Agers on campus. His wife just made an anti-violence speech with their son Mark in front of Sterling Hall."

"Really?" said Rachel. "Mark must be a teenager now. God, he was just a baby then."

"Yeah. He'll undoubtedly go to Madison." Paul started putting his tools away. "And get his degree in Poli Sci."

"Probably" she said.

Paul's face brightened. "Did I tell you, my Tom's taking a double major this semester? Physics and Engineering. He takes a class at Sterling every day. He says they really patched it up since the bombing, but you can still tell."

"Really?" Rachel asked. "What does he say about Agers?"

"The guy who got killed? The usual: him dying and Mark growing up without a father, all that. Young Mark's only fifteen, but wears a beard—a symbol of his dad dying violently like that. His older sister is teaching grade school in New England."

"Why is she out east?"

"Her husband's clan is out there. Guess she never got over her dad dying. Doesn't Jer ever talk about those days?"

"He still has awful dreams."

"Sorry about that."

"Maybe from guilt," Rachel mumbled as she stared at the floor, twiddling her fingers, recollecting how she had come to Jeremy's rescue during the trial with a well-timed, but false, alibi.

"What was that?" Paul asked. "Guilt? Thought he got off legitimately."

"Oh." Rachel tensed. "Guilt by association, I suppose. From being part of the gang."

"Guilt'll cause dreams like that." Paul stood and stretched. "I'm all set for now, Rachel. Be on my way. You can pay me when I come back and put on that dialectic union. I'll shoot for tomorrow, late afternoon, so you won't be out of commission too long. No charge for getting the ring out."

"Thanks, Paul. We'll eat on paper and drink bottled for a day. Be okay." She walked him to the door. He pulled it open and the snow swirled in.

"Phew, look at it out there!" Paul said.

"I'd never get anywhere," Rachel said. "Don't know how Jeremy does it. Probably being a boy scout in his youth."

"Now he has a fancy phone in his car, right?" he asked.

"Yeah. He'd call if he got stuck."

"Where's he coming from?"

"Milwaukee. Client dinner," said Rachel. "Has them pretty regular. He's a VP over at Archer now. I guess I've got to take the bad with the good. That's what Jer always says."

"I guess," Paul said. "Well, catch you later, then." He nodded as he barely tipped the brim of his well-worn Brewers cap.

He's always wearing it, Rachel thought. Tom Ersham used to say his dad never saw the Brewers or even cared about baseball; just liked getting that hat from his son.

"Bye, Paul. Thanks." She waved and closed the door behind him. *Nice man*, she thought. She leaned her back against the door, intrigued that he thought she might be more his type. *Hardly*, she thought. *Although . . .*

She walked over to the stereo. Earlier she had put out her favorite Katia cassette to listen to later. She put it in the tape player, raised the volume a little since Jeremy wasn't there to complain, and began to move with the music. She closed her eyes and the familiar Latin beat began to surround her:

Prah-mises . . .
Can't you see . . . the possibilities.
Love is contagious . . .
You will see my love . . .
I am closer . . . let's use it or we'll lose it.

Rachel started spinning as she danced faster and faster.

Go and ask anyone,
They will all say the same — everyone.
Love is contagious and it proves
We are part of a chain.

Words and Music — M. Litecki, K. Polankski © 1984 PLS Records

"Yes!" she called out to no one as the trumpets blared and Katia's background singers answered her with perfectly blended harmony. Rachel spun herself into a trance as the music slowed and she sang along, swaying back and forth dramatically, as if she were dancing with an imaginary partner.

Out of breath and sweating, she fell into Jeremy's recliner. When she walked upstairs to the bedroom, she was still unable to dismiss thoughts of Paul. She undressed, threw a quick thought to Jeremy, and stepped into the shower.

Kettle Moraine National Forest, southern Wisconsin

Jeremy sat in his car on the ledge for an hour. He was freezing and fuming at the same time. Already, with the heater off, the Coke that Lana spilled on him had turned to a thin, icy sheet. He regretted not having seriously taken the advice of whoever had recommended he store a candle and matches in the car. They said that one candle could keep a closed, four door sedan a steady fifty-five degrees, even if it was below zero outside. If that was no exaggeration, he'd be reasonably warm by now. But, in this case, the candle probably wouldn't have worked anyway since his left rear car window had been punched open, and a continuous stream of frigid air was rushing directly at him. He figured he'd better get out of the car and check out nearby options for shelter or he might freeze to death from the steady arctic blast.

Jeremy turned and looked down the slope. As the moon cut through the clear night and the flurries slowed, he spied a huge tree fifty feet away. In the trunk was a large cave-sized hole at ground level, so the tree could undoubtedly protect some hibernating animal. Then, Jeremy noticed that the hole faced away from the wind. He decided to check out the tree-cave.

As he opened the car door, the car creaked ominously from the shifting weight. He climbed out and moved carefully until he was crouched, ready to jump. He counted to three. Then, as the car creaked again, he jumped down four feet to the adjacent slope. He landed with a soft thud. The snow puffed up and sprayed in his face. He steadied himself.

He clamped down on his rattling jaw and hopped down to the tree as quietly as possible in case the trunk was occupied. When he was ten feet away, he became frightened and returned to the car. He carefully climbed inside, despite a few creaks, and pulled the door half shut. He shivered as he honked his horn repeatedly for two minutes while scouring the area. The pitch of his horn sounded lower with every beep, but he detected no activity down the slope by the tree trunk.

He concluded that if something had been hiding in the tree, it would have heard the racket of his fading horn and emerged by now, angry at having been disturbed. But, there was no sign of life.

He turned on his barely operating hazard blinkers and opened the car door. He jumped to the slope again, hopped down to the tree-cave, and poked his head into the opening in the trunk. As he had surmised, the space was vacant. His superior logic hadn't failed him! Roughly four feet in diameter at the base, the trunk was large enough to accommodate him.

"Man-oh-man." He snuggled into the tree-cave. "This is perfect." The minute the wind disappeared he felt warmer. To retain the thirty to fifty percent of his body's heat that was emanating from his head—a fact he always found amazing—he rearranged his stocking cap over his ears, taking care not to enlarge the openings between the woolen strands. As he shifted his weight, he felt himself sitting on something cold and hard. He tried to reposition himself.

Leaning aside, he pulled out a thin, three-by-five inch rectangular piece of metal. "What the hell is this?" He reached into his pocket to pull out his keys. He turned on his key-chain flashlight. Even that was dim.

He shined the flashlight on the metal thing. It was beautiful. It was solid metal, taller than it was wider, and made of what looked like bronze with inlays of copper and silver. At the top were two tiny holes, each a half inch from the outside edge and a quarter inch from the top. On the front, was a beautiful but worn, bas-relief image of a woman, her legs crossed, apparently praying. To the woman's left, rays of light shot out from atop a pole. To the right and behind her was a Buddha, his legs crossed, hands perched on each knee, palms up.

Angular script was cast into the back of the metal thing, nearly filling the entire space. At the bottom, more script was etched into the surface. Jeremy surmised it must be a good luck charm of some sort.

He stroked the smooth metal. With the strange script, the etchings of the woman, the Buddha, the light and pole, and the overall worn look of the thing, he wondered what he might get for it at the Milwaukee museum if it proved to be some misplaced ancient relic.

He puffed on his hands and put his gloves back on. For the next half-hour, he tinkered with the thing and wondered what would happen to him. He glanced out as the snow tapered to a halt. If he were to fall asleep, he hoped his coat would trap his body heat and keep him warm enough to prevent serious frostbite, or worse. He recalled Jack London's "To Build a Fire," which gave him hope that survival was possible, though he lacked the companionship and utility a dog had brought London's hero. He wished he had a dog to kill for its internal warmth, but was glad he had found the tree.

Drowsy, he thought of Rachel and felt a little stupid. Why had he ever strayed from her? She was actually an intriguing woman, full of what seemed to him like contradictions—confident, yet naive; reserved, yet joyous; passionate in anger, yet demure otherwise . . . and absolutely deferential. Most of all, he appreciated her steadfast loyalty. Her submissive qualities turned him on at times, but they also annoyed the hell out of him at others—when they smothered him beyond belief. Admittedly, she had always had good reason to suspect him of infidelity, but he had never doubted her faithfulness, not for a moment.

Now, his winter night plight seemed almost punishment for his night with Lana, another playmate that he hadn't been able to resist, even though nothing had happened tonight. Lana wasn't too bright, but he forgave that. Her social climber attitude—always driven by her embarrassment about the lower class way she was raised—bugged the hell out of him. In fact, if it wasn't for her poor white trash status, she might not be pregnant and he might not be losing her.

Were all women so complicated as the two he had chosen to make part of his life? He felt like a pig for the way he had treated Lana . . . and Rachel. If he died tonight, what kind of legacy would he leave? How would each of his women remember him? *Rachel would probably never marry again,* he mused. *She'd undoubtedly die of loneliness. Lana would no doubt find another benefactor, though not as caring as me.*

Shit. So, in either case, my effect on the human race will be exactly zero.

"Man. I should've listened to Rach, and had kids. Naw, they're just little pains in the asses." Jeremy chattered and snuggled into the gnarls of the tree's inner trunk. He prayed—something he hadn't done in ages—that someone would pass by, see his fading hazard lights, and call the police. He realized that if he listened hard enough, he could actually hear the snow-laden woods whispering all around—the high-pitched hiss was as constant as his breath, yet as solitary as his thoughts. It was the same winter world that had existed in every one of his thirty-five years, but he hadn't ever really noticed its wonder.

He drifted off over and over, but jerked awake each time. He closed his eyes, then forced them to stay open until it was more comfortable to let them fall shut.

The darkness shifted from black to sky blue. Jeremy felt himself becoming lighter. Soon the hushed sounds of the woods faded into sleep.

"Jeremy, let's go. The coast is clear." Ken Nordberg echoed like he was speaking in a cave as he led the way out of the VW van, through the darkness and into Sterling Hall, the building at school that housed the MRC, the Department of Defense's Math Research Center. Frank Monda pulled the other van, a white Ford *Econoline*, into position, according to their plan: off the street, up a ramp, close to the front door. The vehicle was packed with ammonium nitrate fertilizer, blasting caps and fuel oil—a massive explosion waiting to happen. All four intruders wore black. Even their faces were smudged—real commandos.

This operation would make up for the embarrassment of dropping that dud bomb. It would re-instill the reputation the gang had begun to garner. Jeremy had been the one who suggested taking out the MRC, the most blatant symbol of the establishment on campus, with a powerful ammonium nitrate bomb. It was a daring plan, but eventually the other guys agreed.

The commandos looked around, ran in the front door of Sterling Hall, and, after climbing a half flight of stairs, silently and swiftly checked each of the classrooms on the first floor.

"Jeremy," Frank whispered. "All clear here."

"Right," Jeremy nodded back. "Let's head upstairs. You sure checking like this matters?"

"Ken insisted." Frank shrugged and pointed back at Ken Nordberg. "He is taking the role of leader, after all."

"I guess," Jeremy said, and shook his head. "Then, let's hurry."

Now Jeremy led the way. They rumbled up to the second floor. Jeremy looked back. Besides Frank and Ken, Ken's brother, Harold was also involved. Larger than Ken, Harold had been assigned the honor of lighting the fuse that would ignite the fuel oil to trigger the blasting caps that ignited the fertilizer—ultimately and permanently scarring Sterling Hall and destroying a large chunk of the MRC.

Jeremy pointed left, then right—a question to Frank.

"Go right," whispered Frank. "Meet you at the end of the hall." They ran harder now, looking, searching, looking, searching. The faster they moved, and the more they sweated, the more it seemed as if they were actually running in slow motion—intruders floating through the dark.

"This is stupid," Jeremy mumbled. "We're wasting time. There's nobody here."

They had agreed, or Ken had insisted, that they search the building before they blew it up in order to spare innocent lives. It was the least they could do, Ken had said. He had endorsed this violent act to shake the very foundation of the pro war UW administration; not to purposefully murder blameless civilians. They met at the end of the hall and streamed into room #240.

"All clear?" Jeremy asked, scouring the lab.

"Clear," Frank said as he ran in panting. "Let's do this thing!"

"Wait!" Jeremy squinted.

A high-pitched noise. They all looked up. Whistling was coming from down the hall.

"Shhh," Ken whispered. "What's that?"

They all froze, listening to the approaching whistle getting louder and louder.

"It's somebody," Harold whispered. "And not one of us."

"No kidding," the others giggled.

"Shh. Stay still," Jeremy said, and gestured in the near dark.

The whistle got louder.

"Shit," Frank said.

"Don't move," Jeremy whispered. "Ken, get by the door."

"What if it's the watchman?" Ken slinked to the door.

"He only comes at twelve and two," said Harold. It's past four."

Suddenly, the whistling stopped. Clanging began. Then talking.

"Wait. He's talking to himself," Jeremy whispered as he raised his index finger.

Then the voice burst into the room, the lights flashed on.

"Ken! Get him!" Jeremy said.

Ken was larger than the man, who was in his forties and wearing work clothes. Ken threw his arms around the man and clung tight.

"Hey, what is this?!" the man shouted. His dark red hair flew across his face as he tried to wrestle himself free.

"Dan, you got that rope?" Jeremy said. "Tie his hands."

"Harold, grab that cloth." Jeremy pointed to the lab table.

"Hey, what's goin' on?" the workman shouted.

Jeremy grabbed the cloth from Harold; he ripped a handkerchief-sized piece off and crammed it into the man's mouth.

"Uh!" The man struggled as Ken pushed him to the floor.

"It's the damn janitor. Nobody told us about a janitor," Jeremy said. "Damn Charlie. He was supposed to check this stuff out."

"Wait, you guys," Ken said, "We aren't gonna do the janitor, are we? We're just above the van here. We'd blow him sky high."

"Uh." The janitor mumbled and squirmed with wide eyes gesturing down to his pants.

Ken said, "He wants us to look in his wallet."

"All right. Pull it out," Jeremy said, looking at his watch. "Just hurry."

Ken pulled the wallet from the janitor's pocket. "There's no money in here."

The janitor shook his head, then mumbled again.

Jeremy urged, "All right, thumb through it, Ken. But hurry!"

Ken thumbed through the billfold and tossed various papers, a driver's license, and receipts on the floor. "God, this guy's incredibly organized."

"Just hurry," Frank said.

"Look, he's got two kids," Ken said. He held up a snapshot. "See, this one's just a baby."

The janitor nodded excitedly and mumbled. Ken walked over and pulled the rag out of his mouth. Tears dripped down the janitor's face, "Please don't do this. I want to be there for them . . . and he's my first son."

"Sorry, Timothy Agers," Jeremy butted in, reading the name badge on the janitor's shirt. "You're just part of the equation. The pigs pay your salary, don't they?"

Timothy Agers hung his head.

"Well, Tim?" Jeremy said.

"But Jer—" Ken said. "They're just kids. And the little baby boy? We shouldn't do this."

"Sorry. Timmy roasts."

"Hey, I'm the leader, Jer," Ken growled. "I say 'no'."

"Fuck leader." Jeremy yanked the rag from Ken and stuffed it back in the janitor's mouth. "Hurry. Harold, tie him to that pipe. *Do* it!"

"Harold—" Ken said.

Harold hesitated, then looked up at Jeremy.

"I said 'do it', Harold!" Jeremy said. "Ignore your pussy-ass brother."

"But—"

"The janitor's a fucking pig, guys. They're all pigs," Jeremy whisper-shouted. "He was in the wrong place at the wrong time. Now, let's get out of here!"

The janitor mumbled a protest as Harold tied him securely to a pipe. Agers' eyes flared; his pasty-white face glowed in the sparse light as tears dripped from his eyes.

"Sorry, Tim," Jeremy said to him. "Like I said, you're part of the equation."

"Let's get out of here," Frank said as he rushed toward the door.

They went back the way they came, this time running as fast as they could. They ran down the hall and into the stairwell, jumped every third step down the stairs, and flung open the door to the outside.

"Where's Ken?" Jeremy looked back.

"He stopped at the pay phone," Harold said. Just then, Ken came springing out of the building.

"What the fuck did you do, Ken?" Jeremy asked.

"Just called the Police. Warned the pigs they should clear the building."

"You pussy!" Jeremy shouted. "We just did that!"

"But, what if we missed somebody?" Ken pointed out. "Maybe they'll free the janitor."

"It'll be too late for that anyway." Jeremy yelled. "Harold, it's your turn to be a man! Go do your thing."

They ran to the white Ford van. Harold jumped in for a second, then sprang back out. "Let's get out of here before this thing blows!"

They ran over to the VW van, jumped in, and squealed away. They turned the first corner on two wheels when—

Blam!

The explosion echoed up and down the street so loudly it shook the van. The sound must have reverberated for miles.

Just then, bits of rubble banged onto the van's roof.

"Man-oh-man!" Jeremy yelled. "All the way over here!"

"Shit!" Harold hooted as he swerved the van around the next corner. "Hey, you guys, wipe that shit off your faces. There's a rag back there."

Ken was silent as he started wiping off the soot. "Jer, we didn't have to do that," he said.

"Shut up, pussy!" Jeremy hissed. "Give me that rag when you're done."

Ken handed Jeremy the towel.

Suddenly, a police car appeared behind them, red and blue lights flashing. Its siren blared as it approached rapidly.

"Shit!" Jeremy shouted. "What the fuck now?"

The police car pulled the van over. The officer got out and walked up from behind.

"You guys hurry and clean up," Jeremy pointed at the others.

"Shit. What're we gonna say?" Frank mumbled as he wiped his face clean.

"Let me handle it," Jeremy said.

Frank stashed the towel just in time.

The officer walked up to Harold's driver side window. "So, where's the fire, son?"

"We just gotta get back to the dorm, officer," Jeremy said, leaning from the passenger side, across the front seat.

"Sure you do," the officer said suspiciously. "Say, you guys hear that explosion?"

"Yeah," Jeremy answered. "Sounded like a huge gas explosion or something. On campus, too." He pointed his index finger skyward. "Better check it out, officer. Maybe you'll be the first on the scene." He winked.

"Any of you make a call to the station a minute ago?" the officer asked.

"No, sir," all but Ken said in unison. He sat in silence, shaking his head.

"So, you weren't over that way? By Sterling?" the Officer asked and pointed.

"Oh, no sir," Jeremy said and saluted. "Came from the other direction."

"You boys haven't been doing any drugs, have you?"

"Oh, no way, sir," Jeremy retorted. "That's hippy shit."

"Your hair is as long as any hippy I seen around town." The officer cocked his head curiously. "Why all the black clothes?"

"We were at a party tonight; just keeping up with the fashion, sir," Jeremy said.

"Right." The officer snickered, then leaned into Harold's window, sniffed and pulled back. "Well, I guess you fellas can move on, then. But, you're heading straight back to your dorm, right?" He pointed.

"Oh, yes, sir," Jeremy said. "We're tired. Need some sleep."

The officer waved them on, then walked back to his patrol car.

"Shit," Frank said, "that was close! Nice job, Jer!"

"Shut up, asshole," fired Jeremy. "He'll hear you."

"Jer, this isn't good," said Ken, shaking his head. "I swear, this isn't right. That janitor—-"

"You chicken shit," sneered Jeremy. "You could've gotten us busted with your goddamned phone call. You gotta do what you gotta do. Don't you get it, Ken?" Just then, the cop glanced at them as he climbed into his squad car. Jeremy felt the cop's eyes boring into him. "Shit! He's on to us."

"Maybe we should go park up by Devil's Lake tonight—you know, lay low," Harold said. "Baraboo is pretty close."

"You guys do what you want," Jeremy shrugged. "Harold, drop me at Rachel's."

"Rachel Martin's?" Harold asked. "I thought you were coolin' it with her. Something about her girlfriend."

"You know Rach," Jeremy said. "She's forever obsessed with me. "Besides, I could use her snuggling tonight. She could give me the perfect alibi, too!"

"So, you don't wanna go to Devil's Lake with us?" Harold wanted to know. "They'll never find us there."

"Jeremy, doing the janitor wasn't right," Ken said. "We could've avoided it."

"Ken," Jeremy began, "after that dud bullshit we needed to show 'em the Easter Gang's got some real balls!"

"I guess." Ken hung his head.

Minutes later, the van pulled up to an old building on Mifflin Street. Jeremy jumped out. "See you assholes."

"Jer, call me tomorrow," Ken said.

"Right." Jeremy ran up to the front door and banged on it. In a minute, lights flicked on and the door swung open.

"Jer!" A pretty young woman with ivory skin and short, raven hair threw her arms around him. "I thought it was over with us, baby. Because of Ginny. But you came back."

"It's never over with us, Hons."

He hugged her ceremoniously, then pulled away. "Wait, Rach. I gotta use your phone."

The van drove away. "Where're your mates going?" she asked.

"I don't know," said Jeremy. "Somewhere."

Jeremy walked into the old dining room, picked up the receiver, pulled open the phone book, and dialed the Madison police.

"Police," a voice said.

"I know where you can find the guys who blew up Sterling."

"Where's that? Who's this?"

"Devil's Lake. A VW van," Jeremy said, fiddling with the phone cord.

"Wait. Who is this?"

"You never got this call."

He hung up the phone.

Rachel walked up. "Jer, honey, your hair looks such a mess and your face is dirty." She ran a finger across his cheek. "What happened? What was that boom? Something you guys did?"

"Better you not know," Jeremy said softly. "As far as you're concerned, I was here all night, okay?" He flicked Rachel on the nose with his index finger. "Cutie."

She cocked her head forward in a barely noticeable bow. "Sure. Anything you say, Jer. Now, let's get you out of those clothes."

Jeremy shivered as he tossed back and forth against the roughness of the tree-cave's knotty wall. Over and over he recalled the janitor's pasty-white face, big jaw, and pleading tears. Then, he screamed so loud he woke up, and the numbing cold returned.

Fond du Lac, Wisconsin

Miles to the north, Rachel Lucas lay naked on her back in bed, fresh from her shower, occasionally stroking her soft, fresh-bathed chest with the backs of her modest fingernails. The light was faint, and the temperature indoors too high for a good sleep. The sparkling snow shower fluttered against the window and accumulated at the bottom of each sill, lit by the porch light next to the kitchen door.

She reached over and felt the empty sheet next to her—Jeremy's spot. It was twelve-thirty. He wouldn't be home for at least an hour.

Rachel thought about Paul. She enjoyed having such a nice serviceman for all their plumbing and other handyman chores. He charged a fair price and told the funniest jokes, too. He said those jokes used to make his Claire—who had died of breast cancer four years earlier—laugh until she couldn't make any noise, just hold her stomach and open her mouth, trying to catch a breath.

For a slightly older man (Rachel guessed in his late forties or early fifties) he was incredibly vital . . . and treated her so normally compared to Jeremy. Like she was a real person. He respected her; that was the difference.

Now a self-taught plumber and forever the frustrated gourmet cook, Paul was elected last year to the board of the Fond du Lac Loyal Order of the Moose. In a year, he had single-handedly refurbished the lodge, transforming it into the premier service organization in town, and he was even asked to take the coveted first position in last year's Veteran's Day Parade.

Paul had convinced his brothers at the Lodge to head up a $20,000 charity drive to build a heliport at Waupun Memorial Hospital: the new home base for Winnebago County's only Lifecopter, which was already responsible for saving the lives of two small children after they nearly drowned in the lake last summer.

Rachel wondered. Maybe Paul—so compassionate and easygoing—was, in fact, more her type than Jeremy. Jeremy wanted to control everything, even if he didn't care much about it—he simply needed to dominate it, to control it—at home, at work, with their families—whatever. Maybe that was why he was so successful in business—at least that was what he always contended.

Paul didn't have that need to control the world around him at all. Instead, he cared about everything in a gentle sort of way. *Care versus control*, Rachel thought. Like a grandfather, Paul loved the little neighborhood kids and affectionately chided the teens when they hooted at him as they rode past his house. He'd call out, "You're all grown up now. Why don't you go get a haircut and a job?"

He attended and helped at every pancake breakfast, no matter what the sponsoring organization, and he offered a safe haven for any confused youth who just needed to talk to an adult with an objective ear. Throughout Fond du Lac, Paul had earned a reputation as a man of wisdom and compassion.

Rachel leaned over to take her can of Diet Sprite from the nightstand. She took one last sip and thought back over her years with Jeremy. She realized that for only a few years, at the beginning of their marriage, had the relationship been joyous; then his control was fun. This extension of the college years made Rachel feel safe. And, she trusted him implicitly.

But, after Jeremy became Marketing Manager, everything changed. He was often gone at night for dinners or meetings. Then, when he made VP, on Wednesdays, the regular client dinners began. Finally, when she pointed out that "her clock was ticking," Jeremy decreed that kids weren't in the picture for them because their presence would undoubtedly "crimp his executive style." All those client dinners would take him away from his children, so what kind of father could he be? So, while Rachel had relished Jeremy becoming the success her father never was, she felt she had experienced the costs associated with that success.

Now Jer's inheritance be damned! It had been so important to her years before—her ticket to a normal American life. The inevitability of having a chunk of six million dollars seemed as though it had stopped her from living a normal life. She had been so attracted to the money that she had also bought into Jeremy's treatment of her and her own willing compliance. *Was it worth it?*

In fact, when she was brutally honest with herself, Rachel realized she actually felt incredibly lonely, and not just when Jeremy was gone. She felt lonely when he was around, too—a sort of futility, as if she were standing at the corner waiting for the Fond du Lac bus to arrive to whisk her away, but knowing in her heart that it would never show up. Had she been waiting for something that would never arrive?

She wondered at times if she had made the right decision to marry Jer, and the year before began seeing Dr. Hart to sort out her feelings. Maybe she had been too quick to respond to her mother's pressure. Mum hadn't been so blessed with Daddy, so she had told Rachel endlessly that Jer was the right choice for her. After all, he was a steady company man with a fortune behind him! "You can't beat that!" she always said.

Maybe, Rachel thought, being absolutely honest, she had supplied Jer with the alibi on the night of the bombing in order to land him as her husband—perhaps that tact had been bolstered by her fear that if she hadn't, Jer would've ended up in prison and she'd be a poor old maid from Australia.

Listening to her mother had probably helped Rachel set her course more than she'd ever admit. After all, Mum convinced her that she shouldn't marry someone like her father, an off again-on again pro bowler from Perth, forever looking forward to a big tournament win, a sterling season, a three hundred game. But, instead of living amidst trophies from her dad's career, Rachel had grown up watching her mum dust a mostly empty shelf in the shabbily paneled knotty-pine den.

She shook her head, remembering how her father had moved the family stateside to supposedly find the land of milk and honey, only to settle on Las Vegas as his favorite family vacation destination.

On the family's arrival night in Vegas one year, while Rachel and her mum were snoozing, Harry gambled away all of their vacation money playing blackjack, undoubtedly clamping his cigar between his teeth and smoking it down to a stub, as he pursued his dreams.

The following morning, as they left, her unshaven dad proclaimed, "Next time . . . " and her mum looked out the window at streams of people. Maybe Mum thought she was protecting Rachel from that kind of pain when she encouraged her daughter to marry Jeremy.

Now, after ten years of marriage, Rachel wondered if she might have been happier marrying a lovable, dependable sort like Paul. At least he'd be home every night, even if he never rolled a three hundred game, successfully introduced a toy product in his life, or became a Vegas high roller. Paul would even share in the cooking . . . and enjoy it!

And there'd be kids. But instead, Rachel was living Jeremy's idea of a life, and catered to him endlessly like he was her king. She had gotten so used to that behavior, it felt normal now. Actually, being herself, like Jan always suggested, felt like a foreign concept.

As soon as Rachel let those marital doubts surface, she rolled over in bed and pulled the sheets tight around her shoulders. She wiped away a tear as she imagined herself a young bride seconds before her wedding ceremony, pushing away thoughts of the first love she didn't marry, and what that alternative future might have brought her. Rachel thought about Paul again, and peered into the dark.

4

Kettle Moraine National Forest, southern Wisconsin

Jeremy woke with a start. *Is that the sound of machines?* No, it was cars, male voices, machines. The morning light flickered through the opening in the cave-tree.

In a hoarse voice he called out, "Here! I'm here!" He felt like he had been asleep for a hundred hours and speechless for a year. "Brrr." The vapor from his breath floated onto the brightness of the morning.

"It sounded like it came from over there," a voice called through a bullhorn.

Jeremy looked out of his tree-cave. Up the hill he saw a rainbow of blinking lights from three squad cars, a tow truck, and an ambulance. Workmen attached cables as they climbed around his car. The car leaned askew on the ledge, pointing skyward, resting six feet lower than the level of the road.

"I'm here!" Jeremy cried.

"Dumpy-dum, Dumpy-doo," a policeman sang, then spied Jeremy in the tree. "Here he is!" he said. "Hey, you okay, son?" The man wore a trooper's hat and a khaki uniform shirt mostly covered by a puffy black jacket. He spouted steam as he hopped sideways down the slope, kicking snow.

"I think I'm okay," Jeremy called gruffly. At that moment he tried wiggling his toes. "I feel pretty frozen, though."

"Lord. What the hell happened?" the officer asked. "That car yours?"

Jeremy pointed. "It slid backwards down to that ledge. Pretty spooky. Man, am I numb."

"I get it," the deputy said.

"A branch busted through the car window when I landed on the ledge. So I came down here to get away from the wind."

"Oh, uh-huh," the officer said as he rubbed his chin.

"Damn car phone was useless in these woods."

"Yah," the officer said. "Not a bad idea, gettin' in that tree like some old bear, I s'pose. Oh, by the way, Frank Chambers here."

"I'm Jeremy Lucas. Officer Chambers, I sure am glad you found me." Jeremy slowly stood and stretched.

"Feeling okay, Mr. Lucas? Got all your fingers and toes?"

"Barely. Maybe some frostbite." Jeremy took off his gloves, and wiggled his fingers. "I can hardly feel 'em."

"Still, you must be some kinda Boy Scout, I guess," Chambers said. "You might have some hypothermia, losing all that heat."

"I did some winter camping a long time ago. But, it was a lot warmer than this."

"How long you figure you was out here?" Chambers' bushy eyebrows bounced. He looked at his watch.

Jeremy drew in a deep breath. "Going on seven hours, I guess."

"Wow. Good thing old Nate saw your car. He's the one that gave us a call. Thank the Lord, huh?"

"No kidding. Real service." Jeremy pointed to his car being towed up onto the road with multiple cinches. "Looks a mess." Jeremy steadied himself, and he and Chambers climbed a few steps up the slope.

"Oh, that there's Bob Menard," the officer said. "Nice fella. He'll charge you fifty bucks or so to get 'er up on the road; see if she'll drive. That okay?"

"You kidding? That's a steal." Jeremy held up his index finger and turned back to the tree. "One minute."

"He also can recharge the battery if she's worn down."

"That'd be great."

Jeremy leaned over next to the tree-cave and looked around for the metal charm. It lay in the snow at the base of the tree, flakes almost covering its shiny metal. He reached down, picked it up, and dusted off the white powder.

"What's that?" Officer Chambers asked. "Weird looking gizmo."

"Something I found last night." Jeremy held it up. "Look familiar?"

"Probably some junk a teenager left behind," Chambers shrugged. "Looks like that ritualistic hocus pocus they play with nowadays—dungeons and crystals. Maybe good luck. Oughta take it."

"Yeah. I hope it's not *bad* luck." Jeremy laughed as he stuffed the metal thing in his coat pocket, patted it, and stiffly climbed up the hill. "I'll keep it as a memento."

"Yah, you sure were lucky, I guess. Say, gotcha some hot coffee up here."

"Sounds great. Thanks."

"Don't guess you'll be needing the paramedics," Officer Chambers said.

"No."

"Better ask 'em on the frostbite, hypothermia, though. Have 'em get you a blanket."

"Right."

Minutes later, battery charged, Jeremy drove away in his crippled car. He realized Rachel was probably scared to death. He dialed home once, but, still being in the Moraine, he couldn't get a good signal. *I'll just drive home and take her crap once I get there.*

Fond du Lac, Wisconsin

A half hour later, Jeremy rolled up the snow-covered gravel of his driveway. His white, three-bedroom bungalow sat there among the Spruces. The house was charming, but needed new paint. Along the driveway, a couple of horizontal fence planks hung from their uprights and leaned on the ground, waiting for repair. Jeremy parked and dodged ice patches on his way to the front door. He grabbed the cold, aluminum handle.

The suction from the inner door popped as it flew open. "Jeremy! Oh, thank God!" Rachel cried. "Where have you been?"

"I'm okay," Jeremy huffed. "I blew off my client and went over to Sheboygan with some of the guys—Lance and them—late yesterday. I cut through the Moraine on my way back, got caught in that storm, and slid off the road."

"Oh, Hons." She knelt before him and carefully brushed the snow off his pants. "What about calling? I was so worried."

"Phone wouldn't work in the damned woods."

She stood up, grabbed his head, and kissed him all over his face.

"Rach, cool it. I need a little space right now."

"But how did you stay warm?"

"I slept in the trunk of an old tree."

"I've been petrified all morning, calling all the police departments . . . " Rachel knelt again and tugged on Jeremy's pants legs, wiping off the remaining snow.

"Easy does it, Hons," said Jeremy. "You'll probably get an all-clear call any second. They found me a couple of hours ago. Nice guys."

"I even called Mum and Daddy and . . . "

"Listen, could you run a warm bath for me?"

"Oh, Jeremy." Rachel hugged him hard. "I was so scared. Hot bath comin' right up."

"I said warm. That's what the paramedics said."

"Of course, of course, how stupid of me. Warm."

"I had my dream again," Jeremy said. "Even while I was freezing in that tree trunk. Can you believe it?"

"Oh, Babe," Rachel said. "My poor baby."

"Just start that bath," he commanded. "And not hot. Just warm."

"Sure, sure, I will. Anything you want." She pulled away, her eyes wincing concern.

"What is it, Rach?" he asked.

"Ooo. I'm just thanking God that you're okay," she said. She squeezed his numb cheeks and kissed him wet on the lips.

He lightly pushed her away. "The bath?"

"I'm going." She bowed her head as she turned and walked upstairs.

Jeremy wiped his mouth. He fancied for a moment that his storybook rescue had something to do with the metal pendant he had found. *Maybe it really is a good luck charm!* he thought. *Could it be?* After all, it looked like an old mystical sort of thing. He pulled the cold metal rectangle from his pocket and tossed it back and forth, hand-to-hand.

"Damn thing already brought me good luck."

A half hour later, Jeremy sat in his bath water, still fondling the metal thing. His extremities tingled, then burned, as they came alive. He hadn't realized how numb he still was. He splashed the lukewarm water onto his face.

Rachel walked in the bathroom. "Better, Hons? What's that stain?"

"What stain?"

"In your suit," she said.

"Just Coke. It'll come out."

"Not so sure." She swirled the water, testing the bath temperature. "Is the temperature okay?"

"Perfect," Jeremy said. "I screamed at the normal time in the dream, too. Woke me the fuck up. Damn near jumped out of my pants. I saw Agers' big, square face crying at me and begging, and his dark red hair. Jeremy shook his head. "Mumbling about his kids like he always does—especially his son."

"Oh, Jeremy," Rachel cooed. "Won't the dreams ever stop? Why don't you go to a counselor? Dr. Hart'll see you."

"I don't know, maybe when the rest of the guys are out of prison—that is, if they don't kill me for turning them in. Or, I could always go to my grave with Timothy Agers' red hair and sniffly voice haunting me."

"Paul says that Mark Agers is speaking on campus these days with his mom," said Rachel. "He's only fifteen, but quite a good presenter. It's been fifteen years."

"How does Paul know all that? He does the kid's plumbing?" Jeremy splashed warm water on his legs.

"No, silly," she said. "Paul's son Tommy is over at Madison, remember? Paul said Tom's taking two majors . . . and Mark was speaking to a crowd across from the library."

"Listen, can we drop the Madison stuff now, Rach? I might go shoot myself like my old man. So, give me a break."

"Jeremy!" Rachel raised her index finger to her lips.

"Well," Jeremy sniffed, "between this bullshit trivia and the dreams and almost dying out there, I just might. Thinking about the inheritance helped give me strength."

Rachel frowned. "Didn't you think about me?"

"I always think about you, Rach. In so many ways."

She smiled and picked some of the ice out of his hair.

"Wait till Mom kicks the bucket and I get part of her loot; then I'll buy a goddamned helicopter—skip this woods drive! That's unless Mom spends it all before she dies." He sneezed.

"Bless you, Jer," Rachel said, and started toward the door.

"Rach," he said, "Stay right here. After last night, I could use some company. Just don't hang all over me, okay?"

"Well, okay. What's that metal thing?" Rachel asked and sat back down.

"I found it in the tree."

"The car looked real bad," she said.

"Yeah. Got me home, but it looks like shit—two grand worth of bodywork—easy. After a while, it got so cold in the damned car I cuddled up in that tree, where I found this thing."

"It couldn't be that valuable then. In a tree?"

"I suppose. Say, Rach, you got a towel for my hair? First time I've ever had frozen hair."

"Sure, so this thing happened in the Moraine?" She handed him the towel.

"Yeah, I cut through the camping part; that was my mistake."

"Isn't that out of the way from Sheboygan?"

"Just a shortcut I've found," he said.

"Why Sheboygan?"

"Chuck Roberts' anniversary. Lance came up, so it was almost the whole

Central Region." Jeremy held up the dripping wet metal charm. "This is a pretty nice looking thing. I could clean it up a little, maybe spray paint it so it won't rust."

"Jeremy, you have no taste!" Rachel cried. "Keep it metal. Paint would hide the shine, and the differences in all those metals. Maybe you should just wipe it off, or polish it with some wax. It'd be a perfect paperweight for the bills in your office at home. Or you can wear it around your neck; it doesn't look that heavy. Just put a chain or some string through those holes. Betcha that's why they're there."

"It looks like a good luck charm, doesn't it?" Jeremy asked. "That's what the cop thought."

"Really. Looks like it came from outer space or the Orient or some exotic place. May I have it, please?"

"The cops thought some kids left it," said Jeremy, "you know, while they were hanging out."

"I guess." Rachel walked out of the bathroom, twiddling the medallion, and called back, "I'll figure out something to do with it. I like your office. Or maybe the necklace thing. What do they call these? Amulets?"

"Yeah, protect you from evil spirits." Jeremy sneezed. "That cop was right, probably some kids . . . "

"Bless you," Rachel said. "Jer, that's one nasty cold. Maybe you ought to stay home tomorrow. It's Friday anyway."

"No can do. Have to wait till Saturday to sleep it off." He slumped in the tub and swished the warm water over his lean body.

"Oh, by the way, Mom and Dad want us to come over Sunday. Their anniversary."

"Do we have to?" Jeremy whined. He didn't relish whiffing Harry Martin's cigar smoke and listening to his off-color jokes all afternoon. Jeremy couldn't see how his sweet mother-in-law, Margaret, had put up with Harry over the years.

"Jeremy, you never want to go any place," Rachel called.

"Well, I have this financial planning seminar all day Monday, so I have to go in tomorrow, do my mail, and let Bob know I'm alive. Then, I'll rest over the weekend. That okay after my little ordeal?" he asked sarcastically.

"It's just like we're hermits or something," she said. "That is, except for your client dinners. They're regular enough."

"Wrong, old wise one," Jeremy said, and opened the drain in the tub. The water gurgled as it emptied. "I'll be cutting back on them now. At least, for a while."

5

Fond du Lac, Wisconsin

Friday morning, Rachel drove into Dr. Janell Hart's driveway for an early session. She had been seeing the famous psychologist to resolve the futile feeling she had about Jeremy and his dominance issues, her absolute submissiveness to him—a dynamic born in their college years, and its resultant effects on their marriage a decade later. Were her misgivings more commonplace than she might expect? Were they issues that slip into any relationship after a decade or cling to a relationship after the courtship years? Rachel had so many questions, she ruminated constantly over their answers.

Rachel sat on the couch across from Dr. Hart, seated in an old armchair.

"Rachel, you look exasperated again."

"I just don't know what I should expect out of the marriage."

"We've talked about this before," said the doctor. "The love in a mature marriage is not the same as the romantic falling in love fervor that you have at the beginning. It's certainly not the same as the fantasies we act out in college."

"Then, what else is there, Jan?" Rachel asked. "You know, what makes it go? We don't have kids, so what's the engine?"

Dr. Hart raised a hand. "Like I said before, the marriage becomes all about trust, respect, honesty, and companionship—all wonderful things you discover as you mature. At the same time, as you grow older, love becomes an act of will. It is not an act of submissiveness, catering to his every whim, becoming his object, becoming the total woman."

"Wait. You said act of will?"

"In a way you have to *want* to love him," Dr. Hart said, "so you *decide* that you do—it can become new all over again, just in a different way. You adopt a state of mind. Whatever he says or does, it's all right—unconditional. You love him that much. You forgive him for his humanness."

"But Jeremy is already the center of my world."

"Sorry, that's not the idea, Rachel," Dr. Hart said. "Your submission to Jeremy may make him the center of your life, but it is based on a your *need* to have him there, not your *choice*. That's where the will comes in. It's unconditional love

I'm talking about here. Instead, your brand of love actually pushes him away."

Rachel laughed, surprised. "Oh sure! How could that be?"

"By needing him so completely, your catering behavior smothers him. That's why he always has an eye out for other women. For room to breathe."

"That's just my Jeremy, always the flirt."

"Oh, I beg to differ, Rachel," Dr. Hart said. "That's a Jeremy *you* helped create."

Rachel hung her head and twisted her ring around her finger. "I don't know if I buy that—an act of will? Unconditional? Smother? To be honest, I'm the one who feels trapped by the choices I made back in school. So, from my viewpoint, my love for Jeremy is unconditional, but his love for me is loaded with conditions: what I do; how I dress; how I talk; how I act. It's always been that way. From the time he first whispered to me in a movie theater at college to not move an inch while he touched me all over, even if people were close by."

"Rachel," the doctor said, "don't you see, that's a model for total submission that he's continued to this day. He needs it and you need it; that's virtually the only thing that holds you two together."

"But I love having him be the center of my life. Don't *you* see, I totally trust that he'll do what's right for me."

"Except that if you smother him with your unconditional love, he'll scurry to someone else. Don't you say you have inklings of that all the time? His Wednesday dinners?"

"I guess you're right," Rachel said.

"Rachel, you just can't put yourself in the position of having to *earn* his love by being the perfect woman."

Rachel laughed. "Jan, that's easy enough for you to say. You have beautiful hair, a lovely figure, and killer legs. I hope you don't mind me saying that."

"No problem. What a nice compliment."

"But I have to work at it constantly to please Jeremy," Rachel said. "Or else he's disappointed in me in some other way."

"You may see it that way, but let me ask you: Can you imagine a life where you *decide* what to do instead of automatically conforming to Jeremy's wishes?"

"Hmmm." Rachel paused in thought and looked down. "Funny you asked that, Jan. Recently I've wondered about that—if I was absolutely free to make my own decisions. I can hardly imagine that."

Dr. Hart shook her head. “If you can’t imagine willing your love to Jeremy, you may need to will yourself more in a direction of free choice . . . for your own good.”

“How would I do that?”

The same day, across town, Fon du Lac, Wisconsin

Jeremy’s tires crunched the compressed patches of snow between rows of vehicles that filled the parking lot surrounding the one-story office and plant building. He parked in his assigned space near the front door. He stepped around a few slippery piles as he walked to the entrance of the Archer Toy Company. He pulled the front door toward him, stamped his feet on the mat in the airlock, and grinned as he opened the interior door.

“Morning, Betsy, you look absolutely astonishing,” he hailed the receptionist. Betsy had been at Archer most of her adult life and was now entering her seventh decade on this earth.

“Oh, Mr. Lucas, good morning yourself,” she said and straightened her silver wig. “You’re so sweet. Feeling any better since your accident? How dreadful."

"Yes, thanks, Bets," Jeremy replied. "Bob in?"

"Just got in. If you ask me, he's looking a little peaked. See what you think. He wants to see you."

"Right." Jeremy mirrored Betsy's concerned wince. He walked down a short hall, then turned left to enter the marketing and sales area. The bullpen was filled with beige-colored desks occupied by people he only glanced at.

But his assistant wasn't about to be ignored. "Morning, Jer," Lana called as he approached. "Heard you had a great time the other night," she said sarcastically. "What was that? Winter payback?"

Jeremy snickered. He flexed his right arm. "You know me, Lana. I can survive anything. Even the cold. Even you."

"Ha-ha, you asshole," she whispered. "Oh, Bob wants you. Maybe he wants to fire you. Ha, ha."

"In your dreams. Betsy gave me the heads-up." Jeremy leaned over and spoke to Lana in a low tone. "Speaking of head, her wig looks particularly gruesome today, doesn't it?"

Lana didn't smile. "Not funny, Jer," she said and looked away.

"Humph?" Jeremy hung up his coat behind his office door.

"By the way, Jer," she said, "I need to talk to you, too."

"I bet." *That figures*, he thought. *Now Lana's going to put on the full-court press and make my life miserable.*

He walked across the bullpen area, dodging desks, and saying 'morning' to his staff like a flight attendant.

Jeremy passed Mary Coltrain, whose desk, on the other side of the bullpen, conspicuously guarded Bob Townsend's office.

"Morning, Mary," he said.

"Good morning, Mr. Lucas." Mary called everyone Mister or Ms., even the janitorial and service crews.

Jeremy walked around Mary and knocked on Bob's doorjamb.

"Entrée, Jeremy," Bob Townsend said in a resonant voice, receiving Jeremy with his standard greeting—like he imagined his office was some kind of castle. "So Jer, I hear we almost lost you out there in the woods."

"You need me too bad, Bob," Jeremy joshed. "I couldn't go and die out there." He walked in, saluting. "What can I do for you today?"

"Sit, sit," Bob said. He sipped from his cup with the gold leaf border and stretched his compact frame, then spoke as he yawned. "Hadley wants me to interview a candidate for him: future marketing manager."

"Oh? Marketing? Why wasn't I asked if I needed a marketing manager?"

"Sort of a favor thing, is all. She's the daughter of Hadley's old school chum, Horace Dunne. You've heard of him? CEO of International Data."

"IDS? The old man knows him?" Jeremy asked. "What's her background?"

"University of Chicago. Smith undergrad. Take a look at her?"

"Sure, sounds like a heavyweight. When?"

"Monday at two?" Townsend adjusted his stiffly starched shirt, breathed on his cufflinks, and shined them.

"Oh, great," Jeremy said. "Is Monday the only day?"

"Problem?" Bob Townsend said in a low roar.

"Just that I was planning on going to that Kettering financial planning seminar all day Monday. It's an off-site in Milwaukee."

"It'd be a tremendous favor for the old man." Townsend leaned forward and switched to his *how-low-can-I-talk-and-you'd-better-say-yes* voice. "Jeremy, he'll roast me if we don't give this gal a good look-see."

"But, Bob—"

"It'd be tough for me to say no," Townsend shrugged as tiny pearls of sweat began to bead up on his forehead and temples.

"You okay, Bob?" Jeremy asked.

"Just a little tired. A game today'll do me good. I have our court reserved for noon." He dabbed his brow. "They'll be having this Kettering thing again, won't they?"

"Actually, this is supposed to be the last one—budget cut-back."

Townsend wiped his face with some tissue. "Don't know what this is. A touch of flu? Maybe I can sweat the damn thing out at the club." He looked at his watch. "Say, Jer, don't let me down on this Dunne woman thing. Hadley told me Dunne's trying to straighten out a rift he had with the kid. We wouldn't want to stop progress on that kind of thing, would we?"

Jeremy knew Townsend had a way of persisting until he prevailed—this was an example. "Okay, okay." He turned away and steamed out of the office.

"Jeremy? Come on," Bob called after him. "Let's not get upset, okay?

Remember, we have a game at noon. Meet you over there?"

"Right," Jeremy muttered as he continued walking. This was what things were really like at the Archer Toy Company. His boss was always acting out his more important role as son-in-law of the company's founder.

Rachel didn't have an ounce of appreciation for the bullshit he had to endure just to bring home the paycheck. All she did was complain about him not living up to his wedding vows—perpetually flirting and slouching around, too tired to do anything except grill some ribs on occasion. He weaved across the bullpen into his office and slammed the door.

At a quarter to noon, Jeremy rushed into the club's locker room of endless blue-wire cages where Bob, already suited up, was stretching. "I'm all set for you today, buddy."

"You always say that." Jeremy put on his gym shorts and a ragged T-Shirt. "Let's get this over with."

"See my new racquet?" Bob pointed to an inlaid gold stripe above the racket's handgrip.

"Nice. But what if you break it?"

Bob laughed. “Just get another one.”

Midway into the second game, Jeremy slowed his pace. He had won the first game 21-8 and wanted to make this next one more of a contest. Bob panted, out of breath.

“Think this’ll help that flu bug?” Jeremy joked.

“Oh, yeah,” Bob said, “Just need to sweat it out.”

“I can oblige you there.”

“So, you’ll see that Dunne woman on Monday?” Bob asked.

Jeremy served. “I said I would. Anything for ol’ Hadley.”

“Speaking of Hadley, Mary mentioned your inheritance again the other day? Goin’ okay?”

“Well, I only get it once Mom’s gone, whenever that is, six million will be split between my brother and sister and me. So, it’ll be a nice little nest egg.”

“Just make sure you invest it wisely—make it go a long way. I’ll have the same issues when Hadley passes on.” Bob looked flustered or over-heated or some combination of the two. “And once you become the newest millionaire around here, I wouldn’t want to lose you to a life of leisure.”

Jeremy stopped the game, and held the ball. “No worries about that. I’d hate the thought of sitting around on my ass all day."

"You really make a major contribution to Archer, Jer. Your ideas are golden."

"Then why do we need to interview this hotshot Dunne babe for a marketing spot? I'm doing fine."

"Listen, you know Hadley. He's always talking about us being deep on the bench."

"As long as he doesn't have any personnel replacements in mind," Jeremy said. "He's always thought marketing was a waste. Say, Bob, let's just stop. You're looking pretty tuckered."

Bob served the ball. "Just one more point—winner takes a hundred."

Jeremy dived at the ball and purposely missed. "See, you won this one. Satisfied?"

"Well, look at that. I feel like shit, but I won."

Later, back at the office, Lana Holub walked into Jeremy's office and closed the door. "Well, Jer, what are you gonna do to help me?" she snapped.

"Jesus." He kept writing a memo without looking up.

"Well—" she said. "You *owe* me, Jer."

"Man. Right, I owe you." He tossed down his pen. "I knew you'd start pressuring me. What the hell are you doing? Blackmailing me?"

"I could sue you for sexual harassment, ya know?" she said.

"That a threat?" he asked.

"I just want you, Jeremy," she said, "that's all."

"Lana. Please don't start this. Once and for all, it's not going to happen." Jeremy picked up his pen and signed more papers. "Boy, I about killed Bob at racquetball—literally."

"That's one way to get his job." She snickered, then pouted audibly and mumbled, "I don't know why I keep trying to get you."

"Then, why don't you stop?" he asked.

She walked up to his desk and slammed her hand on it. He looked up.

"Jeremy, I need your help here!"

"Shit," he said. "Like what?" He reached in his pocket.

"Someday you'll cave in." She sniffled. "I'm not ready to be a single mom."

"Oh, Lana, you're just upset," Jeremy said. "Like I said before, do the big A; here's another hundred." He threw two fifties on the edge of the desk.

"Damn! It's not the money. Don't you realize I would do just about anything for you, Jeremy Lucas. You can't buy that kind of devotion."

"Take the money, Lana," he said. "It'll help."

She started talking and crying at the same time, and picked up the money. "Every other guy I've ever dated, we go to a show, they use me, they drop me. I need somebody like you . . . somebody higher level, you know. Now, with the baby, I'll be at the end of my rope. Hell, aren't you even the slightest bit interested?"

"Lana, I don't think my life has room for both you *and* Rachel anymore. It just won't work."

Lana slumped, standing there, her eyes red. "Damn."

Jeremy started signing an approval routing, then looked up. "I guess I have to draw the line. I just can't keep fooling around on Rachel." He tossed his pen down. "You can at least respect me for that."

Jeremy was on his way home when he got a call on his portable phone.

"Mr. Lucas, it's terrible." Mary Coltrain's flustered voice crackled over the little speaker. "It's Mr. Townsend."

"Another emergency? What's so urgent?" Jeremy joked and tried not to sound too put out.

"He had a heart attack," she sobbed.

"My God." Jeremy spoke with his teeth clenched.

"He's gone, Jeremy," she said. She inhaled another sob. "He's gone. What are we going to do?"

For a moment Jeremy celebrated amidst his shock and her sorrow. This would undoubtedly propel him to the presidency.

After dinner, Rachel Lucas called from the kitchen. "Paul's going to have to come back and add a thingamajig to the sink. He says that mixing metals is tricky, but once you get that thingy on, it'll be solid. It's because the house is so old and we're updating."

Jeremy sat with his legs elevated on his cushy black fake-leather recliner, reading *Newsweek*. "I wonder if I'll get it. Mary said I'd get a call tonight, probably from Hadley."

"Bob ate horribly at the parties," Rachel said. "Always into those sour cream dips." Rachel's favorite Katia tape played in the background. "Get what?" she said.

"The presidency, of course." Jeremy flipped a magazine page and looked at his watch. "I wonder if that charm I found was good luck after all."

"Jeremy, that's awful to say," said Rachel. "Let them bury Bob first."

The phone rang.

Jeremy got up and walked to the phone that sat on the knick-knack table outside the kitchen.

"Hello?" he said. "Oh, Carl. Hello . . . I know it's awful. Mary said I'd get a call. Hold on a sec, Carl." He held a hand over the receiver. "Say, Rach! Turn that shit down!" Rachel scurried into the living room, over to the stereo, and turned down the volume.

" . . . Oh?" Jeremy went on. "Oh, I see. . . . No, I understand . . . Congratulations, I guess . . . " Jeremy looked around the room impatiently. "Sure, I promised Bob I'd talk to her Monday. Could be more important than ever." *Wonder why,* he thought. " . . . Yeah, I'll schedule a lunch with each of the DMs to calm things down. Right . . . bye." He put the phone down. *Carl sure sounds presidential*, he thought.

"Fuck!" he shouted and stomped into the kitchen.

"What is it?" Rachel asked.

"*Carl* got it!"

"So what?"

"I thought I'd get it for sure!" Jeremy retorted. "Now that old monster'll really take charge. He's been storing it up for me."

On Sunday morning, Jeremy and Rachel drove to Sheboygan, an hour or so east. Sheboygan was a well-established, rather shabby, primarily blue-collar town. They pulled up to a row of old townhouses, dodged dirty ice mounds, and parked on the street.

"Let's not stay long," Jeremy said flatly as he opened the car door.

"Here we go again," Rachel said. "You always say that."

"Well—" He looked down. "I hate his smoke smell."

Rachel carried her fruit salad to the door.

"It's funny, you bring that every time, Rach. They never eat it. Then you bring it home." He laughed and tapped the door with the brass and rust doorknocker. "Are you ready to go into the taxicab?"

"Jer, be good, okay? They're retired, after all."

"Right." He rang the doorbell twice. "They're also real classy and love to eat well."

Harry Martin opened the door, a dead cigar in his mouth. "Jer!" Margaret Martin stood behind him, fussing.

"Hi-hi-hi. Happy anniversary," Jeremy said. As he walked in, Rachel saw him sniff at the smell of stale cigar as he shook Harry's hand, then give Margaret a kiss and a hug. "Hi, Mom," he said. Rachel was glad Jeremy got along with her mum.

"Oh, Jeremy," Margaret Martin hugged him back hard, "Glad to see you're okay, Dear. Sorry about your boss. Rach told me."

"Hi there, sonny boy," Harry Martin barked. "How's the office? Or do you prefer the woods now?" He laughed. He always called Archer the office.

Jeremy laughed. "Just fine, Dad." Jeremy slapped him on the shoulder. "Except my boss died."

"Maggie told me," Harry said. "Thought she was joshin' at first. So, you the boss now?"

"Missed it this time, Harry," Jeremy replied. "My new boss is an asshole. Knew the old boss real well."

"Bloody connections," said Harry. "That's what you need over here in the States. But, you're still selling lots of toys and games and stuff?" he asked seriously.

"That'll get you promoted next time, I bet. Hell, you're the star over there, right?"

"Daddy," said Rachel, "Jer doesn't sell the toys and games, just plans the programs and manages the sales group."

"Sure, don't you think I know that?" Harry grumbled.

Jeremy smirked at Rachel and imitated Harry behind his back.

"Want a drink, Jeremy? Bourbon?" Harry turned and asked.

"Some wine?" Jeremy answered, "Cabernet, if you have any? Any red is fine."

"My fancy son-in-law always wants the fancy stuff," Harry said. "Sorry, ain't got as usual." He laughed loudly, and belched.

"Daddy!" Rachel said.

"Don't sweat it, baby," Harry said. "Jer?"

"Beer, then, Dad? I know you always have some *Foster's*."

"Right, Jer!" Harry headed to the fridge. "Rach, you want one, too?"

"Sure, Daddy." Rachel handed her mother the fruit salad.

"Oh, thanks, honey." Margaret took the bowl and grimaced. "We'll have it today or you can take it home with you."

"Jer, my boy, happy you're still with us." Harry slapped Jeremy on the shoulder again and handed him the beer. “Little tough in the cold, eh?”

“Yeah, but I’m fine, Harry, really,” Jeremy said. “Just had a little frostbite.”

“I’m cookin’ on the Jenn-Air today,” Harry said. “You want a juicy steak?”

“Sure,” Jeremy said. “You remember about the seafood.”

“Right. Right,” Harry said. “Rach, you?”

“Fish, if you have some.”

“My daughter, the health nut,” Harry said. “Maggie, you got any of that halibut?”

“But keep the damn fish away from my steak,” Jeremy said.

“Fussy, fussy,” Harry said.

“I’ll have that chicken breast in the freezer if you don’t destroy it.” Margaret pulled Rachel aside. “So, pumpkin. What is it? You said you were going crazy.”

“Oh, Mum,” Rachel said, “I’m just upset about Jer, always flirting with the ladies and his secretary and that. You should’ve seen him at the Archer Christmas party. I even smell lilac on his shirt after his Wednesday client dinners. That’s sure suspicious.”

Margaret prepared a salad as she leaned over and whispered, “Nonsense, Rachel! You should be relieved he’s around after that accident out there in the woods. He's still a good lookin' one, he is." She glanced over at Jeremy. "And, don't forget the inheritance—quite a catch, this one."

Rachel stood close, hung her head, and mumbled, "I know, I know."

"Your daddy loved the ladies, too," said Margaret. "But you learn to put up with it, you do. I swear, they always come back." She winked.

"Sure?" Rachel asked.

"Sure. Jer's quite the catch, but so are you!"

"You always say that, Mum. Ever since Madison."

"Well, you could've *prolly* done a lot worse," Margaret said. "Big fancy exec, Rach." She eyed Harry as he turned a steak on the grill, scratched his bristly gray beard, and chomped on his wrinkled, dead cigar. "Harry, now don't you be burning that."

"Just well done, Maggie," he said, "just well done." He laughed loudly and slurped the head on his beer.

"You know how to kill a good piece of meat, Dad," Jeremy said and laughed. "I'll give you that. Just make mine medium rare or medium? How are the lessons going?"

Harry said, "Yank kids, mind you. Don't have any sense about throwin' a damn ball. And forget the damn hook! Gutter every time they try."

"You'll teach 'em, Harry," Jeremy said. "You're the old pro."

"Friggin' kids. I'll wear 'em down, maybe." Harry started to light his stub.

"Stop it right there, Harry," Margaret said.

Harry froze.

"You know how the kids hate all the smoke," Margaret said.

"Oh, all right." He put his match down and chewed his cigar harder. "Just be getting cancer of the lip, then."

"Rach?" Margaret said. "How'd Jer's ma like that door hanging you did?"

"I didn't give it to her yet," Rachel replied.

"That rich witch!" Harry put down his beer and wiped the air. "She hates everything. Sorry, Jer."

"It's okay, Harry." Jeremy shook his head.

"Harry, you hush," Margaret said.

Rachel mumbled, "She'll find something wrong with it, I bet."

"Rach, she'll love it," Jeremy said. "Honest."

Rachel frowned at Jeremy as she toyed with the silverware and napkins.

Margaret Martin leaned over to her daughter and said, "Now, don't you fuss about Jer and his little flirts, Rach. Besides, you don't have a choice, Pumpkin, do you? He's such a good catch, he is."

"Whatever you say, Mum," Rachel said. "Hmmm, choice." She stared in thought, recalling her appointment with Dr. Hart. Now, she realized that with her mum always championing Jeremy, she never felt like she had much of a choice.

"You'll get over this, Pumpkin." Margaret patted Rachel's hand and looked over at her husband. "Harry? You 'bout killed that *joey*? Want me to take 'er over?"

"See," Harry said and chuckled. "My Maggie's always there to fix things."

They all laughed, but Rachel shook herself out of a thought about Paul and dropped a fork on the floor.

6

Fond du Lac, Wisconsin

Jeremy invited Carl Dietrich to lunch in the company cafeteria on Monday. He hated the thought of it, but he figured he'd better try to make peace with Carl, now that the old guy had become president of Archer.

Jeremy studied the man. Carl had been a rough and ready operations type, but overnight had taken on the look of a company president: sonorous voice; dark gray suit; crisp, white shirt; a club pattern in his tie. *Carl has picked up a few ideas from Bob Townsend over the years*, Jeremy thought. In fact, except for several mannerisms like picking his nose and ears, belching randomly under his breath, and using working class diction, it was clear that Carl had taken good notes on dress and voice.

His bumpy nose was gargantuan and contrasted with his smooth, mostly bald, rectangular head that perfectly reflected four fluorescent trapezoids from the ceiling above. Jeremy thought it comical, how Carl's head and his oily nose gave him an overall shiny appearance. Maybe he should be applying pancake makeup all over!

"So, anyway," Carl said. "That Dunne woman coming at two?" He rubbed his nose and looked at his finger, then wiped it on his pants. "I hear she's pretty sharp, Jeremy. Hadley sees her as your back-up, ya know?" He snickered as his trim little mustache bounced. "Just in case we lose you out there in the woods sometime."

Jeremy looked up. "Just in case, Carl?"

"We'll see." Carl snickered.

"You realize that I'm *your* back-up, don't you?"

"Don't plan on that one real soon," Carl said.

"You never know. Meanwhile, of course I'll try to make you look good."

"I'm sure you don't have to worry about getting bumped, if you see what I mean . . ." Carl paused. "That is, for now. At some point we might find a need to adjust things depending on G & A expenses." His bloodshot eyes looked directly at Jeremy and his shiny forehead creased fivefold. "See what I mean?"

"Hmm." Jeremy wondered. Hadley had always wanted back-ups in every position. Now, he'd use Bob's unfortunate death to guarantee that Carl would execute his plan. "Is Hadley really close to this Dunne woman?" Jeremy asked.

"Treats her like a granddaughter, I hear. They used to ride horses out west. But, don't let that worry you. If we hired her, I'm sure she'd be a big help to you." He smiled.

"Thanks, Carl," Jeremy said and sipped his cold coffee. "Should I be floating my résumé?"

"We shall see," Carl laughed. "If you don't mind me being completely frank about this, I think maybe you've been flying a little high around here, Jer." He slurped his coffee and looked at his bulky watch. "We need to get things back in balance so that marketing doesn't get such a free ride around here. We can't afford to spend money like it's going out of style."

"What do you mean by that?" Jeremy asked.

"Just don't go courting the old man to get your way. Your ass'll be grass faster than you can say *Boomers*."

"That sounds like a threat. But you won't keep me down forever." Jeremy smiled.

Carl flushed, holding back, then slammed his knife and fork down. "Jeremy Lucas! Frankly, I'm sick of you makin' everybody think you're so damn perfect."

"What?"

"It's time you had somebody like this Dunne woman around," Carl said, "just to keep you honest, shall we say."

Jeremy fumed. "Did it ever occur to you that my performance—especially if Hadley was aware of it—could reflect on *you* . . . one way or the other?"

"Is it my imagination, or do I have a feeling you're planning on trying to make me look bad?"

"I'll try my best not to." Jeremy smiled as he stood, then threw his napkin down. "I have to get back to work."

Jeremy strode past Lana Holub's desk on the way to his office. He swung a full coffee cup in his hand, spilling some on the carpet.

"Jeremy!" Lana exclaimed. "You're making a mess again. H. R.'s sending that candidate over now, by the way—that Dunne lady."

"Great," Jeremy said sarcastically, sloshing more coffee on the carpet. He looked at his watch; it read two o'clock. *This won't take too long*, he thought. "At least the bitch is on time." He grabbed the résumé Human Relations had sent over, walked into his office, and sat behind his desk.

"Carl's on Line 1," Lana called.

"Carl? What now?" he asked, swung around, and picked up the phone on the credenza.

"Hi, Jer," Carl said, "Sorry if I riled you at lunch."

"You didn't. Not at all."

Silence on the other line. "Just don't go eliminating the Dunne woman from consideration, okay?" Carl said. "Let me know how it goes."

Jeremy sipped his coffee and looked at his door. Lana was talking politely to someone. "She's here now, Carl," Jeremy said. "Gotta go."

"Right," said Carl. "Call me later."

With his back to the door, Jeremy hung up, glanced at the résumé, and wrote some notes in the margins. He looked over his shoulder. Lana stood in his office doorway, frowning and looking to her right. "Jeremy? This is Catherine Dunne."

Ms. Catherine Dunne appeared. "Good morning, Mr. Lucas," she said in a silky voice.

Jeremy flinched. That voice—she had said it in a low, resonant tone, smooth and precise; a voice that sings like a morning dove and makes you take notice.

She spoke again. "I'm so-o-o sorry to hear about Mr. Townsend."

Her face was ivory, flawless, and sculpted. "Father said Uncle Hadley and Mr. Townsend were very close," she went on. "And, the effect on the company, of course—"

"Uncle Hadley?" Jeremy stood and gulped.

"Just a nickname."

She stood in front of his desk, statuesque, gracefully posing her hands in front of her like a model. Then she nodded and her lips formed an almost-smile. Her jiggling, amber bangs were long and swept to each side of her face. Her short hair caressed her cheeks and made her dark eyes—violet-blue with heavy top lids—flash from beneath stylishly thin tortoise glasses, oversized for her face.

"Jeremy?" Lana called from the doorway, interrupting his trance.

"Yeah? What?" He couldn't take his eyes off Ms. Dunne's simple silk blouse—how it caressed her shoulders and traced her breasts. He glanced at her skirt—cut slightly long, clinging to her willowy form and accentuating her calves, which appeared slightly large, maybe because of her stubby heels or because she partook in regular aerobic sessions. He instantly pictured her in four inch spiked heels. "Hmm."

Lana cleared her throat.

"Oh, yes, excuse me, Ms. Dunne," Jeremy said. "This is my assistant, Lana Holub."

Lana said, "Hi. We met."

"Outside," Catherine said and gestured to Lana's desk.

"Uh huh," Lana said, but didn't smile.

Catherine Dunne took a step closer to Jeremy's desk. Her bangs jiggled.

Jeremy began, "So, Ms. Dunne. I've heard a lot about you. We finally meet."

They shook hands, then Jeremy walked to his door and closed it. As he did, he caught Lana frowning at him. He sneered back at her, then returned to stand behind his desk.

"Of course, do call me Catherine," the woman said properly.

"By the way, thanks for your sentiments about Bob," Jeremy said. "His death was a major loss, personally and for Archer. Please—" He motioned to one of the two chairs on the other side of his desk.

"Thank you," Catherine Dunne said in smooth slow motion, like a classical music FM DJ. "You certainly have a splendid working environment here at Archer."

She took her glasses off and propped them carefully on Jeremy's desk. Instantly her eyes blossomed.

Man-oh-man, Jeremy thought.

Catherine's eyelashes fluttered visibly. "What is it, Mr. Lucas?" she asked and smiled.

"Oh, nothing. Just call me Jeremy—or Jer." He felt frozen and tried not to stare.

"Fine, Jer. But there's something bothering you, I can tell."

"Oh, hardly *bothering*. It's your voice. It's so . . . smooth."

"Oh?" She laughed and put her hand to her mouth. "Thank you. You know, everybody mentions it."

"You should really be a voice-over talent or something," he said. "Commercials, the works."

"Thank you. People have told me that. I've even recorded a demo tape."

"Where'd you get your voice?" he asked. "Hereditary?"

"I can't explain it." She shrugged. "Just have it."

"Really incredible. Guess we should talk about your résumé." He pointed to the paper.

"Of course," Catherine said. Her eyes sparkled as she flashed her Mona Lisa smile.

"Wow," said Jeremy, studying the résumé. He looked up at Catherine and noticed her sterling Movado sport watch. "Smith, University of Chicago, Hasbro, Mattel. From the looks of your résumé, I expected—"

"A squeaky dweeb or a nondescript friend of the Archer family, right?" she asked.

He laughed. "Well, something . . . "

"Sorry if I disappointed you."

"Disappoint? Hardly." He raised his hand. "Scout's Oath."

"I'm glad you approve." She smiled, then looked at her watch again.

"In a hurry?" he asked.

She looked up. "Oh, no. I have another appointment is all, and I still have to see Mr. Dietrich."

"Hmm." Jeremy looked at his watch and thought, if Carl got a good look at Catherine, it could spell the beginning of the end of his own career at Archer. "Carl's pretty tied up," he said. "Maybe you'll need to come back."

"Oh?"

"Well, he's busy with his new presidential duties. You understand."

"Of course. Perhaps you can forward my résumé to him."

Jeremy looked down at the résumé again. "I'm not disappointed," he said, "in your background, or anything else." He fiddled with the edges of her résumé and felt himself flush.

"Thank you." She held back a laugh.

He noticed that she seemed to like his awkwardness. "Your résumé's very impressive, Ms. Dunne," He studied her face inquisitively. "But—"

She nodded. "My appearance? I know, I probably don't look the part, right?"

"Well, that's okay, really," said Jeremy. "I mean, good looks along with the brains, if you don't mind me saying so. So, why are you interested in the little Archer Toy Company in Fond du Lac, Wisconsin? We're small potatoes. You should be seeing Kimberly Clark, S. C. Johnson in Racine, or Quaker in Chicago."

"SCJ's actually my late afternoon appointment. But, I'm only doing that one for reference, you know. Racine's not far, is it?"

"No. Within an hour."

"Father insisted that to understand how to operate a company from the inside out, I should start small, dig in for a few years, and learn the marketing, sales, and operations sides. He's insistent that I not slide through life based on his position. Being pegged a rich bitch can distort people's impression of you, as you might imagine."

"Hmm. Wise advice," said Jeremy. "I've been there with the burden of an inheritance." *God, she seems so absolutely reasonable and even honest*, he thought. *No doubt the other folks at Archer will like her. The best I can do is postpone her meeting with Carl.* "It's certainly our good fortune to have a shot at you."

"You're so kind." One side of her mouth barely turned up in a hint of a smile.

He gulped. "I'm really impressed."

She closed her eyes, then opened them . . . slowly. "Thank you, Jer. It's so nice to see that we seem to be connecting." She licked her lips. "Will that help my chances at Archer?"

Their eyes locked.

"You could say so." He stared. "I mean, you do have the perfect voice, after all, and a wonderful résumé."

They laughed. She looked at her watch. He studied her—he wanted her to stay because of her beauty, but wanted her out of his life, because Carl would surely find a way to oust him once he met her.

"What is it, Jeremy?" she asked.

"Oh, nothing. Just nothing."

"Are there any other quick questions you'd like to ask?"

"Sure." Jeremy scanned Catherine's résumé again.

After more routine questions about her various positions, her honors paper at the University of Chicago, and her travels to the Eastern bloc, Jeremy noticed that she lived on the north side of Chicago. "It says here you live at the 2650 Lake View building?"

She leaned forward, wincing concern. "That a problem?"

"No, but your last job was at Mattel in LA. I don't get it."

"I've just stayed in Chicago for the last year to get my head together. I love the Lake View area."

Nice if you can afford it, Jeremy thought. "That's a pretty nice address."

"You have friends down there?" she asked routinely.

"No, but I know the area. Gold Coast, right?"

"No—Like I said, Lake View. The Gold Coast is only a mile away, though," she said.

"Listen," said Jeremy. "I have a lunch set up in Chicago, I think for next week. Maybe we could pick this up then?" Part of him was saying this was a stupid thing to pursue, but maybe something would come of it.

"That appropriate?" she asked.

"Of course." He smiled back. "Wait, let me just check my schedule." He leaned back, picked up his phone, and pressed the com-line button. He held up his index finger. "Besides, maybe I could warm you up, so to speak, for Carl. Give you an up-front on what some of his typical questions would be."

"Wonderful."

"Lana?" he talked into the phone. "I just wanted to check. I'm seeing Brad next week, right? That's what I thought . . . No, staying over one night." He laughed, then whispered, "Sorry, Lana, I said it's over." He hung up, shook his head, and turned to Catherine.

"Something wrong?" Catherine asked.

"Oh, nothing. She says I'm booked to be down there next Thursday."

"Oh, really?" Catherine said and smiled her smile. "Where specifically, might I ask?"

"Sure," said Jeremy. "I'm meeting Brad Coleman—our Chicago DM—District Manager—for lunch at the Chéz Paul on Dearborn. You know it?"

She answered: "Oh, yes. That's just south of—"

"Your place," he said. "Right?"

"Uh-huh. A short taxi." She tapped her fingertips together in a praying posture. "It's a favorite place of mine. Maybe we could meet for a drink or afternoon coffee?" She pressed her fingernails into her cushy lower lip as she said it.

"What?" he asked.

"Nothing," she said quickly. "Listen, I really must go."

Just then, Lana leaned in and whispered, "Remember, Jeremy. You have a three o'clock meeting." She disappeared in a huff, leaving the door ajar.

Catherine saw the exchange and pointed at Lana. "Something wrong?"

"No, I'm sure it's nothing," Jeremy said. "Just her."

She nodded. "Here, let me take your card." She reached forward and took a business card from the little plexiglass tray on Jeremy's desk. "We'll try to keep this appropriate."

"Try?" Jeremy was a little taken aback. He pictured himself as an insect being wooed into a Venus flytrap. *Am I really getting signals from this babe or just fantasizing?*

Wait, he thought. The only reason Catherine Dunne was acting this familiar with him and had jumped at the chance to see him again was to improve her odds of landing a position at Archer. That must have been her modus operandi all along, he figured—get close; snag bait. Suddenly, Jeremy felt infinitely naive in Catherine Dunne's presence.

She unfolded her legs and her skirt hiked up. "Whoops," she said. "Damned skirt. Always happens."

He glared at her, surprised at her sudden profanity.

"What?" she asked innocently. "Did I do something? I know, I swore. Bad habit. See, I blew it."

"That's okay," Jeremy stated. "Just makes you human."

She smiled. "Listen, I better go, Jer. I'm enjoying myself, but I do have other commitments." She tapped her watch and walked out. "My apologies to Mr. Dietrich. I will see him another time then."

"Of course." Jeremy smiled. "Oh, Catherine?" he called after her. He felt his stomach gurgle. "Now, don't you go taking any instant offers at SCJ." *Maybe she should,* he thought. "Unless they're incredible." Then, she could be his lover, not next in line for his job.

"Bye-bye, Jeremy." She turned and fluttered a graceful, royal wave at him.

"I'll see you . . . I promise." Her wave lingered as she floated away.

Jeremy sat down and fanned himself with the résumé. "Man." He swore that, as she drifted off, she was a breath short of throwing him a kiss. *Man, what am I going to do?* he wondered.

A second later, Lana walked in and closed the door. "You're going to hire her, I can tell."

"How the hell can you tell that?"

"She's so beautiful," Lana said. "I wouldn't trust her though."

"Why?"

"Well, she was sexy in a mysterious sort of way. She's smart and rich, too. And I can tell she really likes you. Meanwhile—"

"What?"

"I get pregnant and I'm history. I bet you she'll be your new honey."

"Oh, Lana. I doubt I'll ever see her again. Except—"

"What?"

"Oh, nothing. I was just thinking about my trip next week."

"It's just routine with Brad, right?" asked Lana. "You aren't planning to see that Dunne woman, are you? Jeremy, truth?"

"Don't be silly," he scoffed. "Why're you so suspicious?" God, now Jeremy was imagining how he could cheat on his wife *and* his former lover.

"Come on Jeremy, I know you." Lana nodded with her hands on her hips. "Don't forget. I've been your secret on the side for three years."

He looked at his watch. "Listen, I have that meeting to go to." He walked out of the office.

One hour later, Jeremy was back in his office and calling Carl.

"How was she?" Carl asked.

"Aw, I don't know," Jeremy said dismissively. "Her résumé reads pretty well on the surface, but, if you ask me, she looks a little book smart and stuffy."

"Shame I couldn't see her. Not too good, huh?"

"No, but I might follow-up with her to check out the chemistry, you know? Then, you can see her if I think she's worth another look. Sound good?"

"Fine," Carl said. "Keep me up-to-date so I can get back to the old man. Got a lot on my plate right now."

"Right, boss," Jeremy said purposefully, and hung up.

At about six-thirty that evening, Jeremy began packing his briefcase to head home. The phone rang. He picked it up.

"Lucas here."

"Jer?" Catherine Dunne's voice said.

"Catherine, what a surprise!" he said. "How was your interview at SCJ, or should I ask?"

"Archer's still on top of my list—if you'll have me. I think you'll have me, won't you?"

"Was my assessment that obvious?"

"Listen," she seemed to hesitate for a moment before she continued quietly, "I don't want to be too forward here, but since you're heading down to Chicago next week, I thought maybe—"

"Catherine, honest. I'm glad you called. Maybe we can—"

"Meet?"

As Jeremy drove up his driveway that evening, he was still thinking of Catherine Dunne. He had never been so instantly taken by a woman, but afraid of her at the same time. Her mysterious demeanor and teasing familiarity was terribly attractive. But, she was also a perfect enough candidate that he could imagine Carl moving her into his job in no time at all, which would, no doubt, please the hell out of Hadley. On balance,

Jeremy had to admit to himself that the occupational risk made her even more of a turn on.

He looked forward to seeing Catherine during his Chicago trip, but wondered for a moment about the dangers of allowing his libido to rule his decisions once again—if only he could find a way to experience the attractive part of Catherine and eliminate the threatening part.

Jeremy got out of his car, walked to the door, and opened it. "Yo, Rach!"

"Coming!"

As she skipped down the stairs, Jeremy gazed out the front window. He thought back to his first dates with Rachel. They hardly knew each other then, but enjoyed going to the movies together. While she watched the screen, he kissed her and touched her all over without a sound, and she loved holding back as if he weren't fondling her. They were both seduced by the eroticism of fooling around as other students sat nearby. For him, his absolute dominance over her blew him away; for her, her total submission to him, maybe in the presence of others, made her helpless in a way, like she didn't have to take responsibility for her actions—Jeremy was taking responsibility. That's probably why he felt exhilarated at the idea of getting to know Catherine Dunne—new prey, but not as deferential or smothering.

Rachel slipped her arms around his waist.

Startled, he asked, "Rach, where were you?"

"Cleaning up. Till just ten minutes ago, the kitchen was a mess, so dinner's not quite ready."

"Bad girl," he said as he hung his coat.

"Well, I'm sorry, baby," she said. "Paul was over again, working under the sink, that union thingamajig. Dinner's your favorite—pasta. So, I hope that'll make up for it."

"I swear, Paul *lives* over here. Are we his only customers?"

"Jeremy, he really takes care of us. He's funny, too."

"I suppose that's why we hire him—the funny, paternal plumber. Next he'll be doing stand-up at the Laff Stop in Milwaukee."

"He said the pipes—"

"I know, I know." Jeremy held up his hands. "I'm sick of the pipe talk—important details of your life-domestica."

"Well," Rachel spouted, "I used to work in a lab, drawing blood, but you were the one who told me to stop so I could take care of you."

"Well, I was sick of hearing about needles, hematomas, and Complete Blood Counts. Jeez—" Jeremy picked up the newspaper and walked into his office. There, on a stack of bills, sat the metal charm, polished so that all the different metals glowed—bronze, copper, and silver. It was beautiful. For a moment, he pondered how the talisman must be some kind of good luck charm, first saving him from his cold weather accident, then bringing him Catherine Dunne, so captivatingly perfect and someone who acted so familiar toward him, as if she'd known him for a decade. An affair with her was definitely the next lucky gift the charm might bring his way.

He sat and thumbed slow motion through the sports section, which consisted mostly of a Milwaukee replay. Fond du Lac's rag sheet wasn't too bad; at least it tracked the Bucks and Brewers pretty well.

"Dinner!" Rachel called.

Jeremy glanced at the charm as he left his office, then walked into the kitchen.

"Thing looks pretty cool."

"What thing?" she asked.

"That charm thing."

"Shined up pretty nice, eh?" She stood at the stove, then deftly turned to the table, serving dish in hand, sending her short-cropped hair flying.

"Wonder what the hell it is," Jeremy pondered out loud. "The charm."

"Julie came over today," said Rachel. "I showed it to her. She says I should bring it over to the Madison campus." She shrugged. "Maybe it's some valuable old thing." She scooped some pasta onto a plate, then added sauce. "She's gonna ask Gus at dinner. He's good at that stuff."

"Julie, the neighbor with the big ideas," said Jeremy sarcastically. "I found it here in central Wisconsin in a tree trunk, but she's thinking it's a real archeological find. She'll verify that notion when she talks to Gus at dinner. Being a roofer, he's bound to know all about it."

"Jeremy." She sighed.

"Ooo, why can't we have this pasta five times a week instead of four?" he asked.

"Jeremy! What's wrong with you? I shine your charms and make your meals. What more do you want?"

"Variety," he said. "Just a little variety, I guess."

After dinner, Rachel poured coffee as Jeremy listened to her talk more about Paul and the pipes, then he decided he should lay the groundwork for his upcoming trip. "Oh, I forgot to tell you, I'm going down to Chicago to see Brad at the end of next week."

"I don't want you cutting through the Moraine till the snow clears," she said.

"No worries, I'll drive major roads. Maybe I'll stay at that little hotel off of Michigan Avenue, the Delaware House."

"I remember that," said Rachel. "Pretty nice. I'd love to go there again."

As she said the words, Jeremy stared through his glass, thinking of Catherine Dunne. He shook his head to clear his thoughts.

"Jeremy, come on, what is it?" Rachel looked at him with her eyebrows raised. "It's like you're somewhere else tonight."

"It's nothing. Guess I'm thinking about my Chicago trip."

"Important business with Brad?"

"Yeah, I suppose. With Bob gone and Hadley giving Carl the reins, I have to help the troops adjust to the change."

"I thought you were convinced you were going to get Bob's job."

"I'll be next," Jeremy sneered. "Don't worry. I'll nail Carl's ass. Only a matter of time. I'm about right for next in line. Probably interviewed my damn successor today. Bob found the bitch. That's all I need."

"A female?" she said. "You could kill her to eliminate the competition?"

"Very funny."

"Well, you sound so upset."

"I'm not," Jeremy said. "She just has a perfect background—Smith, University of Chicago MBA, Hasbro, Mattel. Daughter of the CEO of IDS—about the perfect credentials."

"How old?"

"Thirties."

"Hmm," Rachel sighed, "a knock-out, I bet. Some rich beauty, no doubt." She primped at her mousy brown haircut.

"Why'd you say that?" Jeremy mused to himself for a second about how accurate Rachel had been. *If Rachel knew the details*, he thought, *she'd really be nervous*.

"Well, since Bob found her," she said, "she has to be a social climber, right?"

"Yeah, but she's different, I think," said Jeremy. "Glasses, bookish. Hadley knows her, too."

"I bet she can't dance like me," Rachel said, straightening her posture.

"Rach, nobody moves as well as you do, except Katia herself. And her back-up singers. How'd she ever get that Latin influence, living in Poland?"

"Probably like me," Rachel said. "She's Polish, I'm Australian. When we were kids in Perth, we used to get tapes smuggled out of Cuba: Tito Puente and Celia Cruz. I played them all the time. *La Clave* grew on me."

"*La Clave*?" he asked.

"You know. 'The Key', that Afro-Cuban rhythm, like Desi Arnez."

"Big deal."

"Or *The Mambo Kings*," said Rachel, "remember the movie? They all have it: *La Clave*."

Jeremy sipped on his coffee and looked away. "Interesting," he mumbled and yawned.

"Oh, Jeremy! It's in my blood. See?" Rachel hummed and bounced her hands in a mock-mambo beat as she craned her head, rocking it back and forth and squeaking the kitchen chair right on beat. "Once you've got it, it's part of you forever."

"I think I understand," he put his cup down and said. "You and Gloria Estefan and Katia and Tito whoever?"

"Puente! The King! You *do* understand." Rachel kept bouncing and humming. "You must have things like that too—things you couldn't get rid of if you tried."

"Yeah, I suppose," Jeremy said, and looked down. "By the way."

"What?" she asked. "What's the matter?"

"Why aren't the damned walks cleared of all that snow?"

"Oh, Mabel told me that little Clark's been sick with a really bad sore throat and cold. Just be careful when you walk up to the front door."

"Oh, Rach, you know I'm always careful."

"Yeah, I guess you are."

7

Chicago, Illinois

Jeremy pulled his loaner car, a Corolla, up to the waiting valet on Dearborn Street in front of Café Chez Paul for his lunch with Brad Coleman.

Brad stood there on the curb like a Viking god. His bright white shirt, tropical tie, and latent tan popped out of the opening of his long leather trench coat.

"Jeremy!" Brad yelled. "How you be? Hey, new wheels?"

"A Corolla? Hardly. Just a loner."

Jeremy took his ticket stub from the valet, stuck it in his left pocket. He and Brad shook hands. "The Volvo's in the shop, getting a second life after my accident—two grand worth."

"Ughh."

"At least I got out alive," Jeremy said, holding up his fingers, "with all my digits."

"No kidding," Brad frowned. "Cold out there, huh?"

"Brad, it's been what, four months?"

"Too long," said Brad. "Hey, really sorry about Bob. Loved the guy. I know he thought the world of you."

"Yeah, I think he did. I guess I was sort of his right hand man."

"Really," Brad said. "You always made him look great to the old man."

Jeremy nodded and smiled. "Part of the job."

"How'd all the old timers take it at headquarters?" Brad asked.

Jeremy shook his head. "A real shock."

"Boy, looks like we have our pick." Brad pointed to ten cloth covered tables that sat under the rust-tinted glass of the restaurant's sweaty atrium, which jutted out onto the sidewalk.

They took a table, and after they sipped chardonnay for a few minutes, the noise level in the place approached lunchtime levels. The waiter reappeared. "So, what will it be today, gentlemen?"

"A Caesar," Jeremy said. "You can make it without the anchovies, right?"

"As you wish, sir." The waiter scribbled on a pocket notepad.

"Completely—no traces of anchovy sauce either," Jeremy said. "I'm allergic."

"Yes, sir. Of course. How about we toss some fresh Romaine for you? Add a little Parmesan, a touch of Caesar Dressing?" The waiter scribbled again.

"No, I'll have Italian dressing," Jeremy said.

"As you wish."

"And I'll have the Veal Marsala, too," Jeremy added.

"Yes sir." The waiter turned to Brad. "And for the gentleman?"

"The sea bass," Brad said, "and more chardonnay, please."

"Yes, sir." The waiter reached onto the cart passing by and grabbed a basket, then flung it through the air, caught it with his other hand, and placed it at the center of the table. "Some warm bread, perhaps?" Impressed with his own acrobatics, he allowed himself a tiny grin and then retreated.

"Great, nice and warm," Jeremy said as he reached into the breadbasket.

"So, Carl got the nod, huh?" Brad asked.

"I thought this might be the big move for me," Jeremy shrugged. "Maybe the next time someone dies." He flashed a cool grin.

Brad snickered. "Sure. Here's hoping." He raised his glass.

Jeremy answered the toast. "So, Operations'll feel most of the changes since that's Carl's thing," he said. "At least, more than Sales. He doesn't have a clue about that."

"That means he'll keep his hands off our area," Brad said. "Boy, I hate change, though."

"I'm talking to each of the DMs, filling them in."

"Good," Brad said. "You know what the word is in the ranks, don't you?"

"No, what?"

"Carl's after your ass," Brad said.

Jeremy looked up. "What?"

"Word is he wants to replace you with somebody less threatening . . . and less costly." Brad sipped his wine. "He's no dumb-ass."

"Hmm." Jeremy tapped his finger.

"He probably wants to get back at you. You haven't exactly been kind to him."

"The asshole." Jeremy quickly reviewed his history with Carl. "He's always been a real pain. My plumber's more sophisticated than he is. I hate how Carl picks at his various bodily orifices."

Brad laughed. "Say, what's with this year's Toy Show? It's normally on the East Coast."

"I'll probably go with Carl. This year it'll be here in Chicago at McCormick Place."

"So, I'm going, too, then?" Brad perked up.

"Local DM always goes," Jeremy said.

"Great. I haven't been to one since Phoenix in '77." Brad munched on his bread and winked.

Jeremy tried to stifle a grin.

"You remember Phoenix, right?"

"Oh, yeah." He snickered.

"I'll never forget you and Regina shacked up for a couple days in that casita," Brad said. "You won that bet!" He reached across the table and mock-punched Jeremy in the shoulder. "All we did was swig Margaritas for a week while you had all the fun."

Jeremy shrugged, and sipped his wine.

"Jer," Brad smiled, "there are winners in this world, and there are lucky dogs, but you take the cake."

They clinked glasses again.

"It'll come out of your budget," Jeremy said.

"What?"

"Going to the show at McCormick Place."

"Rip-off."

They laughed.

"Jeremy, you are one cunning hombre. You always come out on top, as it were."

"It's just the way I look at life," Jeremy said.

"You're something, I'll give you that." Brad toasted him again.

A few minutes later, when the waiter brought their food, Jeremy pointed to his salad. "See, Rachel's after me to lighten up on the red meat."

Brad pointed to the salad. "Still gotta watch the bread. Anything white converts easily to simple sugars."

"True," Jeremy said. "That's right, Brad, you're a health nut, too. You sound like Rachel. Hell, like my *mother*."

"Enough to drive you nuts, I guess." Brad turned to the waiter walking by. "Say, could I have another glass of this Stag's Leap? Excellent chardonnay."

"Yes, sir." The server bowed.

Jeremy gazed out the window for a second. He thought he saw a tall, amber-haired woman striding up the sidewalk next to Dearborn Street. Some lunchtime walkers instantly obscured his view.

"What is it?" Brad asked and turned.

"Oh, nothing. Thought I saw someone I knew."

Brad chewed his food hungrily, mouth half-opened as he talked, gesturing with his fork. "So, Corporate was pretty shook up, huh?"

"Man," Jeremy said. "Place hasn't been worth shit since. Like we're all on vacation."

"You never realize what someone's worth till they're gone," said Brad. "Even Bob."

"Yeah. Bob the climber," Jeremy jibed.

They laughed.

"But, really," Jeremy shrugged. "He always treated me fairly, even though I wasn't family. Looked out for me, too."

"True."

"He respected competency, that's for sure."

"Yeah," Brad said. "And, entitled ones like you—the inheritance and all."

At that moment, Jeremy glanced over at the hostess stand. Catherine Dunne was being seated at a table not more than fifteen feet away. She sat, looked his way and raised her index finger to her velvety lips. "Shhh," she whispered.

"What is it, Jer?" Brad asked.

"Oh, nothing," Jeremy replied.

"Well, you think Corporate will be able to meet our deadlines for sales aids on *Boomers* this spring?" Brad wondered. "It'd sure help us stay in the game with Parker and Lego . . . "

"Parker?"

"Yeah. They're making waves like a son-of-a-bitch—stocking allowances—the works—like a new company."

As Brad talked, Jeremy's eyes drifted over to Catherine. Every time they did, she stared back, unrelenting, devoid of blinks. At first, he felt uncomfortable, but then he thought back to her interview. There was even more to this woman than had originally met the eye. Now, she had arrived here as she had promised and was playing with him. He felt himself start to tremble as he looked away.

Seconds later, he glanced back at her. She wasn't looking anywhere near his way. Then, suddenly, she turned toward him and smiled her subtle smile. His stomach rolled over.

"Who do you keep looking at, Jeremy?" Brad looked back at Catherine. She looked away. "Oh, that babe? Not bad. That's right, you like 'em on the classy side."

"Whatever."

They laughed.

Jeremy kept staring at Catherine off and on as he and Brad finished their lunches with cappuccino. Every time he stared at her, his stomach churned.

Jeremy vaguely heard Brad continue: "Jeremy, being competitive on the street is what we need now, so if you guys could come up with some good deals on existing items, then a really hot one on the *Xers* intro. When'll we be ready for the *Xers* rollout?"

Jeremy looked back. “Soon. We’re looking at late spring.” Jeremy’s latest new product was Xers, a Trivial Pursuit-type game targeted at Generation X. He hoped it would be as big for Archer as *Boomers* had been.

“Perfect,” Brad said.

Jeremy shot a look back to Catherine. She was staring back at him. Jeremy gulped. He looked away, sipped on his glass of water, and cleared his throat.

“I’m really excited about *Xers*,” Brad went on, “it’s more my age group.”

“Yeah. We think it’ll be pretty good.” When Jeremy looked back at Catherine, she slowly, almost imperceptibly, licked the edge of her lips.

Jeremy picked up his glass and slurped some water.

“You okay, Jeremy?” Brad asked.

“Yeah. Why?” He wiped his brow with his napkin.

“You look a little flushed.” Brad’s brows knitted. “Should I call somebody?”

“Oh, it’s nothing, Brad. Probably the food.” Actually, Jeremy was surprised anything as simple as Catherine’s stares had sent him reeling.

“Just a salad? What could be wrong?” Brad asked.

“It’s my cappuccino,” Jeremy said. “Pretty hot.”

"Oh, right," said Brad. "Ever since Bob died, I've been extra careful to notice if anyone looks a little off."

"Right." Jeremy glanced back at Catherine. She was lightly tracing the inside of her thigh with long, ruby-painted fingernails. Or was he just imagining that? Maybe she was doing it, not necessarily for his benefit, but for no other reason than because her damn leg itched.

Brad broke Jeremy's trance. "Well, listen, guy." He looked at his watch. "Hate to cut this short—really do—but I better split." He wiped his mouth with a napkin and rose, reaching for his wallet. "Got a three o'clock back at the office—second quarter quotas."

"I'll get it, Brad." Jeremy fumbled for his wallet. "Besides, you'd better get going. Oakbrook's a bit of a trek down the Eisenhower this time of day."

"Say, thanks, Jer. I'll catch the check next time."

"Deal." Jeremy rose. He and Brad shook hands. Brad glanced back at Catherine and smiled. "Quite a stylish lass, Jer. Good luck." He mock-slugged Jeremy in the shoulder.

"Yeah, right."

Brad walked away.

Jeremy laughed to himself. He sat back down and took another drink of water. He was feeling the same way he had years ago with Rachel—like this was an important conquest, except he wasn't sure this time if he was the hunter or the hunted. He suddenly felt manic, like he wanted to lose control—like whatever he did now didn't matter—everything was a game. And, because this game was obviously Catherine's idea, he didn't feel responsible for how he might react.

The waiter walked up. "Anything else for you, sir?"

"Another cappuccino," Jeremy said.

"Yes, sir. Non-fat, right? Was the last one to your liking?"

"A little hot . . . no, on second thought, it was perfect." Jeremy looked at his watch, then Catherine—staring at him again—and recalled the old charm sitting on his desk at home. *It must be bringing me more good luck, all right*, he thought. The waiter brought the cappuccino and Jeremy sipped it slowly. He avoided direct eye contact with Catherine, just to play along with her game. It was painful, but he lasted almost five minutes without looking her way.

Then, out of the corner of his left eye, he noticed her stand up. Not even looking at him, she abruptly threw down some bills, put on her coat and walked out, stopping to talk to the maitre d' for a second, then glanced at Jeremy for even less time.

"Man-oh-*man*," he muttered. *Is this part of the game?* Had he lost? Once outside, Catherine walked down the ice-patched sidewalk along Dearborn without looking back even once.

Jeremy slumped in his chair. Were all of her overtures just his imagination? With his naturally horny mindset, he was prone to erotic imaginings, but now he felt stupid. He shook his head, wiped his brow, and swore under his breath.

Catherine had left, probably because she was impatient with his playing hard to get. He wondered if he should have at least walked over and said hello. She had walked out and not even looked back. She was probably pissed.

How stupid can I be, he thought.

"Sir?" The silver-haired maitre d' appeared next to him, hand outstretched. "For you, sir."

"What?" Jeremy put down his cappuccino and looked up.

"From the lady." The maitre d' smiled and pointed toward the table Catherine had occupied.

He handed Jeremy a yellow matchbook.

"What's this?" On the shiny smooth surface of the *Chez Paul* matchbook, written at the top in tiny blue script, Jeremy saw his name. Then below it: "5PM, Apt. #1904, 2650 Lake View," and easy directions.

His stomach flip-flopped. He turned and strained to look outside as the melting snow dripped down the amber-tinted window. Through the plants and drips on the window, he could make out the dark, willowy figure of Catherine, a block away, crossing the street quickly.

He looked down at the matchbook.

5PM? He sucked in a breath, then looked back down the street. She was gone.

"Un-effing-be*liev*able." He slumped back in his chair.

Jeremy thought about the practicality of going to the 2650 building. As he sipped the last of his cappuccino, he considered his situation. If he accepted Catherine's invitation and anything happened, he'd be cheating on his wife all over again—with an employment candidate at that—his probable replacement, too!

"This is crazy," he said under his breath.

He read the matchbook again. His face flushed, imagining the possibilities with this fox. Never before had a woman pursued him this directly.

He wondered if she had any other tricks up her sleeve, things that could weaken him in the knees beyond belief. Maybe she could take him places he'd never been. She might be able to fulfill him like other women never had, even Lana or Rachel, who had submitted to his every wish; so, he basically controlled those relationships completely. This was different.

He became nervous and decisive at the same time, like whenever he made a major purchase. He signed the credit card receipt, wiped his mouth with his napkin, stood to put on his coat, and walked outside to the Illinois Bell phone booth. He took off his right glove, plunked in a quarter, and dialed his home number. He deposited more coins and got Rachel's prerecorded message. He tapped his fingers on the cold, scratched, stainless steel surface and waited till her recording ended. "Rachel, remember, I'm going out with Brad and a client for dinner. Then, I'm staying over down here at the Delaware Place, I think. Sorry I missed you. Love you." He hung up and sighed, relieved he didn't have to talk to her.

He reached into his right pocket for the valet's ticket and felt around—not there. Then he tried his left pocket. *There!* He pulled out the ticket, then the yellow matchbook with the tiny blue message. As the valet retrieved Jeremy's car, he felt himself sweating as he fooled with the matchbook. "Amazing woman," he said out loud, thinking back to her interview.

His Corolla pulled up and the valet got out.

Jeremy handed him the three-dollar fee plus a dollar.

"Oh, thank you, sir. Need any directions?" he asked.

Jeremy drew in a deep, cold breath. "No, thanks. I know exactly where I'm going."

8

Chucago, Illinois February 13, 1985

In the small marble lobby of the 2650 building, Jeremy walked across the cushy carpet and passed a rushing waterfall. To his right, a chubby guard with beady eyes quickly stowed a chrome flask and stood at attention behind a marble podium.

"Can I help you, sir?" he asked. His speech slurred.

"Yes, nineteen. Ms. Dunne? My name is Lucas."

The guard burped. "Excuse me, sir," he said, pencil in hand, and studied a list in front of him.

Jeremy looked down at the list. "That's right." Jeremy was repelled by the stench of alcohol on the guard's breath.

The guard smiled and wobbled as he looked up and down the list slowly. "Lemme see. Lucas, Lucas."

"Jeremy Lucas."

The guard picked up a phone and dialed. "Miss Dunne? There's a man down here to see you. Name's Jeremy Lucas." He put down the phone. "Sorry, Mr. Lucas. Can't be too careful these days. You don't look familiar. Well sort of, I guess."

"Right," Jeremy said. He turned and walked toward the brown elevator.

"Oh, s-sir?" the doorman called.

Jeremy stopped and turned. "Yeah?"

"Wait," the guard said and giggled. "That brown one's for freight. It's in a bad place. Take the chrome one."

"Right." Jeremy did an about-face, stepped to the chrome doors, entered, and pushed the nineteen button.

During his ride up, he examined his reflection in the elevator's chrome walls. *I'm still a pretty dashing guy,* he thought. He smoothed back his longish hair. Soon, the doors opened and he walked out.

He preened as he walked down the plush carpet to apartment 1904. The brass knocker echoed down the hall. *There's still time to call this off,* he thought.

But, at that moment, the apartment door eased open. Catherine stood there in subdued light and smiled her almost-happy smile. She was wearing what was either a naughty red nightie, or the sexiest dress he'd ever seen, complemented with a sterling silver circle pin that gathered the silky material invitingly across her breasts.

"Hi," Jeremy said. "Made it."

"Right on time," Catherine said in her incredible voice. She looked down at her nightie-dress, then up. "You like?" she asked. "I hope it's not too much for the follow-up to our interview."

"Perfect." He laughed nervously.

She took his coat, turned, and hung it in the entry closet next to the door.

"Some wine?" she asked.

"Sure. That guard downstairs sure had a little of something."

"Roy? Every once in a while I catch Roy nipping, but it still makes me feel safe to know he's watching out for me."

Jeremy laughed. "Said I looked like one of your friends."

"Merlot okay?"

He nodded.

"Daniel," Catherine mused. "You look a bit like him, I think."

"That good?" he asked.

She smiled. "Sure."

He looked around. Her apartment was immaculate—not a scrap of paper or a magazine anywhere.

"Looks like you have a live-in maid," he said.

"Not live-in, but weekly. Why?"

"I don't know, it just looks so perfect—like you barely live here."

"Thanks. Janina's great." Catherine walked away, then returned and handed

Jeremy the glass of wine. He felt so nervous, he just gulped it down.

"Hey, easy." She laughed, poured more wine in his glass, and put the bottle back in the kitchen.

"Sorry, I guess I'm thirsty," he called.

Catherine pulled open a drawer, lifted a hand-rolled cigarette from it, and returned to the entry. She lit the cigarette and took a few short drags mixed with air, held her breath for a second, and smiled. "You indulge?" she half-asked, half-coughed, and offered Jeremy the marijuana.

"Grass?" Jeremy asked. "On occasion. But, I never inhale."

They laughed.

He was already feeling a buzz from the wine. He glanced at the joint one more time. "What the hay," he said.

She exhaled. "Don't overdo it with this stuff—pretty outstanding weed." She toked once more and handed him the joint.

He sucked in a breath and coughed. The joint went out. He reached into his pocket, pulled out the yellow matchbook. "Oh, by the way, Catherine." He held up the matchbook. "Nice touch."

"You're here, right?" she said.

"Right." He precariously held his wine glass, struck a match and relit the joint.

"Man, that smells *rich*," he said, "if that's the right word."

"Told you—potent."

She led him over to an antique table in the dining room.

He tossed his matches down on the table. She led him to the couch nearby in the cozy living room. "Man, I can't figure you, Catherine."

"What?" she asked. She cuddled close to him.

"You're obviously trying to turn me on like crazy, but you also want to work for me." He shrugged. "Is this the new age businesswoman approach?"

She laughed. "I thought about it at first, and wondered if I might create an incredibly nasty feedback loop all the way to my father. Whoops!" She got up and walked back into the tiny kitchen.

"And—" he called.

"Then, I sensed you were different and I was safe."

He watched her scoop some tossed salad into two bowls and point to the dining table. "Have a seat, dinner's almost ready. Start on your salad," she said and carried the bowls back to the dining room, the light shining through her nightie-dress, revealing her willowy form. "Hope you like pasta," she said.

"Rachel makes it several times a week. My favorite as long as the sauce doesn't have seafood—bad allergy."

"That's too bad," she said. "I love fish, go to *Buck's* all the time—best in the city." She paused a second. "Oh, by the way."

"What?" He looked up at her from his salad.

"No 'wife' talk, okay? Unless she's going to be joining us," she said.

"Wow. All right," Jeremy said and laughed. "Say, this antique furniture's outstanding."

She smiled. "My great grandmother's. Vintage 1880 or thereabouts."

"Wonderful."

She smiled and returned to the stove. Stirring the pasta, she looked maternal—a side of her he had never imagined.

He recalled how he had married Rachel a couple of years after the bombing. She had given him the alibi that saved him from prison. He wondered if he had really married her as some sort of unspoken agreement to keep her quiet about his activity at Sterling Hall that night.

The microwave suddenly beeped, startling him. Catherine reached over and pulled out a ceramic tub of steaming sauce.

"Ready?" she called, and reached for a hot mitt.

"All set," he said. He rubbed his hands together.

Standing at the sink with her back to him, Catherine dumped the pasta into a shiny copper colander. She carefully drained the hot water. Rising steam ensnared her body. She jiggled the colander, shaking off the excess water, asher breasts jiggled invitingly. She emptied the pasta into a serving bowl. Jeremy was mesmerized by her grace as she brought the steaming pasta and the sauce tub to the table.

"Here you go. More wine?" She ladled ravioli onto her plate and his.

"Sure," he said.

She picked up the bottle of merlot and poured from just the right height to create scores of tiny air bubbles.

"Impressive," he said.

"Helps aerate the wine."

By mid-meal, Jeremy's head was spinning from the grass. He rose and staggered over to the couch. "Ooo." The walls of the room seemed to be moving up and down.

She sat next to him and cuddled him. That felt safer.

"That's a boy," she spoke in a soft, smooth voice that seemed far away.

"You're okay, Jer. Just ease down. You'll be okay. You know what day it is?"

"Thursday?"

"Yes, that's right. You'll be fine."

Jeremy felt so high. The room was spinning, he was freezing and shaking, and he couldn't conceive of the idea of sitting up straight.

She pulled him to her and stroked his head. "Take it easy, Jer," she said. "You feel better now?"

"Better."

"I was hoping I wasn't losing my new lover?"

"Oh, Catherine, when you come on to me like that, is that sincere? You sound like you really care—in a sexy sort of way." He felt like a schoolboy again, vying for his sweetheart's affections. Or maybe he was walking into a trap.

"I do care," she said matter-of-factly. "But I'm into passion, I have to admit, and you really turn me on."

"How?"

"Most guys act like major macho fucking machines off the bat. I'm not into that. But you like, uh, *cognitive* sex. I can tell."

He felt lucid for a second. "Say, Catherine? Tell me your deepest darkest secret." He thought that sounded particularly cognitive.

"See, I like that." She laughed. "Let's see—like the time I made it with my girlfriend—Diane Hightower—over and over one summer out at the Cape. We were seventeen and horny as hell."

"Made it?"

"Oh, we were hot. You name it; we did it."

"Really? You know that turns guys on? Two chicks together." Jeremy felt himself come down from the scary crest of his high to a cruising ebb. "I mean, if two women can express a tender act of love, how is that any less legitimate than a barbaric heterosexual mating ritual, right?" *Poetry,* he thought.

"Thanks, stud," she said, "Your turn, Jeremy: tell me your biggest secret. You feeling better now?"

"I think." But the crest of the high was returning.

"Good, come on, then," Catherine said.

"It'll blow you away," he said. "I warn you."

"Really?" She tenderly kissed his forehead.

He smiled. "Really. I hope you can take it."

"Try me." She ruffled his hair. "I love your hair."

"Okay. In SDS, at school?" he said.

"Students for a Democratic Society?"

"Yeah. U. of W. at Madison. Pretty wild anti-war campus—the wildest," he said, "in the whole country."

"Got it. You were there. I'm impressed."

"I helped blow up some bombs, even a building."

"Really?" she said. "Wow."

"We used a fertilizer bomb to blow off the side of this building. Killed a janitor in the process," he said and sat straight up, "and damaged other buildings, too."

"Oh, my God, Jeremy."

"It was my fault, Catherine. Honest. You're the first person I've ever said this to. I was the leader and ordered the blast. It was my fault the guy died. My buddies went to jail for me."

"Buddies? I'll say."

"Man." He held his head and shook it.

"Go ahead," she said. "Who?"

"My friends."

"Why not you?"

"Uh . . . uh . . . uh." Jeremy shook, unable to answer. "I ratted on them and Rachel lied for me."

Catherine nodded. "So you felt indebted to her and married her?" She laid his head on her lap and stroked his hair.

He nodded. "Yes. But two of 'em—brothers—got out five years early."

"Thank goodness for small favors." Catherine shook her head. "How long were they in prison?"

"Fourteen years," Jeremy answered. "I'm so fucked up."

"Aren't we all. The rest of your friends are still in prison?"

He nodded. "Shit," he said and half laughed, his hand against his forehead. "Ooo, man. Your damn grass."

"I warned you," she chided.

They pawed at each other, then started hugging.

"Hey!" Jeremy exclaimed. "You're not s'pose to swear, Ms. Dunne."

They both giggled.

"Makes me human," she said.

They laughed again.

"Jeremy," Catherine said, "if you hire me, we can fool around all the time."

"What?" He laughed. "You really are a shrewd bitch, aren't you? I knew I should be wary of you."

They laughed and rubbed their faces against one another, kissing.

"Just good business skills," she said, and winked. She kissed him on the cheek—her soft lips lingered there in the hollow for a moment.

He turned to meet her lips, but stopped. "Man-oh-man," he said softly.

She pushed his shoulders. "Will you stop saying that!"

"Part of the job requirements, Ms. Dunne—you have to emulate my speech patterns."

"That all it takes?"

"There is a down side . . . for me." He laughed.

What's that?"

"Archer'll hire you; then you'll take my goddamned job."

She laughed and sipped some wine. "Never can tell," she said. "At least, now I know there's one guy out there who appreciates the sexy things I do."

"Who might that be?" he asked.

"You, dumby!" she said.

He shook his head. "Sorry, I'm still so fuckin' high. I mean less, but still a lot."

"Like I said, potent weed, *mon*."

They laughed.

She continued, "Being with someone like you—who shares my turn-ons—legitimizes mine. Makes me feel okay about myself."

"Really?" Jeremy said happily. "Well, between you and me, having someone with the same turn-ons as me is a dream come true. I didn't know anyone like that even existed. I always thought I was the horniest guy in the world . . . and very alone."

"What about what's-her-name?" Catherine pouted.

"Rachel? She really got to me when we were dating, but she doesn't seem the same anymore. Like the marriage covered her with this cape of . . . *domestica* or something."

"You don't have kids?" she asked.

"No."

"Your problem?" she asked.

"We sort of decided against them a long time ago, but it was mainly my idea." He sipped more wine.

"Ooo. Bet she was pissed about that. I want to have kids some day."

"Rachel constantly brings up the life we could've had."

As they blabbered at each other, they gestured sloppily and their touching became more familiar.

"Man, I still feel *incredibly* buzzed," Jeremy slurred slightly. "Is that the right terminology?"

"That's okay. Say, Jeremy?" She hung on his shoulder, unbuttoning the buttons to his shirt and stroking his chest hair. "After being near you just a couple of times, I have to be honest."

"What?"

"We're really connecting, don't you think?" She moved closer and toyed with his hair.

"Like at the restaurant?" He leaned over and kissed her lightly on the neck. "Say, you don't mind if I kiss you, do you? Your skin is so soft. I just feel like doing this."

"I've been waiting for you," she said.

"I'll do it again, then." He did.

"Ooo, yeah," she said. "That gave me incredible butterflies. Really on the edge—"

"Oh, you like getting kissed on the neck?"

"No, stupid." She laughed. "The restaurant. I like the subtle stuff. It got to you, I could tell."

He pointed an index finger toward the sky. "Accurate assessment, Ms. Dunne."

"I was totally overwhelmed, like a night I spent with Daniel," she said.

"Who's Daniel?"

"A friend since we were kids. A real soul mate I still see once in a while. At the restaurant, my stomach had that gulpy feeling, could you tell?"

"You concealed it pretty well," Jeremy said. "Man, I don't think I did."

"You're one passionate stud, Jer."

"I don't think I've ever heard a woman talk to me like that. Ever. Well, maybe Rachel at the beginning, but I think she always felt guilty about it."

"I'm glad you like it. There's more where that came from, especially if you hire me." Catherine leaned over, clutched his head, and pulled it to within two inches of her face. "Jeremy, now that I've had part of you, I want all of you."

Yeah, including my job, he thought. *Then my career's a blow-out.* "I don't know if I can trust you."

She smiled. "Oh, Jeremy, I can be your tramp, your whore," she said, and snuggled him.

"Oh, *God*!" he sighed.

"*Take* me, you fucking animal. I want to *experience* you. Totally." She kissed him all over his face.

"Man." He laughed nervously. "I know I can say anything to you. Absolutely anything." He grinned. "You know how that feels? Like absolute freedom."

"Hmm," she said. "I do want you. I'm not just saying that."

"Okay? So, when?" he said.

She laughed. "Tonight, Jeremy. Why wait? Why not christen us working together. Just think, Jeremy. Again and again."

"Right. No better moment than the present to get started." He chugged his wine and held out his glass.

She poured the rest of the bottle, put it down, pulled him to her, and kissed him again. Her manner was rough, but her tongue, soft, and her taste, sweet. She moaned as she moved her head and glided her lips back and forth on his. She leaned over and rubbed her breasts against his chest. She pulled back for a second. "I'm glad I found you, Jeremy Lucas."

"Man-oh-man," he said. "Ooo, sorry. I said it again." He suddenly waved his hands in the air. "Wait, Catherine, I have to admit this. I don't think I've ever admitted this to a woman!"

They laughed.

"What?" she asked.

"I think I'm totally ruled by my penis."

She laughed.

"Really, I think I need the conquest so bad, I can't resist temptation. I've never been able to. But, I suck when it comes to the commitment."

"Well, commitment or not, this is a lot of fun, you have to admit," she said. "The restaurant . . . seeing you like this."

"But," he said, "I know Rachel wouldn't find this funny at all.

"Actually, she's probably home sacked up with the milkman."

"Probably our plumber, Paul," he said. "He lives next door."

"Paul?" she said. "Then, let's toast to Paul."

"To Paul!" they both said and laughed harder. Jeremy tipped his wine glass, and spilled some red wine on the ivory carpet.

"Oops. I'm sorry," he said.

"Leaving your mark?" Catherine said and laughed, "If you're trying to dissuade me, Jeremy, you've failed miserably." She pulled him to her. "I still want you."

"Then take me, you heavenly goddess," he breathed, staring into her eyes. "That's right! I noticed that before, your eyes are that violet color. What are you? A new age Liz?"

They laughed.

Then she kissed him hard and pulled away. He mimicked her.

They kissed each other again, this time longer. Their laughing tapered to a whimper.

After a minute or so, they stood, keeping their lips affixed.

They pulled off each other's clothes and moaned urgently. Then they groped at each other's bodies, he in his underwear; she, naked. He yanked off his Jockeys.

"Wait, Jeremy," she said temptingly. "Come over here." She signaled him with her index finger, pulled open the sliding patio door, and led him out onto the balcony, twelve-by-twelve foot concrete square, bordered on three sides by heavy gauge wrought iron. Outside was wet, but strangely, no snow had fallen. The cold night breeze instantly chilled Jeremy to the bone. Then, he saw a seven-foot-tall propane heater blasting hot air from glowing blue jets.

"What's that?" he asked and pointed.

"A toy Daniel gave me. Come on." Catherine pulled him farther onto the balcony. "You should've seen the looks in their eyes when the guys delivered it!"

"Hey, wait! It's really cold out here." He started to pull her back inside.

"No. Please, I promise. Come over here. You'll warm up. We'll do it while I'm flying." She led him near the heater. "Interested?"

"Flying?" he said.

"Yeah. You'll see. Wait." She ran inside, then reappeared a minute later.

"Where did you go?"

She gave him a condom. "A habit."

"Ooo, I hate them."

"Sorry. Until we're tested and regular, it's a must."

She lay down a cloth napkin on the balcony's railing. She turned around and, facing him with both hands on the wrought iron, she hoisted herself onto the railing, wobbling as she did. "Whoops, it's cold." She scooched over till she was well balanced.

"Wait. Are you crazy?" Jeremy looked over the edge. He still felt high and the tiny, snow-covered front lawn of the apartment building seemed to move nineteen floors below. For a moment, he laughed to himself, thinking that this could be one way to rid himself of her as competition for his job.

"Relax, Lucas," Catherine said, not looking down. "I'll have you know I've done this quite a few times. It's perfectly safe as long as . . . "

"What?"

"As long as you help me keep my balance. I call it flying. Pretty cool, huh?"

"Man-oh-man, but we're already high."

They laughed.

"Just watch," she said. "Gymnastics was good for something." She raised her hands off the railing until she was balancing on her butt, teetering back and forth like a high wire pro. "See. Just help me balance, okay?"

"Sure. I'm impressed," Jeremy grunted, reaching forward to steady Catherine. "Now, you'd better get down. Come on, you're scaring me."

"No, no," she purred. "Just wait. I'm okay. I told you Daniel and I have done this before. It's your turn."

"Turn?" Jeremy said incredulously. *On the other hand,* he thought, *she'd be a perfect replacement for me at Archer: impeccable credentials, horny persona.*

"You know, *your* turn to do it with *me*," Catherine explained, and quickly glanced down. "Besides, I'm sure this will have a favorable effect on my employment potential; that is, as long as you don't try to get rid of me." She glanced down again.

"Catherine, stop saying that. You're such a goddess, I don't know if I could ever hire you now. I'd rather love you." He pondered for a second the inevitability of her taking away his life and career, and he quivered.

"They'll make you hire me, Jer. After all, Hadley *is* my adopted uncle."

Jeremy said, "That's probably true." *My career is over for sure,* he thought. *Why am I doing this flying nonsense then?*

"*Do* it to me, Jeremy," Catherine sighed, "*then* hire me. Then, do it to me again and again."

"This does look interesting," Jeremy nodded, and looked up at the propane burner as sweat dripped from his forehead and steam shot from his mouth.

Making love in this flying position began to appeal to him. "But, I don't know if I can stay hard out here." He laughed. "Can you help?"

"Come closer." She laughed and beckoned him with pendulous arms, floating gracefully in the air as she teetered.

He slithered between her warm, soft thighs. Then, she clamped him tightly. She kissed his mouth, stroked him with her hands, and rubbed him against the baby-softness of her inner-upper thigh.

"Ooo, that feels so good," Jeremy said. In seconds, he hardened. While he steadied the woman, she took the condom, unwrapped it and expertly slipped it on him. Seconds later, he grabbed her by the hips and plunged into her.

"Ah! That's outstanding," she said.

"Ooo, *yeah*. Not bad," he panted. "It feels incredibly good—like velvet. I knew you'd feel like velvet. Are all Chicago MBAs this smooth?" He rocked back and forth.

"Just the female ones."

They laughed.

"See, I told you," she said. "Magnificent out here, isn't it?"

"Oh, yeah," Jeremy murmured.

"Ooo, and see how the railing's the perfect height." She arched her back, rolling her hips back and forth at him.

"Oh, yeah." He pounded harder. "But, please be careful."

"Oh, baby!" she shouted. She started flicking her hips, swiveling at her waist with quick jerks while she waved her hands in the air. "See . . . I'm flying, Jeremy!" He steadied her as she seemed to float before him in the vapors from their breathing.

"God, you're the most beautiful woman I've ever seen," Jeremy yelled. "I knew we'd be good together, but not this good."

"Oh, it's won-der-ful!" Catherine cried. "Harder, please?"

"I love that voice, how you say 'wonderful.' " Jeremy couldn't stand it, he was on the verge of climaxing. "I want this to go on forever." He still felt a little tipsy from the grass. "Ooo, I'm so high." He briefly readjusted his hold on Catherine. Then, he heaved up and back.

"Whoops!" She lost her balance for a second. She nervously adjusted herself on the railing. "God, that was too close."

He looked down. "I told you, now, be careful!" he cried, panting steam. "This is one of those things we can't make a mistake on. You sure you want to keep doing this?" For a second, he pictured her making a mistake and how that would protect his turf at Archer. *What a thought!*

"Oh, yeah." She leaned farther back and waved her arms gracefully through the air. "This is heaven!" she said. "Look at me, Jeremy!"

"Beautiful!" He ogled her, then glanced around at Chicago's near north skyline, peppered with dots of light from a thousand windows in a dozen high-rises all around, like little candles pasted onto the midnight blue sky. "Think anyone can see us?" He panted.

"Oh, God, I hope so! Can you imagine them seeing us and loving it? Not knowing who we are? Even calling their neighbors?"

"Man." Just for a second, Jeremy pictured Catherine falling, away from him, and how then he would be absolutely secure at work, probably even taking Carl's job at some point. But, then, he flashed to the opposite alternative—losing his job to this beauty. *My God!* With his near-criminal past, he absolutely had to maintain his position at Archer. He'd *never* be able to replace his job with something comparable. He felt weak and helpless for a second—

She suddenly slipped six inches down off the railing. "Dammit, Jeremy!" she snapped as he pulled her close. “Are you trying to eliminate any future competition?”

For a brief second, he was angry she’d said that, maybe because he had thought the same thing. “Here, let me control you,” he said.

She relaxed. “But, I love the freedom, you know?” After a minute of kissing, she pumped at him even harder.

“No! Don’t move.” Suddenly, the sex felt particularly good for Jeremy.

“What’s going on?” she asked.

They stopped talking. He felt a surge of highness and when he looked at her, she was stiff as could be, not moving a muscle.

“Is this how you like it, Jer? Controlling me. Well, okay.”

“Don’t say a word.” Her breasts swelled in the soft shadows created by the blue propane glow. “That’s so good,” he said. “So beautiful.”

“Whoops—” She slipped down half a foot. “Wait. Help!”

“But, I can’t hold—” he said. He grabbed at her hips, but his hands were slippery with sweat and he scratched at her. He knew, as he clawed helplessly, almost in slow motion, that something futile was about to unfold. “Catherine—”

She slipped further.

"Jeremy! This isn't—"

"Your weight—too much."

"No!" she said. "Wait!" Her legs kicked high into the air. He felt his manhood shrink. Her head flopped back and her shoulders yanked away from him. He reached for them, but his hands slipped loose. His body pitched forward. To save himself from toppling over the railing, he pushed against her. At that moment she grabbed at his hair, tearing some out, and then slipped from his grasp.

"Catherine!"

"No-o-o!"

She fell.

Jeremy watched her plummet away from him. Almost unreal to him, she gaped in silent shock as she drifted down. Her pendulous arms and legs floated in space, as if her graceful flailing might help. As he watched in horror, he knew by pushing her to save himself, he had created this moment. Then, as she floated downward, her arms stopped moving, like a beacon signaling the moment she must have given up. Jeremy watched her frozen eyes fix on him till they faded into darkness as the image of her body got smaller and smaller.

What seemed like a lifetime later, she hit the frozen snow nineteen stories below. Only an inconsequential, muffled *thud* echoed through the apartment's courtyard and back up to Jeremy.

Her naked body lay sprawled and still on a blanket of white snow, illuminated by spherical lights that cast multiple shadows. The winding, shoveled walk, leading to the building's front door, framed the grotesque scene. Jeremy could make out dark liquid streaming from her head and mouth.

Jeremy felt dazed as he stared at the miniature lifeless form. Stunned for a second, he quickly shook himself out of his trance. To run, to hide, to flee from this scene, was suddenly all he could think of.

"My God!" he shouted and glared around at adjacent balconies, all vacant. He shook his head hard to ward off the highness. He pulled off the condom, turned off the heater, and dashed to the living room. He grabbed his clothes and frantically put them on, stuffing the condom in his pocket. He looked around. *Have I left anything?* He wiped his wine glass and utensils with a napkin. Then, gasping wildly and still not sure of his balance, he ran toward the apartment door. He grabbed his coat from the front closet and wiped the closet door handle.

He peeked out the front door, trying to maintain enough composure to wipe both inside and outside knobs; then, flew down the hall, around the first corner. He pushed the elevator button, then wiped it clean.

Wait! The drunk doorman!

He dashed out of the passenger elevator as the doors closed, then scurried around the corner to the brown freight elevator door, pushed the button that would take him to the loading dock, then wiped it clean. With his hand wrapped in the sleeve of his coat, he pulled the doors closed. The elevator slowly rumbled downward toward the dock. Jeremy hoped he wouldn't be greeted by the police, or anyone else for that matter. He sweated profusely, struggling to catch his breath.

The elevator stopped. Jeremy frantically pulled open the door. The loading dock was empty. He ran across the dock's slippery concrete floor and pulled open the ten-foot garage door. The wind froze the sweat on his face to a micro-thin sheet of ice. He jumped off the dock and fell when the slick bottom of his dress shoes hit the icy alley four feet below. He was able to stand, but hobbled down the slippery, faintly lit alley to Clark Street.

He turned right onto Clark and limped one block north to Mike's restaurant. He contained his frantic demeanor as he passed the faces of customers, barely visible through the steamed glass. When a few of them looked at him, he turned away and slowed his gait, acting as nonchalant as possible. He was just beginning to feel straight.

He crossed the street and walked back down Clark toward Eugenie Street, where he saw blinking red lights and heard sirens. When he ran over to LaSalle, an officer stood in the middle of the intersection, directing traffic.

Jeremy looked around and spotted his car across the street and down the block, next to the park. He half-ran and half-walked to the vehicle. He nearly bumped into a babbling old street-lady. With her fingers poking out of her tattered gloves, she was reorganizing her shopping cart full of boxes, blankets, and canned food. She hacked a deep cough.

"So what's the big deal, ma'am?" he asked, and pointed around.

She looked up. "Don't ask me, fella." She eyed him. "Say, where you runnin' to?"

"Nowhere, ma'am," Jeremy shrugged. "Must be some kind of accident."

"Something crazy, I bet." The old woman's head quivered as she pushed her cart away on the frozen, bumpy, unshoveled sidewalk, swearing under her breath. She cleared her throat, then sang in a raspy little voice: "Jesus, my sweet Jesus. Weird kinda people doing crazy things these days . . . " She hacked again.

Jeremy noticed that a crowd had formed near the front of Catherine's building. He reached in his pocket, jangled his keys, and ran to his Corolla loaner. He slid onto the icy, stiff, seats, pushed in the clutch, and started the ignition. First, the engine cranked slowly, then faster. Finally, the car started with a zoom. *Thank God!*

He rolled back a few inches, crunching ice as hard as crystal. He slipped into first gear and stepped on the gas lightly, inching out of the parking space.

Three knocks rapped on the frost-covered driver's-side window. "Hey, you! Stop there for a second," a muffled male voice said.

Jeremy slammed on the brakes and thrust down the window. A forty-something police officer, breathing steam, looked down on him with a scowl. Jeremy recalled the distinctive checkered band on his Chicago Police hat from when his

Easter Gang had protested at the '68 Convention in Lincoln Park with some yippies from out of town.

"What's the fuss?" Jeremy asked.

"Say, buddy, you aren't leaving *that* building, are you?" he asked as he squinted at Jeremy. He pointed to the 2650 building.

"Me? No, sir. Just park here every day. Take the bus from Downtown up here. Saves on parking. You know how expensive it can get," Jeremy chattered nervously.

The cop picked at his left ear. "Gets pretty high all right," he said. He looked back at the building, then back at Jeremy. "Guess you can go." He knocked on the car roof and blew into a little black multi-tone whistle. He turned back suddenly. "Hey, wait. One more thing." He sniffed the air.

"What's that, officer?" Jeremy's heart jumped.

"Naw, you're not the type."

"Type?"

"These new wheels?" the cop asked.

"No, a loaner from the dealer."

"If you park 'em here all day, you might lose 'em," he said. "Corolla's one of the most common steals, you know. Great chop shop stuff."

"Oh, really?" Jeremy feigned interest.

After the cop dismissed him, Jeremy made a U-turn on LaSalle, just to annoy the cop, drove one block south, and made a right at North Avenue. He took North past the projects. He rolled down his window, reached in his pocket, pulled out the condom, and tossed it.

As he turned north onto the Kennedy Expressway, the ubiquitous orange of the solar vapor streetlights flooded through his windshield and lit up his hands. He noticed a blue ink stain on his right thumb.

"What the hell is this?" He spat on it, rubbed it on a remnant piece of Kleenex lying next to him. It wouldn't come clean.

Jeremy looked at his watch. He turned on the radio and dialed in WBBM News Radio 78 to see what the reporters might have to say. Then, he turned on his courtesy light, looked in his day timer, flipped a few pages and dialed a long distance number—no answer.

He sped north. An hour later, after making another quick call, he took Route 57 to the Wisconsin Route 28 exit and headed into Cascade.

Cascade, Wisconsin

He limped up to the door of Building D and rang the bell. It opened.

"Jeremy. You really came," Lana Holub said.

"Yeah, sure." He looked around.

As far as Jeremy could tell, Lana was wearing only a T-shirt. "What, you like? I walk around like this all the time, but you probably forgot that."

"Right, nice." Jeremy was still sweaty. He wiped his brow. "Listen, can I wash up? I'm a mess."

"What's that smell?"

"Just a smoky restaurant."

"What's with the limp?"

"Hurt it. Say, I might need your help, Lana." He knew she could provide an alibi if he needed one. He just had to push the right buttons.

"Jeez. Here, let me take your coat." She took the jacket and opened her little closet, crowded with a palette of different pastel-colored clothes.

"Don't let my coat dirty all your clothes," Jeremy joked.

"Why are you being so nice? It can fit fine." She pushed aside the hangers to make room. "Ma still thinks clothes'll get me a man. Sends me money once a month. Tells me what to buy: 'I saw this lovely blouse at Fields. I tell her, 'Ma, there's no Fields up here.'" Lana laughed. "She just wears out her Keds walking through Fields down in Chicago, then she tells me to buy the same thing over at Tar-jay up here."

He forced a laugh. "Yeah, good old Target." Then he scowled. "Where were you when I called the first time?"

"Oh, after work, I went to the movies. Some cool film was playing. Confusing, but cool."

"Sounds interesting." He shook his head.

"You know, Ma still wants to know if I'm gonna snag you. Can you imagine? She still calls you Jerry. If she only knew about the abort—"

"Listen, Lana, you gotta know how bad I feel about all that. Honest."

"Right. Well, my AA degree from the Milwaukee Business College has done all it's gonna do for me." She laughed cynically. "And you're pretty much outa my life now, I s'pose."

"Lana, don't be so negative," Jeremy said.

"Well, I tell her, 'Some day, Ma. Some day I'll find somebody like Jer. Some day.'"

"Say, you got some water or something?" He looked around. Throw pillows were scattered on the second-hand furniture he had picked up for her a year ago. The little TV was on, showing a rerun of *Seinfeld*; as usual, Kramer was stumbling into Jerry's apartment.

"How about some wine?" Lana offered. "For old times' sake. I'm all healed up now, I just might take advantage of you if your gimp leg can hack it."

"Hmmm." Jeremy grimaced. "It's fine, really. Just a little banged up. Lana, you still have what it takes, you know." He cleared his throat. "Whatever you want, Lana. Tonight, you're the boss."

"Jer, does that mean you're really sorry?"

"Scout's honor, Lana. I owe you tons."

She scurried to the kitchen and called back, "White okay? I still have some of that Kendall Jackson you like."

"Sure."

On TV, George wanted Jerry and Kramer's advice. He had trouble being perfectly honest with his impossible parents, and found himself always lying. "So, you do what you have to," Kramer said, singing and shaking in his usual way. "After all, this is life, Georgy. You gotsta survive!"

Man, that's really true, thought Jeremy as he listened to the canned laughter.

Walking back, carrying two full glasses of wine, Lana continued. "Well, to us." She toasted. "And to me, for helping you out with your situation."

"Right," he said. They toasted. "Say, can I sit down?"

"Sure, here," she answered, patting the seat on the couch next to her. "If you want, you can take a shower. See what happens."

"Sure. Great. But, first—" Jeremy grinned, "let's say we make another toast, Lana. Really. I want to make it up to you. This toast's for you."

She sat down next to him. "Really, Jer? Okay." She leaned her head on his shoulder and sniffed. "If that's the way you really want it," she smiled. "You've always been able to press my buttons." She held up her glass and clinked his.

"To you, Lana Holub," Jeremy announced. "I swear, tonight's for old times' sake. I'll try to make up for being such an asshole."

"Oh, Jer—I like." She smiled coyly.

"And, you never know what might come of it," he said.

PART II

THE REWARDS

9

Fond du Lac, Wisconsin February 22, 1985

A week and two days later, on a Saturday, Jeremy sat reading the newspaper at the kitchen table after breakfast. His right calf muscle had stiffened after the night of Catherine's fall. Then, after a few days, the pain subsided. Today, the winter sun that streaked through the side window flashed rays into his face, like the lamp above a prisoner being interrogated. He adjusted his chair to improve the light—no better. Jeremy had tried to deny his pangs of culpability, but they kept returning even a week later. He tried and tried to convince himself that he had little to do with the dramatic accident that happened in Chicago on the prior Thursday night. But nothing seemed to work.

The news coverage immediately following Catherine's death had been sparse on Milwaukee TV, but it did point out that the strange incident might affect Wall Street analysts' view of her father's ability to lead IDS, so distracted would he be. The reporters believed that her falling to a dramatic death while making love would, at the very least, trigger some unwanted PR for the company.

The Fond du Lac newspaper had only mentioned the incident in passing, and apologized for the skimpy coverage, noting that perverse incidents of this kind usually only occurred in large cities like Chicago, Los Angeles, or New York—certainly not in communities surrounding Lake Winnebago.

That perspective only somewhat echoed Jeremy's personal thoughts on the matter. Catherine's "flying" bullshit and propane toy were the real causes of the fall—certainly not his pushing her as she grabbed for him. Consider first his sweaty hands. They might have been his sweaty hands, but she had made him sweat with that propane torch and her enticing arousal techniques. Also, he wouldn't have been so aroused had she not worn that red dress. And, she wouldn't have been wearing something that alluring had she not wanted to seduce him, starting with her vampish behavior at the restaurant. And so on. Only one person was responsible for Catherine Dunne's demise, and that was Catherine Dunne. Of this, Jeremy was dead sure. He just happened to have been there; it could have just as well been her friend Daniel. *Hell!* It could've been the drunk doorman.

"Jeremy." Rachel tapped him on the shoulder.

He jerked. "Rachel! Don't scare me like that."

"Well, I've been standing here, talking to you, holding this damn pitcher," she said.

"Jesus."

"I said, 'do you want any more orange juice?' " she asked, standoffish.

"*No*," he fired back, "for Chrissake." He pushed his newspaper aside.

"What is it, Jeremy? Something's been bugging you for the last week, I can tell."

"Why do you say that?"

"I don't know. You're so touchy. You just haven't been yourself! And you still look like you're favoring your right leg a little."

"Just leave me alone, okay? Got a lot on my mind—Bob's death and all the changes at work." He pulled back the paper roughly and turned a page as he sipped his coffee.

The doorbell rang. He jumped again. "Jeez."

Rachel giggled. "See, I told you. Stay put, I'll get it." She stood up slowly. "Probably little Clark—wants his shoveling money." She grabbed her purse from the kitchen counter, jangling it as she headed for the front door. "Going to have to clean this old thing out one of these days."

A second later, Jeremy heard low mumbling, Rachel talking to an adult male voice.

"Jeremy!" Rachel called.

"What?" he said.

"Some policeman wants to talk to you!"

Jeremy froze. His gut churned. At once he felt like running away; this had to be bad. He looked around for a casual escape— none to be found.

He stood, feeling shaky in the knees. He peeked around the door into the living room. A Wisconsin State policeman stood just inside the front door, talking to Rachel. A set of incredibly long teeth poked from beneath his upper lip.

Jeremy casually walked into the living room and tossed the folded newspaper on his recliner. With a waver in his voice, he said, "What is it, officer?" He looked at his badge. It said James L. Rainero. *So proper*, Jeremy thought.

"Officer Jim Rainero, here." He shook hands with Jeremy.

Rachel looked bored. "He just wanted to verify that you were in Chicago week ago Thursday," she said. "I told him yes."

"Damn, Rachel. Why are you talking for me?"

The officer frowned.

"Excuse me, sir, you are Mr. Lucas?" he asked. "Jeremy Wayne Lucas?"

"Yeah. What's with the middle name?"

"Positive I.D. is all. You attended U. of W. at Madison, right?" His teeth seemed to struggle to fit in his mouth as he talked.

"Yeah," Jeremy said. "Why?"

"Member of SDS? Arrested in '70 for setting the explosion and fire at Sterling Hall?"

"So?"

"Tried for the death of a janitor, Timothy Agers, killed in the blast? Life's work of Professor Naubasch destroyed—on the verge of some major advances in superconductivity?"

"Whoa. What's with all the details?" Jeremy raised his hands. "I was cleared of all that."

"I understand that, sir. They let you off. I just wanted to make sure you were the right guy. Where were you Thursday night, a week ago, Mr. Lucas?" the policeman asked.

Jeremy's stomach shook. "Thursday . . . hmm . . . the 13th?"

"That's correct, sir."

Jeremy put his index finger to mouth, stalling. "Uh . . . uh."

"I told him Chicago" Rachel blurted, irritated.

"Rachel!" Jeremy scolded her. "Damn you! I said shut up."

"Well, I'm sorry, but you were," she said indignantly, looking back and forth between Jeremy and the officer, hands on hips.

"Is that right, sir?" the officer said, his eyes turning cold. "Where exactly in Chicago?"

Rachel butted in. "At the Delaware Place on the near north side."

"Rachel!"

"Near North side? That right, sir?" the officer asked. "We can check on that." He wrote a note in a pad.

"Uh, yes. I was thinking I wasn't there that Thursday but I guess I was." Jeremy shivered.

"Hmmm. Sure. I'm afraid, then, that you'll have to come with me. You can bring a few things; pack a small bag."

"Uh . . . uh . . . Why?" Jeremy asked. "Rachel, pack my gym bag with a few books and stuff."

"Please come with me," the officer said, his mouth closing and jaw clenching. He reached forward and gripped Jeremy firmly on the left bicep.

"Hey!" Jeremy said and pulled away. "You can't—"

"We can do this naughty or nice, sir," he said. "Your choice, Mr. Lucas."

Jeremy put his hands up. "Just take it easy, okay? Where the hell are you taking me?" He turned and kissed Rachel on the cheek. "I'm sorry, Honey."

"Cook County Jail, sir. Need to check your prints and get a strand analysis on your hair."

"Hair? What's going on here?"

"Just identification, sir. Seeing if you were at the scene of a death. That's all."

Shit, Jeremy thought. *This is for real.*

"Jeremy," she said. "What's this all about?"

"Probably some stupid mistake. You know the system."

The officer looked at his watch. "Well, Mr. Lucas?"

"Okay, okay. I'm ready, I'm ready," Jeremy said. "Rach, don't sweat it, okay? Call Billy and tell him to meet me at the Cook County Jail in an hour and a half or so."

"But, Jeremy," she cried.

"Just call him."

"That your attorney, Mr. Lucas?"

"Yeah."

"Good idea."

Jeremy put on his coat. Officer Rainero led him out to the squad car where a younger officer waited. "Reno, what took you so long?"

"Had to establish a clear probable cause. Inconsistencies did it." Rainero held Jeremy's head down as he climbed into the rear seat.

"You're treating me like a I'm a goddamned criminal or something," Jeremy said. "Can't you see you're scaring the hell out of my wife?"

"Normal procedure, Lucas." He shook his head. "And I thought Nam was a bitch! My grandfather—he was in World War I—would be rolling over in his grave if he saw how nicely we treat suspects!"

"Now I'm a suspect."

"We'll have to see. Haven't you heard a word I've said? The prints?"

The second officer leaned over. "What's his beef, Reno?"

"We call 'em piss-ass blueblood perps."

"I heard that, Officer Rainero."

"So? Just clam up, Lucas."

Rachel stood on the lawn without a coat, trembling in tears, arms wrapped around her body, spouting steam. "Hons, what's going on?" she called.

"Nothing," Jeremy mouthed through the car window, "It's nothing." A second later, as the officer backed down the curvy driveway, Jeremy waved to Rachel. She hugged herself and jumped up and down, still crying.

"I'll call you," he mouthed. As they drove him away, Jeremy looked back. He saw Paul, shovel in hand, walk over from next door. Rachel's breath was visible as she talked to Paul and gestured toward the police car.

"So, what's this all about?" Jeremy asked Officer Rainero.

"Told you. Need to shuttle you down to Chicago," he said.

"I know that. But why?"

"There's a reciprocal arrangement between the Wisconsin State Police and the Chicago force—just questioning."

"Can you do this? God, this is such fascist bullshit. And, what's this hair shit . . . and prints?"

"Like I said, just routine, Lucas. They need to see if you're the same Jeremy Lucas they think was at the scene."

"Well, how the hell did you get my name."

"Matchbook . . . and a print on it. Then the FBI database."

The other officer—a bald guy with short-cropped hair on the sides of his head—was sitting on the passenger side.

"Like he said, the State of Wisconsin has an extradition agreement with Illinois, too."

"But am I charged with something?" Jeremy asked.

"Have to see, sir," Officer Rainero said.

"How?"

"Like I said, they found a fingerprint at the scene of a death. They found your name and a hair . . . and you and the missus couldn't seem to agree where you were last Thursday."

"So."

"That gives us probable cause," he said.

"Cause?" Jeremy said.

"Yah," the second officer replied. "To look a little further. Might be nothing."

"Except my Saturday."

"Listen, they said the print looks pretty convincing," Officer Rainero said. "Found it on some matchbook. I guess the cover was printed with high gloss ink, so the print—a right thumb, I guess—came out real good.

"Jesus," Jeremy said.

"Yes sir—and get this," the second officer said. "That matchbook had your name on it, too. Iddy biddy, blue ink, they said."

He turned and scratched his head. "Can't blame 'em for wanting to see you—

especially if you might've fled the scene . . . and virtually denied today that you were there even though your wife puts you in the area. Doesn't look good."

Fuck, Jeremy thought, *that goddamn yellow matchbook.* He looked down at his right thumb as the light flickered through the trees on Park Avenue on the way to Route 45. It still showed some faded blue ink. As inconspicuously as possible, he licked his thumb and rubbed it hard on his jeans.

"So, you were down in Chicago week before last, then?" Officer Rainero ventured, bobbing at the mirror, exposing parts of his eyes, then teeth.

"Yes, I guess," Jeremy mumbled. "Business." He could feel his heart racing. He slapped one fist into the other palm.

The second officer turned. "Does the missus know about that bombing way back?"

"Of course," Jeremy mumbled.

"What'd you say, sir?" Rainero craned his skinny neck to see Jeremy in the rear view mirror.

All Jeremy could see was his long teeth. "Nothing. I was just thinking I'm glad my lawyer'll be there."

An hour later, as they exited I-94 and merged onto the Edens Expressway,

Jeremy looked at the side of the road, stark all around. Leafless, gray trees, piles of dirty snow, solitary patches of ice jutting through puddles that reflected a charcoal gray winter sky. He hadn't ever seen the Edens this desolate. "We're going to Cook County Jail, right?"

"Yah."

"Shit," he mumbled. Jeremy pictured the jail, full of hardened criminals. For the first time, he could imagine being one of them, not ever getting out of this mess—sentenced and put away. He shivered. That charm on his desk wasn't giving him any lucky favors this time.

Cook County Jail, Chicago, Illinois

"I really need your help. This isn't happening," Jeremy said excitedly to Billy Stokes, his lawyer. He glanced down the row of seedy-looking people sitting on an adjacent wooden bench against the wall—a man who hadn't bathed in a month with gray whiskers popping out of cavernous wrinkles; a black hooker who kept yapping about her rights; and an indignant teen with a James Dean pout who kept flicking his greasy hair away from his eyes.

"Hey, Jer." Billy Stokes reassured. "Relax, now. Let's just take this one step at a time. I would suspect the DA will be looking to make this murder two if he can uncover a motive."

"Murder two? Motive?"

"Well, we could try to convince him to go manslaughter right away, but I'm guessing that's not how a DA would think. He'd go for the biggy first to establish a solid bargaining position."

"But, Billy—I can't believe this!"

"Hey, what do you expect?" Billy's voice crackled. "A lady's dead here, right? She was smart, a looker, and had a big-shot daddy. It's a shame, but people don't like to hear about a rich, pretty lady dyin' from a messy fall while she was doin' it. Somebody has to pay."

"Sure. Hmm," Jeremy said. "Billy, have you handled these kinds of cases before?"

"You're kidding? Defended the Jones twins who were accused of killing their daddy with a shotgun."

"Really? You can handle something like my case—not so clear cut?"

"Well, I went to Southern Carolina Law. That was the place to go back home."

"Great. What happened to the twins?" Jeremy asked.

"Lethal injection," Billy said casually.

"Billy! Lethal injection?"

"Jer, listen, I look a lot dumber than I am." He laughed. "Did I say that right?"

Jeremy instantly calmed down. He covered his mouth to hold back a laugh.

10

Chicago, Illinois

Stokes went on, "Listen. After the Grand Jury convenes to determine if you'll to be arraigned—which I expect based on what you've told me—the judge'll determine if you can post bail, which I wouldn't count on because of the severity of the case, the damn fingerprint, your name, and of course, with your bucks, the flight risk. So, y'all gotta know, we're lookin' at some jail time here, could be from now till after the trial."

"Jail? That long?"

"Yup. Depending on the arraignment and trial dates, it could be two or three months."

"Can they do that? Seems like forever."

A brutal-looking seasoned detective walked up. "You're Lucas?"

"Yeah."

"In this case, it's just the law. A woman's dead. It's how the system works. Sorry."

"I'm sure you are."

Billy tried to reassure him. "Listen, Jeremy, after arraignment—which'll take four-six weeks—I'll see if I can move us up on the calendar for an early trial, but I can't guarantee anything."

"Great," Jeremy said sarcastically. "Rachel will have to call work to tell them something. I'm sure Archer'll be able to continue my salary . . . or part of it. God, Carl will love this!"

The detective wore a wrinkled gray suit and perpetual sneer that drooped to the left. "Good for you. That's not something anyone can get." Only the right side of his mouth moved.

"I hope I'm not here that long."

"Don't count on it. Right now we need you," he said. "Line-up. This your lawyer?"

"Yeah."

"We need him, too."

"Line-up?" Billy said. "Let's go, Jer. You don't have to answer any questions you don't want to. Did they read you the Miranda?"

"Yup."

"It's time." The cop looked back and forth from his worn Timex watch to Jeremy, then took Jeremy by the arm.

After the lineup, during which Jeremy stood with several other similar-looking men, he had a lock of his hair cut off by a short Asian man. Then, after he got fingerprinted, Jeremy was led into a small conference room where Billy sat across from the detective, who mumbled as he scratched notes on a little notepad while Jeremy related his story. Jeremy wondered how the cop's suit had gotten so wrinkled. "Detective, how'd your—"

"What?" the detective looked up. "By the way, name's Schmidt." Schmidt licked the pencil. "So, let me get this straight, Lucas," he said. "You met the deceased—this Dunne lady—at an interview at Archer Toys in Fond du Lac where she comes on to you. Then, this past Thursday, at a restaurant on north Dearborn here in Chicago, she gives you some matches with her address?"

"You can answer," Billy whispered. "As long as you know what you say can be used against you in court. This sounds okay."

"Yeah, basically, that's it." Jeremy talked to Schmidt as he looked around the small worn interview room.

Schmidt jotted a few more notes with his chewed-up pencil, carved on the end like it had been sharpened by a pocketknife.

The room smelled like a taxicab. The shiny, old mahogany table reflected four file cabinets standing guard around the room. Jeremy felt increasingly surrounded as Schmidt stood and paced, humming "My Way." Then, he stopped to adjust the yellowed blinds. As he clattered each blind shut, the room seemed to become smaller and smaller.

"What's going on here?" Jeremy asked. "The pressure bit?"

"Easy, Jeremy," Billy said.

Schmidt turned. "So, you can't explain the print on the matchbook?"

Jeremy shook his head. "Detective. Honest, I told you all I know. I have to think about it."

"Not gonna cut it, Lucas," Schmidt said. "Print's as clean as a whistle. Prints are prints—and your name, too. *And,* Roger is testing that lock of hair." He shook his head. "No matter what you say, it looks like you were there . . . period."

A knock sounded on the door's pimpled glass. The door rattled open. A pudgy man with round, flushed cheeks tapped on the jamb with a flashy, gold pen. He wore a meticulous navy suit, starched white shirt, and dark, conservative tie. The Asian man reappeared and stood behind the pudgy man. He nodded at Schmidt and gave him the thumbs-up sign. The pudgy man cleared his throat, and said with as much authority as his tenor voice would muster, "What do we have, Schmidt?"

"He says he wasn't there," Schmidt replied, "but, we have prints . . . a positive ID in the line-up . . . a conflicting statement by his wife *and* Roger just verified we have a positive match on the hair that was found at the scene in Ms. Dunne's hand."

Jeremy turned. "Who are you?"

"Edwin Terrance Butler, Assistant D. A.—the bad guy. You're Lucas, I presume."

"Yes. This is a great way to spend a Saturday," Jeremy said sarcastically. "This is just a big misunderstanding."

"Lucas," Butler said, "in this case, the smoking gun is this damn print. It puts you at the scene. The time written on the matchbook puts you there near the T.O.D. Your conflicting statements about *not* being there makes your story iffy. Now, we have a hair match and some witnesses. I'm afraid we have probable cause."

"What's T.O.D?" Jeremy stuttered.

"Time of death," Butler said.

"But, I could've left before her death."

"True," said Butler, "but why'd you leave your matches behind? In a hurry? And, why were strands of your hair in her hand?"

"Well—"

"The lab guys agree," Butler said, "evidence doesn't get much better than this." He shrugged. "Doesn't look good. And Schmitty, I assume you guys got a thorough lab on the body and scene.

"Like I said, Wong already tested the hair against his.

"That could be your unlucky break, Lucas," Butler said. "Hair strand analysis is only a rough forensic match of hairs—looking at the hair under a microscope. Certainly not conclusive."

God, Jeremy thought, *Butler's cheeks look like Santa's.* "So, Mr. Butler, I could've seen her at the restaurant and headed home to Rachel before this all happened, right? She could've even pulled my hair before she was killed, if it was my hair at all."

Butler slapped his pen in his palm, then smiled. "And so far two witnesses'll put you there at the right time. *After* the T. O. D."

"Witnesses? What witnesses?" Jeremy sat up straight.

"That line-up," said Butler. "Lucas, with a tight case like this, we're undoubtedly going to charge you, probably M-II if we can uncover a reason you'd want Ms. Dunne dead. That's why we're interviewing up at Archer."

"Man-oh-man," Jeremy said. "But—"

Butler cleared his throat. “It may be a stretch for murder two without a motive, but, if your attorney’ll take a reduction to manslaughter, maybe I’ll consider five-to-eight. But, if that plea doesn’t fly, we’ll go to trial and go for the murder two. Then, you could be talking a lot more time.”

“B-but this isn’t fair!”

“You look awfully guilty, Lucas,” Butler said. “The more I think of it, the murder two’ll stick if I can only find a motive.

“Motive?” said Jeremy. “Fat chance.”

“Already have a lead on that,” Butler put in. “Like I said, we’ll be talking to the folks at Archer. That’s where you work, right? Her father told us Ms. Dunne was a candidate there, right? Interviewed with you?”

“Uh, right. So what.”

“We’ll be following-up on it.”

“Sounds like you’re planning on winning, huh?” Jeremy retorted.

Butler chided, “Grand Jury’s tough down here. Hope you’re not playing the odds with me, Lucas,” He snickered. “I wouldn’t if I were you—especially if we’re talking murder two. Could get you eight-to-twenty, depending on circumstances.”

Jeremy gulped. “Eight-to-twenty years?”

"Listen, Lucas, you don't have an alibi, right?" Butler asked.

"Well, actually—" Jeremy said and thought of Lana.

"Don't answer that, Jeremy," Billy butted in.

Butler shrugged. His neck disappeared. "*If* you have an alibi, you might save your butt . . . just like last time."

Jeremy looked up. "Last time?"

"Well," Butler said, "I looked into your FBI record—they sent it to us from the Milwaukee office—you're no stranger to dealing with the prosecutor, are you?" He smiled. "We know all about you and Madison fifteen years ago."

Jeremy looked away. *They must know about the bombing and Agers the janitor,* he thought.

"What do you mean, Eddie?" Schmidt asked.

"Haven't you done your homework?" Butler grinned.

"Oh, his record?" Schmidt said. "Jennifer just gave it to me yesterday. Got partway through it. Why?"

"Well, it seems our friend, Lucas, helped the Dane County D.A. once upon a time," said Butler. "Right, Lucas?"

Jeremy nodded.

Butler continued: "Lucas turned state's evidence. Implicated his buddies in that bombing up at Madison back in '70."

"No kidding," Schmidt said. "I remember that."

"Things looked bad for him till he came up with an alibi," Butler went on. "He made a deal with Paul Kaiser, the D.A. at the time. Lucas' four buddies were found guilty, thanks to their old friend here. Two of 'em were just released early by the govenor—public pressure."

"Boy," Schmidt said, facing Jeremy. "Lucas here is the kind of friend we all should have."

"He got out clean as a whistle," said Butler, pointing at Jeremy.

"No shit," Schmidt said.

"Wait." Jeremy held up his trembling hand. "Who'd you say just got out?"

"The Nordberg brothers, Ken and Harold," Butler answered. "Some people in Madison put together a petition. The Governor bought it, but you were saved from the get-go by your girlfriend—weren't you?"

"There's no law against that," Jeremy said.

Butler tapped his fingers on the table. "Your other buddies are still in the can—five more years, I think, plus or minus."

"Man-oh-man." Jeremy held his head and covered his ears. *Will this ever go away?* he thought.

"Now Lucas is out finding exotic ways to get arrested," Butler said. "Like this balcony bit."

"Haven't I paid enough?" Jeremy mumbled, thinking of years of nightmares, the terror he felt after Catherine's fall, and his flight from the scene . . . and now this arrest.

Butler laughed. "What is it they say? 'Ye reap what ye sow? You've just begun to pay for this one."

"Ha-ha." Jeremy forced a laugh. "Say, why don't you just leave me alone? This must be called badgering the prisoner or something."

Butler grinned. "Oh, I've just begun."

"Right," Jeremy smirked. "Anything else, Mr. Butler?"

"Just that my older brother died in the same war that you protested."

"Man, I'm sorry. Really."

Butler handed Billy a business card and started to walk out. He turned. "Just stay in touch." Arraignment won't be for several weeks.

"What about bail?" Jeremy asked.

"Dream on. For the severity of this case, you're in jail until arraignment, then through trial."

Ten days later he appeared in court, where he was arraigned for murder two. After court, he returned to the jail and was sent through a series of catacombs, where he was, after internment procedures—papers, cell assignment, shower, body check, and a fresh inmate uniform—escorted with his small gym bag of personal belongings—toiletries, a few books, and his good luck charm, approved by guards during his check-in—through an echoey block to his cell. After a few minutes of casual talk, Jeremy found himself laughing at his gangly cellmate's jokes as they lay on their steel bunk beds—Jeremy on the top bunk; Albert Shecklemeier on the bottom.

Jeremy laughed. "Albert! You're making my gut hurt!"

"Well, when you're locked up," Albert said, "you gotta know how to tell good ones." He spat out a laugh that sounded like a cartoon buzzard.

The guard walked up with a couple of dinner trays. "Hey, you guys," he said. "A-number-one cuisine tonight."

Jeremy and Albert sat on the edge of their bunks.

"Berger, you just fattening us up for Monster?" Albert asked. "He'll use that shank on us."

"Say, guard?" Jeremy asked. "What's a shank?"

"Lucas, call him Larry or Berger," Albert said in a whisper. "He hates 'guard.' And a shank is a damn homemade knife."

"Berger, you just fattening us up for Monster?" Albert repeated.

"Say, Larry? Who's this Monster guy Albert keeps talking about?" Jeremy asked.

"Oh, that's Vito," Larry Berger said. "He eats newcomers for dinner. Better watch out, Lucas." He laughed.

"Or he butt-fucks 'em in the shower," Albert said and laughed, exposing a mouthful of rotten teeth.

"Don't worry, Lucas," said Berger. "That only comes after he gets to know you real well." He slipped the food trays through a slot at the bottom of the cell door. "But, if I were you, I'd take heed in the shower, the john and the movies." Berger talked intelligently, like he should've been a teacher or a Ph.D. in biochemistry, not a jail guard. "Now, enjoy."

Jeremy glared at the food. "Say, Berger, is that fish?"

"Fish *sticks*," Berger replied. "Why? Too *plebeian* for your tastes?"

"No. Actually, I have a severe seafood allergy."

"Sure, you do. They all say that when they want a New York Strip or a juicy burger."

Jeremy held up his hand. "No, honest." He purposely flashed a fearful look on his face. "It could kill me."

"You're not kidding, are you?" Berger stated. "They should've caught that when you did your medical."

"They said I had to come back to fill out the forms."

"Whoops," Berger said.

"Almost died last year eating a gourmet pizza with ground crab in the sauce. After that trip to the hospital, the doctor said I was so sensitive I might die the next time."

"Really?" Berger asked. "Anaphylactic shock?"

Jeremy nodded. "I normally carry around a syringe of Epinephrine if I need to inject some into my femoral artery." He slapped his thigh. "You know, if I eat some seafood by mistake."

"What's this eppi-whatever do?" Albert asked.

"Antihistamine. Just enough to get me to a hospital."

"So, where's the syringe?" Albert wanted to know.

Jeremy turned to Berger. "I wasn't given enough time to even think about bringing a syringe, so I didn't bring it."

"Okay, Lucas," Larry Berger said. "You've convinced me. Let me check in the commissary for something else. We don't need any liability." Berger walked away.

"Say Jeremy," Albert whispered. "You serious about all that stuff?"

"Oh, yeah. It's a bitch, knowing you could go at any time. I avoid eating anything that might have seafood in it."

"I thought the Shecklemeiers were the only ones that ate simple."

"What nationality is Shecklemeier?" Jeremy said. "German?"

"Pure hillbilly; proud of it. My Grandpa's German, though. How'd you know?"

"Are you married?"

"Yup. Rosey's super," Albert said.

"Known her long?"

"She's some kinda distant cousin I played with when I was little so I've knowed her forever."

"Cousin?" Jeremy laughed out loud.

"Yeah, what about it?" Albert said, obviously hurt. "What's so funny? Hey, Rosey's the best."

"Sorry," Jeremy said. "How'd you get to Chicago?"

"Moved from West Virginny to Kentucky to Cairo, then East St. Louis, then Chicago."

"Why all the moves?" Jeremy asked.

"Following the work. Mostly factory, a little hauling." Albert stuck his index finger way up his nose.

Jeremy cringed. "So, why are you in here?"

"Stealing a 2500."

"A what?"

"A 2500, Ramcharger—dynamite truck."

"Did you do it?" Jeremy asked.

"Yep. Just didn't get away with it."

Jeremy laughed.

"Fuckola! I needed wheels, didn't I?" Albert laughed. "Why you always laughing like that?"

"Oh, sorry."

"How 'bout y'all?" Albert asked.

"They tied me to the death of someone—like I murdered her because they found a fingerprint and a matchbook with my name."

"Well, did you . . . murder her?"

"Killed her, but not purposely. Let's just say they have a good case."

"Oh, yeah?" Albert snorted. "Know what Monster says, don't ya?"

"What's that?"

"If they have a good case, you're probably guilty." Albert pointed to Jeremy's charm. "And, if you need some kinda good luck . . . " He sucked in his breath, blew his nose into his hand, and casually wiped a fresh wad of mucus on his pants.

Jeremy grimaced. "Yeah?"

" . . . You're *definitely* guilty."

Fond du Lac, Wisconsin - two weeks later

Rachel Lucas popped one of her favorite tapes into the stereo. Whenever she felt tense or bored or confused or down, one of Katia's tapes got her through.

As the first song started, so did she. Slinking on each hip, she danced to the music like it flowed from deep inside her. She always felt this way: she listened to the lyrics and sang along so intently that the music became an extension of her life. She mouthed the words as if she were performing. She danced, traversing the living room floor, throwing back her head, closing her eyes, and spinning easily. Then she imagined some balmy tropical night in Rio during *Carnival* as she glided down a crowded street through a wave of bodies.

The doorbell rang.

She turned down the music. “Shoot! Right when I get going.” She walked to the front door and pulled it open, perturbed. “Paul! It’s you—I was ready to be annoyed.”

“Sorry, Rachel,” he said apologetically. “Saw you through the window. Pretty good dancing. Didn’t mean to peep.”

“Oh, that’s okay,” she said.

“You were pretty darn smooth.”

“Really?” She smiled.

“Claire loved to dance.” He clasped a little plastic tub.

“Oh, come on in,” Rachel offered. “It’s cold out there.”

Paul stepped through the door. “Not nearly the way you fly around though, but she was good at the waltz. Swing—she was great at that, too.”

“I never knew—” Rachel said.

“We even won the cha-cha contest at the Moose Christmas dance in ’76,” Paul went on. “That was the night I asked her to marry me. She said ‘yes’ right on the dance floor. ‘Tonight I Fell in Love’ was playing on the jukebox. Remember the Tokens?”

“Oh, Paul. You really miss her, don’t you?”

"Been four years. Seems like it's been forever."

"Say, you want some coffee? Got some fresh right here."

"Guess so," said Paul. "Black's fine. Came over to check the seal on that union. And, I brought you a present—my latest creation." He looked down at a little plastic tub he clutched. "I'll just put it in the refrigerator. Okay? And, check the union."

"Sure. What's your present?"

"Don't you know you're supposed to wait for a surprise till the right moment?" he said.

Five minutes later, they sat on the couch, sipping coffee and chatting about Jeremy's dilemma.

"That union looks like it's holding just fine, by the way." Paul stood. "Thanks for the coffee. Better get going."

"What's the tab?"

"We'll square up next week." He almost tripped, coming dangerously close to the hutch. "I'll just—"

She laughed and teased affectionately: "Now, Paul! Be careful. That's my china in there, you know."

"China, what—" Paul chuckled as he stumbled to the front door. "So, the trial starts next week already, huh? Boy, that's sure fast."

"It's already been four weeks!" Rachel said. "Seems like forever."

"But, that seems fast for our criminal justice system," he mumbled awkwardly. "Guess Jeremy's lucky he doesn't have to be in there forever."

"At least, I hope not." She bit her bottom lip. All the movies she ever saw, and all the books she ever read, and every *Perry Mason* episode she ever watched flashed through her mind. It hit her all at once. She couldn't contain the welled-up tears.

"Oh, Rachel." Paul wrinkled his brow and stepped forward. "I'm sorry. Say, this jail thing must be awful."

Rachel sniffled. "Paul." Her lip quivered.

"What is it?" he asked.

"I'm so sorry," she said. "I just can't help—" She ran to him. "Please. Just hold me for a second." She snuggled into his soft flannel shirt and wrapped her arms around him.

"Oh, Rachel," he soothed, settling his arms around her. "Poor baby."

She kept crying.

"I don't know about this hug business. With Jeremy—"

"Oh, Paul," Rachel sobbed, rocking in his arms. "You really loved Claire, didn't you? Darn, just hold me for a second."

"Claire?" said Paul, sniffing. "Sure did love her. Still do. More than anything."

"It shows. You're so faithful to her, even after she's been gone for four years. If you'd just open up a little, somebody else's bound to . . . I mean, some day, of course. You know?"

"Oh, not at my age," Paul chuckled. "Nobody else'd want me."

"Oh, Paul, be positive. There's *lots* of love in this world."

"I'm not counting on any of it." He shook his head. Rachel looked up; his eyes hung sadly. "I'm pushing fifty, you know."

"Fifty's not so old," said Rachel. And you're so sweet. You're caring and funny." She reached up and straightened his sparse, curly, salt and pepper hair. "You're so—"

He pulled away. "Rachel, I almost forgot!" he shouted.

"What?"

"Your little bucket of sauce!" he said happily. "I put it in the fridge before."

"Oh, the gift?"

"My latest recipe."

"Paul, I swear!" Rachel exclaimed. "You're forever the closet gourmet."

"You and Jeremy eat pasta, right?"

"Sure."

"It's my latest pasta sauce. Manhattan Style, I call it. Has tomatoes—of course—and onions and just the right spices—oregano and cilantro and basil and a few others—and, then, there's the chopped clams—*mmm, mmm.*"

"Clams?"

"The secret ingredient," Paul said proudly. "I actually make a paste and mixed it into the base."

Rachel held her hands up. "Sorry, can't take it, then."

"But, why?" Paul questioned. "The taste is so subtle, you don't even know the clams are in there."

"Jeremy's got a serious seafood allergy."

"I think I remember that."

"Oh, yeah. Quite serious. Remember him going to the hospital last year?"

"That's right," Paul recalled. "I remember that now, the ambulance. That was just because of him eating seafood?"

"Yeah."

Paul perked up. "Well, then. You and I can eat it for lunch some day."

"Oh, I don't know," Rachel said, fidgeting with her fingers.

"I'll help you finish it off in a couple of sittings," Paul offered.

"Maybe."

"Rachel, listen, I really want you to try it."

"Well, okay. If I keep it here, I'll have to label it real good."

"Perfect!"

"And, Paul, thanks for that little hug. I've felt so alone and frustrated with this jail thing."

"Great," said Paul. "That reminds me, there was something I've wanted to tell—"

"I do feel better now," said Rachel. "Thanks so much, Paul. You're a real friend." She lightly stroked his arm.

"Oh . . . right. Listen, I have to finish stretching those screens for your porch windows. Spring'll be here before you know it. Are you home, say Friday?"

"Next Friday?" Rachel said, thinking. "Won't work. That's the first day of the trial."

"Thursday, then?"

"Thursday it is," Rachel said.

Paul made a hasty exit, and after Rachel watched him march back across the snow to his house just feet away, she walked into the kitchen, opened the refrigerator, and saw the little tub of sauce. She reached into the junk drawer and found a permanent marker. She labeled the tub: "Warning! Not for Jeremy! Contains seafood." Then, she returned it to the fridge, went into the living room, walked over to the stereo cabinet, and pulled out another Katia tape. She sat in Jeremy's recliner and tinkered with the remote. The second song came on:

Always the best of Friends
You do know me too well.
But, I can tell you, there's still more to know.
Listen, I admit I'm just your friend.
But that can change. It really can.
It's true I'm always here for you.
And we're always with each other
When we need a hand to hold.
Right now, there's only so much that we can do.
But we always end up going to the same place.
If not physically, baby, in spirit.
There's no doubt we will find each other sooner or later.
Just give us time, we might be lovers.
But even then, we'll always remain the best of friends.

Words and Music — M. Litecki, K. Polankski © 1984 PLS Records

The song ended, and Rachel sat and thought of all the reasons Paul wouldn't be a good fit with her: his age, fifty-ish; his love of Claire, forever.

Hugging him had felt so natural, though. Rachel pictured being with him, cooking with him, kissing him, even cuddling him. Going to the Moose Hall and dancing with him. Then she tried to picture talking—just talking. That felt comfortable, really comfortable.

She suddenly felt embarrassed that she had those private thoughts, and felt as if they were being broadcast by some large loudspeaker throughout Fond du Lac.

She realized those moments were only her private moments, and no one could intercept the meanderings. So, she let the thoughts fill her again, and settle there for a minute, then two. She walked into the kitchen and pictured Paul under the sink, fixing the next catastrophe. Her fantasies of being with him didn't feel bad. In fact, they felt warm and safe.

She walked back into the living room, picked up the remote, and cued the song to play again. Even though the tune was all about best friends, she let the lyrics fill her with more than that.

Chicago, Illinois

Jeremy Lucas lay in the semi-dark of the jail, having fallen asleep listening to the echoes of grumbling and screaming throughout the cell block. He tossed and turned, reliving the dream once again. At the appointed time, Agers' pasty-white face glared at him and begged for mercy for the sake of his newborn son.

Y-ah-ah-ah! Jeremy's scream echoed. He yelled so loud he woke himself. He sat straight up and bumped his head.

"What the hell is it, Lucas?" Albert leaned over from the upper bunk.

"Nothing. Just a dream I always have."

"Holy shit! Should I call Larry? He's workin' late tonight."

"No, I'm okay, really," Jeremy assured him. "Go back to sleep." He rolled over and stuffed the blankets around his shoulders.

"Man, there must be some kinda hell playin' in your damn head," Albert muttered.

"Something like that." Jeremy stared into the near-dark and listened to the noise out in the block until it quieted down, and he could hear the beat of his own heart.

"What does it all mean?" Rachel's eyes were red and puffy. The next Monday, she sniffled as she stared at Jeremy through the glass at 9:30. She had driven south for a visit prior to trial. The visitors' room window was crisscrossed with wire, and Rachel talked to her husband through a phone. Indignant that his case was proceeding, especially with the murder two charge hanging over his head, Jeremy had defiantly directed Billy Stokes to reject Butler's plea offer for manslaughter. So, he would go to trial and plead not guilty to murder two.

Jeremy wore a blue inmate's uniform. A four-foot high glass panel separated Rachel from Jeremy. A scratched, pale green partition made of sheet metal stretched from the top of the glass to the ceiling. Rachel imagined all the prisoners who had silhouetted their hands with their loved ones' on the glass. "This is just like the movies," she whispered hoarsely. "I've visited you only once a week and just being in this place makes me feel like a damn prisoner."

"Whose problem is this anyway?" Jeremy asked. He held the phone loosely.

Rachel looked down. "They always make me pick a number to get an appointment time to see you. Then, I have to wait along a wall with everyone. They empty my purse on a table and rifle through my stuff. Then, I have to take off my shoes and belt, and walk through a metal detector." She sniffled. "It's awful, Jer."

"God, you act like you're the one in here. Have you seen Billy? He may recommend that you take spousal privelege, so you won't have to testify for the prosecution . . . against me."

"I can do that?"

"Yeah, it's called spousal privilege or something. You could even testify *for* me . . . as a defense witness . . . like at Madison."

"Hmmm. Jeremy, I don't know if I'm up to lying for you."

"Shh, what if they're taping this?"

"Sorry."

'Just be careful, okay?"

Rachel whispered, "Jeremy, are you sure you want Billy to represent you?"

"Honey, Billy's great."

"But, he was in prison, wasn't he?" she asked. "You just met him on some beach in Hawaii."

"Yeah," Jeremy remarked, "but a judge took him under his wing. Billy went back and got his undergrad, then went to law school. It's pretty amazing if you ask me. I mean, the guy paid his dues and climbed back into the mainstream." Jeremy looked at the clock. "And, he's as sly as a good ol' southern boy can be."

She twisted her ring. "Well, only if you're sure."

"He'll be fine," Jeremy said, and looked away at Krause, the guard, standing nearby.

"Well, what's next?" Rachel asked.

"They've already selected the jury. The trial starts on Friday."

"Oh, Jeremy! I'm so afraid of this; what could happen."

"The judge is moving this thing along. Probably brown-nosing Old Man Dunne, too—the big shot. Hell, maybe they're old school buddies. Damn system."

"What else did Billy say?" she asked.

"Nothing. He's trying to keep me relaxed. He says that Rogers, my judge, will be pretty progressive in handling the case."

"What's that mean?"

"He bends the rules."

"Suppose that's good." Rachel fiddled with a Kraft paper bag sitting in front of her.

"As long as it's in my favor!"

"Oh, Jeremy," said Rachel. "Things'll work out the way they're meant to. They always do."

He snickered. “That’s what I’m afraid of. Say, what’s this I hear about Ken and Harold getting out?”

“It was on CNN a couple weeks ago. Folks in Madison formed a committee and petitioned the governor. It worked. He commuted their sentences.”

He shook his head. “It’ll take a while for them to get it back together.”

“Ken was always the strong one,” Rachel nodded. “He’ll make it okay. I don’t know about Harold, being a little younger.”

“Man, they probably hate the fuck out of me.”

She nodded again, then shot him a hard glance. “You blame ‘em?”

10

Chicago, Illinois

Friday morning, Jeremy looked around the Division 10 courtroom. He could tell the place had been recently renovated—the bright, white, easy-to-read clock dial; the contemporary sea-green paint; the dented, buffed linoleum and the shiny brass ceiling fan.

He guessed that the original wood on the judge's bench and the bar separating participants from the gallery had been dark mahogany, because all courtrooms looked that way. But, in this particular room, the richness and intricate carving of old, dark wood had been removed and replaced with medium-toned oak and butt joints. Jeremy looked around and took a whiff. He felt as though he was attending the opening day of a freshly built grade school rather than the traditional halls of justice. He hoped that the progressive jurisprudence Billy had said was this Judge's style would ultimately be positive.

Jeremy listened to the excited murmur in the gallery behind him. The din reminded him of the preface of a city council meeting at the Fond du Lac City

Hall, or the anticipation that preceded the annual Archer Toy Company sales awards banquet at the Milwaukee Sheraton.

By contrast, the jurors looked somber as they followed the bailiff's pacing. Some fidgeted with worried eyes; others glanced around, bored; most looked alert and ready, eyes glued to the judge's bench.

The bailiff sat down, then rose again, seeming to be weighted down by his oversized police uniform and bulky holster. On his head, a sprig of mousy brown hair poked up from a primarily bald landscape. He looked at his watch, darted glances at the gallery, and cleared his throat with a squeal. In response, the murmuring in the courtroom tapered to a hum.

His tinny voice commanded the attention of all: "Hear ye, hear ye. Stay seated for His Honorable G. Kenneth Rogers."

The door opened. His Honor hurried in, carrying a stack of paper. His flowing robes puffed with air. Then, as he sat, the garments settled around him. At first he looked angry, an impression left by his arching, untamed eyebrows, a mixture of black and gray-white, which gave him the appearance of a harsh wizard.

"Good Morning," Judge Rogers said in a gentle tenor voice. He struck the gavel once. There was no answer from the gallery. "I said, good morning."

"Good Morning," the gallery said in bumpy unison.

"I'd like you all to meet the players in case #63097: Mr. Stokes, the defense attorney and his client Mr. Lucas; Mr. Butler, our Cook County prosecutor; Donald, our bailiff; Francis, my clerk; and Cheryl, our brand new court reporter. Say, hello to the folks, Cheryl. Go ahead, dear, this is your big moment." Cheryl turned toward the gallery, beet-red, and waved.

The judge continued: "And, let's not forget the hallmark of jurisprudence, our fine jury." Cheryl began her reporting; she moved her lips in sync with graceful typing.

Francis, the clerk, cleared her throat conspicuously and pointed to the judge.

"Thank you, Francis. I'm Judge Ken Rogers. Let's get on with it, then. State of Illinois vs. Jeremy Wayne Lucas. Case #63097. The charge against Mr. Lucas is murder in the second degree." He nodded Jeremy's way. The eyes of the jury members followed.

"Mr. Butler. You're opening," the judge said.

Edwin Terrance Butler rose slowly, stretching his portly frame, making it appear longer than it was. He tossed down his gold pen, strode over to the jury, and put both puffy white hands on the rail. He talked directly to the members in a rich baritone. "I'm Mr. Butler, Edwin Terrance Butler, the prosecutor; you remember me from selection. How are we all doing this morning?"

The jurors nodded; some answered.

Butler paced for a second or two. Then, he turned and pointed to the defense table. "Mr. Stokes might be planning on giving the briefest opening argument in history, and maybe, if his reputation is valid, the most colorful. You see, he knows that juries like those kinds of openings. If it's short, it must be true—that kind of thing. If it's colorful—humorous shall we say—it must also be true." He paced in front of them, then stopped. "So, I bet he'll go awfully short and give you the impression that his version of the facts is especially true." He faced them. "See how it works?"

A few nodded.

He looked down in thought. He suddenly turned back. "Nonsense!"

They reared back.

Jeremy Lucas turned to Billy Stokes and whispered, "He's undercutting what you'll say."

Billy reached over and patted Jeremy's forearm. "Just part of the game, Jeremy. Let's see what he's got."

Butler stared directly at an old lady in the first row of the jury box. He counted on his plump, little fingers as he spoke softly in an octave higher than his normal speaking voice. "But, all the ploys that Mr. Stokes might pull can't change the fact that, *A*, we have proof that the defendant was at the scene during a window-of-time that includes Ms. Dunne's unfortunate death." He nodded. The old lady nodded back. Then, Butler bellowed as he paced and kept counting: "*B*, we have a clean thumbprint from a matchbook found at the scene that also has the defendant's name on it, *and* directions from the restaurant where they both ate that afternoon, to her apartment . . . and *C*, a hair strand analysis of hairs found in the deceased's right hand shows that the hair roughly matches Mr. Lucas'."

"And *D*—" He stopped pacing and shrugged. "We even have two witnesses who'll place the defendant at the scene—actually fleeing the scene—immediately after Ms. Dunne's death, which we estimate at six o'clock, the evening of February 13th. *A, B, C, D,* that spells *guilty*, ladies and gentlemen." Butler shot a glare toward the defense table. The jury followed.

"Witnesses? Ain't on the discovery list," Billy Stokes whispered behind the back of his gargantuan hand to Jeremy. "Anybody see you there, Jer?"

"Let me see," Jeremy said. Then, he thought back to the old bag lady. *They could have found her. And the cop.*

"And," Butler said, "we also have an *E*. Contrary to what Mr. Stokes might believe, we can establish a pretty convincing motive for why Mr. Lucas would want Miss Dunne out of the way." He looked over at Jeremy. He shrugged. "That's all we need." He sat down.

"What the hell?" Jeremy said softly. "What motive? Wait, could it be Carl? I heard investigators were going to visit Archer?"

"Mr. Stokes?" Judge Rogers said. "Yours."

As the courtromm rumbled to silence, Billy Stokes stood. He pushed back his slick, Elvis-style haircut and cleared his throat repeatedly, as if preparing for his first school play. "Excuse me ladies and gentlemen!" he shouted, then apologetically lowered the volume of his voice. "We shouldn't even be here today." Billy sang his words with a splash of South Carolina drawl, ending each sentence as a question, the last syllable a higher pitch than the one preceding it:

"See, first Jeremy Lucas met this attractive woman, Miss Catherine Dunne, during an interview at work? Then, on another day, they ran into each other at a restaurant at lunch? She invites him over to her place, but he refuses. She even offers him a matchbook with a time and itty-bitty directions on it, but he still says no; he touches it, but gives it back. Says he's gotta go home to his missus. Simple."

With that, Jeremy looked back into the gallery at Harry and Margaret Martin. He shrugged at them like he was hearing Butler's accusations for the first time. Harry was frowning and Margaret's concerned eyes were trained on Jeremy, as though he were her one and only son. Rachel, on the prosecution's witness list, was waiting out in the hall.

Billy Stokes stopped and raised his hands, palms up, like a circus performer expecting applause. "Later that day, the deceased—Catherine Dunne—not getting along with her folks, worried about getting a new job, not satisfied with her career, or some such—leaps to her death. End of story." He paused. "Now, as you review the so-called evidence Mr. Butler presents, just remember my simple story. Why, not a shred of evidence undeniably supports Mr. Butler's pipe dreams." Billy Stokes lumbered away from the jury box, his bulky halfback frame looking as fashionable as it could be.

He threw back the jacket of his khaki suit, exposing a cobalt blue shirt and generous gut, then turned and slung his thumb on his western-style belt. He looked striking compared to the patchwork of subtle winter hues in the gallery. Edwin Butler, with his pudgy form and sheathed in a dark gray Brooks Brothers suit, dominated the prosecution table.

"Folks," Stokes said, poking up his crooked right index finger, supposedly broken five times playing football, "Mr. Butler will have y'all believe that my client, Jeremy Lucas, pushed Miss Dunne—she was naked as a jay bird, mind you—over the balcony railing of her apartment to her death." He turned and sang loudly: "But, why would he do that? My gosh, she was a job candidate for Mr. Lucas' company, too. And *naked*? Doesn't make any sense."

The jury flinched.

"Why, he hardly knew the lady!"

Then, crunching his shoulders, head, and arms and putting his finger to his lips, Billy Stokes spoke in a near whisper. "You see, that's what'll be missing from Mr. Butler's argument—the darn motive. Mr. Butler says he has one, but I kinda doubt it. And, without one, I'm afraid he doesn't have a case." Stokes paused and scoured the jury one-by-one. "As they say down South: 'That dog don't hunt.' " The gallery laughed.

"Okay, order," Judge Rogers said. He landed his gavel once.

Billy ignored the gavel and shrugged at the prosecutor. "Sorry, Mr. Butler." He walked to the defendant's table—the farthest from the jury—and sat next to Jeremy, slapping down his stack of papers.

"Nice one, Billy," Jeremy whispered, and patted him on the shoulder.

"Went pretty good. Even the joke."

Judge Rogers glanced over at their whispers and shook his head from side to side. "Shhh," he commanded.

For most of the morning, the prosecution presented the details of its forensic case: Detective Schmidt, his suit pressed; Roger Wong, a lab technician, who apologized for the inconclusiveness of hair strand analysis as a forensic test; and Dr. Tom Jaros, a physics expert witness, who said that, given the landing point of Ms. Dunne's body and calculated trajectory, she couldn't have been pushed. Then came the waiter and the maitre d' from the Chéz Paul, and Brad Coleman. Together they established that, without an alibi, Jeremy definitely could have been at Catherine Dunne's apartment between five and six—what had become the so-called "window" Edwin Butler continued to reference. They pinpointed the beginning of the window as the time Jeremy supposedly arrived at the 2650 building. The end was pegged as the time of Catherine Dunne's dramatic death—about six.

Billy whispered to Jeremy, "The jury's buying it, the way they're looking over here. Even if the hair strand analysis doesn't implicate you, the fingerprint puts you there; the matchbook and witnesses nail the time."

"But—" Jeremy complained.

"Jer, just try to look unfazed, okay?"

"Oh, right." Jeremy sat up straight, tightened his tie, looked back at the Martins, and shrugged. The judge called the morning recess.

After the recess, Butler stood at the prosecution table. "Permission to approach, Your Honor?"

Judge Rogers signaled for both counsel to approach the bench. Butler and Billy Stokes walked up.

At the bench, the trio mumbled back and forth; then, after counsel returned to their respective tables, the Judge said, "For the record, I'm allowing the next witness from out of town without defense discovery because it would have been impossible and the State has convinced me of his relevance. His testimony is required for the State to try its case adequately. Defense discovery now would just slow this thing down, and, Lord knows, Francis has a long list of cases I have to get to."

Francis, the court clerk, nodded and waved a sheet of paper.

"So," Rogers continued, "for the sake of the State of Illinois and the taxpayers' pocketbooks. Mr. Stokes, instead of discovery I'll allow you significant latitude on cross. Are you okay with this, Counselor?"

"Yes, I s'pose, Your Honor," Billy Stokes said as he huffed back to his seat. He sat stiffly.

"Mr. Butler," the judge said. "I'm warning you, this better be good."

"Yes, Your Honor," Butler said sullenly. "State calls Daniel S. McNalley."

"Wait," Jeremy broke in. The name sounded familiar. Then, it came to him. "Billy, wait," he whispered, turning toward his attorney, "I think you have to stop this."

"Calm down, Jer," Stokes said. "Nothing I can do."

"Problem, Counsel?" Judge Rogers asked.

As Billy Stokes stood, he patted Jeremy on the shoulder. "No, Your Honor. But, we would've liked to depose Mr. McNalley prior to trial. This is highly unusual. We don't even know who he is."

"Counsel," said the judge, "I'm allowing this for the reasons I've stated. Are we clear?"

Stokes nodded. "Yes, Your Honor, of course."

Jeremy leaned over and whispered, "You have to stop this."

"No way, Jer," Stokes said.

"Remember, I'm giving you significant latitude on cross, Mr. Stokes," Judge Rogers said.

"Yes, sir," Stokes muttered. "That's right, sir."

"Please sit, then," Rogers said. "Let's get on with it."

Billy sat, then leaned over to Jeremy. "Well, they said Judge Rogers was progressive. This is sorta throwin' me off."

Donald the bailiff squeaked open the two doors at the back of the courtroom. He called McNalley's name down the echoing hall. At first, there was no sign of anyone. Then, seconds later, a man about thirty-five appeared. He hurriedly entered, and Donald closed the doors behind him. Thin, and dressed in a perfectly tailored conservative navy suit, McNalley strode to the bar.

"Ever seen him, Jer?" Stokes asked.

Jeremy shook his head. "No, but I think I'm remembering his name."

The man had sandy blonde hair and tortoise-shell glasses. He walked with purpose through the gate at the bar. He glanced coldly at Jeremy.

He stepped quickly to the witness box. The clerk approached him. "Please raise your right hand, Mr. McNalley."

He did and sat at attention, eyes straight ahead.

"Swear to tell the truth, the whole truth, nothing but the truth, so help you God?" the clerk said.

"I will."

"State your full name for the record."

"Daniel Sterling McNalley, the third."

"Your address?"

"305 E. 71st Street, New York."

Edwin Butler rose and walked up to the witness box. "Mr. McNalley, please state your occupation."

"Investment banker."

"That involves what?" he asked.

"Working with clients—companies—acquiring funding for projects, acquisitions, buy-outs, IPOs, and so forth." McNalley looked down.

"I see," Butler said. "And, you knew the deceased, Ms. Catherine Dunne?"

"Yes." McNalley sent a scowl Jeremy's way. "For years."

"What was your relationship with her?" Butler asked.

He sniffed. "Catherine was a lifelong friend and, on occasion, my lover."

The gallery rumbled.

"Oh, no." Jeremy shook his head slowly.

Judge Roberts slapped his gavel twice. "Order."

The courtroom became instantly quiet.

"Do you know the defendant, Jeremy Lucas?" Butler asked.

"No, I don't," McNalley replied.

"Then, what might you add regarding Ms. Dunne's death that would enlighten us?"

The witness sniffed again. "Well . . . "

"Just take your time, Mr. McNalley," Butler said, glancing sideways at Jeremy.

"Well," McNalley began, "on several occasions—five or so—I visited Catherine at the 2650 building in Lake View on the near north side, where she lived."

"In Chicago on business?" Butler asked.

"Yes," McNalley said.

Butler shrugged at Billy. "Go on, Mr. McNalley."

"On several of those occasions, we made love."

"Yes? How might this be relevant to the current case?" Butler faced McNalley.

"Catherine loved to take chances. She parasailed, mountain biked, and even climbed some fairly rugged mountains out west."

"And?" Butler said, impatient.

McNalley hesitated. "She engaged in some pretty inventive sex games, too."

The gallery rumbled.

"Go ahead, Daniel," Butler nudged. "Enlighten us."

"Well, out on the balcony of her apartment—" McNalley said.

"Yes?"

"She liked to balance on the railing when we made love."

"Really?" Butler said, rubbing his chin. "Hmmm."

McNalley cleared his throat. "She called it . . . 'flying.' "

"Eh? Now, this was during the warmer weather, correct?" Butler paced back and forth.

"Last time, it was winter," McNalley said.

The gallery's murmur escalated.

"Order, *order*!" The buzz calmed quickly.

"Winter?" Butler asked.

"Yes," McNalley said. "Last Christmas I got her a propane heater for her balcony so she could fly anytime." He snickered self-consciously. "She loved it—Making love on the railing."

Jeremy leaned over to whisper in Billy's ear, "He's going to make sure I burn in hell."

"Jeremy, relax."

"In fact, I think she got to liking flying *mostly* during the winter," McNalley said. "The steam, the sweat, the heat from the propane."

"On *what* balcony, exactly?" Butler said, tapping his pen on his hand. "So we have it straight."

McNalley looked uneasy. “You know, hers.”

“Yep,” Billy said under his breath.

“What is it?” Jeremy asked.

Stokes nodded knowingly. “Butler explained how it might’ve happened; now he’ll use his witnesses and try to put you at the scene, with a motive.”

“Shit,” Jeremy whispered, “That sounds bad.”

Stokes frowned. “Yup, pretty bad. I wish Rachel was on *our* witness list.”

“That’s it, Mr. McNalley,” Butler said and returned to the Prosecutor’s table.

“Mr. Stokes?” the Judge said. “Yours.”

Billy Stokes rose. “Your Honor? Request a fifteen minute recess.”

“Fifteen minutes, then,” Judge Rogers said. “Mr. McNalley, you may step down, take a break. Stick around, though. We’ll need you for Mr. Stokes’ cross.”

“Yes, Your Honor.” McNalley stood.

“Billy?” Jeremy leaned over.

“Say what?”

“I got an idea,” Jeremy said. “Can you make a call?”

Stokes looked irritated. “What now?”

As Jeremy whispered in his ear, Billy’s eyes widened. “Lana?”

Jeremy said, “Tell her I’ll leave Rachel for her. Tell her anything.”

"Shoot." Billy rose and lumbered out to the hall. Minutes later, he strode back up the aisle that split the gallery. A grin spread across his face and he flashed a victory sign with two gargantuan fingers.

Billy explained: "Not only did I call Lana, but I talked to Rachel out there. She really doesn't want to testify against you."

"So?"

"So, she'll assert her spousal privilege which allows her not to testify against you—that's good news. Then, we can add her to our list."

But, Jeremy wondered. The news about Rachel might be good. He knew getting Lana Holub to testify could backfire.

Just then, the Judge hit his gavel and said, "I'm looking at my watch and thinking we should break a little early today. So, if there are no objections from you fellows, we stand adjourned until nine on Monday. And, Donald, please let Mr. McNalley know we'll need him at that time."

Monday morning, after the preliminaries, Billy Stokes lumbered back and forth, head down, in front of Daniel

McNalley, who was sitting in the witness chair. Billy turned, stunning him. "So, Mr. McNalley, you've stated under oath that you've made love with the deceased, Ms. Catherine Dunne, at her apartment, out on that railing?"

"Yes, I have," McNalley replied.

"And, when was that?" Billy questioned.

"Several times over the last few years," McNalley said.

Billy turned. "Oh, but not *this* February?"

"No."

"You sure?" Billy asked. "Definitely not February 13th?"

"Definitely."

"But, Mr. McNalley, did you see my client with Ms. Dunne on the night of February 13th."

"No, I didn't. But—" McNalley folded his arms tightly across his chest.

"Any communication with her that indicated she was visiting with my client that night?"

"No."

"So, as far as you're concerned, you might just as likely have been there that night as my client?"

Butler shot up. "Objection."

"Overruled," Judge Rogers said. "Go ahead and answer, Mr. McNalley."

"Yes, well. I guess," McNalley said, readjusting himself in the witness chair. "But, I *wasn't* there."

"You haven't changed your hair color recently, have you?"

McNalley stuttered. "No, sir."

"Can you prove that?"

"I don't keep a record of my hair color, if that's what you mean."

"Ever color your hair."

McNalley snickered.

"Well, Mr. McNalley?"

He paused, then answered. "Well, once maybe."

"Fine, that's it, Mr. McNalley." Billy shrugged and smiled at the jury. Hmm, reasonable doubt?"

"No editorializing, Mr. Stokes. You can step down now, Mr. McNalley," said the judge. "Thanks for making the trip. Make sure to fill out all those vouchers for staying over."

"Yes, sir. But—" Daniel McNalley looked pleadingly at the Judge. Then, he stepped down.

Edwin Butler rose. "State calls Carl Dietrich."

Jeremy looked up.

"What the hell can he add?" Billy asked Jeremy.

After swearing in Carl, Butler paced in front of him. "So, you were just promoted to the presidency over there at Archer Toy Company?"

"Yes, sir." Carl rubbed his huge nose. "After Bob Townsend died."

"How do you think the defendant, Jeremy Lucas, reacted to you getting the job?" Billy asked.

"Objection," Butler said, "Calls for a conclusion of the witness."

Judge Rogers spoke, "Let's let him answer that. I'd like his point of view. Go ahead, sir."

"I think if he was smart, he would've expected it." Carl looked coolly at Jeremy. "But, I don't think he was pleased."

"After you were promoted," Butler said, "did you get a specific instruction from your boss, Hadley Archer?"

"Yes, Hadley wanted back-ups in all positions. Always wanted that."

"Even for Jeremy Lucas' position?" Butler asked.

"Sure."

"Safe to say Mr. Lucas was a star over there at Archer?"

"Supposedly," Carl said. "At least, Bob Townsend always thought so."

"And, who specifically was interviewed for the Lucas back-up?" Butler asked.

Carl swallowed. "Ms. Catherine Dunne."

Scattered mutterings filled the courtroom.

"Did you have a chance to interview her, Mr. Dietrich?" Butler pressed.

Carl shook his head. "No, funny thing, never did, but I did see her résumé after she interviewed with Jeremy one day. Outstanding."

"Is it safe to say, then, that you would have endorsed her for hire?"

"Absolutely," Carl said. Her education and experience was perfect."

Butler raised his hand. "Then, she would have been a good back-up for Jeremy Lucas should he leave for any reason, or if you chose to replace him, say, to lower Archer's overall executive salary exposure?"

"True." Carl looked at Jeremy.

"So," Butler said matter-of-factly, "you could say, had you hired her, she would've most likely been a threat to Mr. Lucas' career? She'd be a superstar at a lesser salary, right?"

Billy Stokes butted in, "Compound, Your Honor."

"Witness will answer the first question," Judge Rogers said.

Carl looked at Butler.

"That's the one about Ms. Dunne being a threat to Mr. Lucas' position?" Butler continued.

Carl stuttered, “I guess she would be, sure.”

Grumbles resounded throughout the gallery.

“Fine. Sounds like a motive to me. Yours, counselor.” Butler walked to his seat, wiping his hands.

Billy stood. “Mr. Dietrich?” he asked.

“Yes?”

“Who’s your back-up in the chain of command?” Billy asked.

Carl stretched his neck, wiped his shiny nose, and snorted. “Jeremy Lucas,” he replied.

Billy paced back and forth. “Hmmm. Is it fair to say that, over the last few years, Jeremy has outshone you at Archer?”

“But, I got the promotion, didn’t I?” Carl spouted. Suddenly, he looked vulnerable, wiping his forehead with his handkerchief.

“Still, does it bother you that Jeremy is your back-up?” Billy asked, unfazed. “Might he make you look bad, say, to Hadley Archer, the founder?”

Carl half rose uneasily, his mustache twitching. “Just what are you saying?”

“If he was convicted, it would be one less problem for you to deal with?” Billy drilled.

"If you're implying—" Carl stammered.

"That you might slant your testimony to make my client look bad?" Billy's eyebrows shot up. "Could it help protect your job if Jeremy was out of the way?" Billy went on. "Let you shine in the founder's eyes?"

Carl's face flushed. "I resent—"

"Non-responsive, Your Honor," Billy said.

"Just answer the question, Mr. Dietrich," Judge Rogers ordered. He looked at Billy. "Perhaps you'd like to restate it, Mr. Stokes."

"Could it help protect your job if Jeremy Lucas was convicted?" Billy repeated.

Carl squirmed. "Jeez, I guess. But—"

Billy paused and glared at Butler, then strutted back to the defense table. "That's it."

Butler made some squiggles in his notebook. A colleague whispered to him.

"Mr. Butler?" Judge Rogers said, "Your next witness."

"Yes, Your Honor." Butler stood. "State calls Officer James Kelly."

Jeremy turned around and looked about the buzzing courtroom.

"Order, now!" His Honor said, and slapped his gavel once.

Billy sat. The courtroom quieted.

Butler raised his pen. "Oh, Your Honor?"

"Yes?" the judge said.

"Sorry to say, we can remove Agnes Schumacher from our list. I've been informed of her sudden and untimely passing." He looked over at Jeremy.

"That must be the bag lady," Jeremy whispered to Billy, and smiled.

"Jer, wipe that grin off your face," Billy whispered. "Show some remorse. Hear?"

"Right." *See*, he thought, *I always seem to get out of everything.*

Officer Kelly took his seat in the witness stand and completed all the preliminaries.

"Officer Kelly?" Butler asked.

"Yes sir?"

"Where were you on the night of February 13th?"

"Working second shift that night," Kelly replied. "Got called on a disturbance up on LaSalle in Lake View."

"Describe that disturbance, please."

Kelly took a deep breath, then said, "Catherine Dunne, the deceased, allegedly jumped or fell from her apartment balcony on the 19th floor of the 2650 building. Soon pedestrians gathered and traffic snarled, so I was sent to the scene—routine, at least the traffic control was."

"And you saw the defendant leaving there?" Butler asked.

"Objection!" Billy Stokes rose. "Leading."

"Sustained," Judge Rogers said. "Mr. Butler, just an open-ended question please."

"Sorry, Your Honor." Butler shook his head. "Officer Kelly, what happened next?"

He pointed at Jeremy. "On LaSalle by Lincoln Park, I saw the defendant—that man—getting into his car. It was a Corolla, I remember that for sure."

"And what time was this?" Butler asked.

"A little after six p.m.," Officer Kelly said.

"Immediately proximate to the time of death?"

"Slightly after, according to the lab."

Jeremy sank. "Shit, Billy," he whispered.

Billy put his hand up and mumbled, "Don't forget, we got Lana."

"Right," Jeremy remembered, but his gut churned.

Billy stood and approached the stand. "Officer Kelly?"

"Yes, sir."

"Lights up there on LaSalle?" Billy asked.

"Some."

"Pretty dark at six this time of year?"

"I suppose."

"Lights directly over where you allegedly saw my client?"

"Well, not exactly," the policeman replied. "Every half-block or so."

"So, it wasn't awfully bright, then?" Billy said and gazed into the air, looking out the side of his eyes at the jury. "Yep, I can picture it."

"A little dim, I guess," Officer Kelly said. "But I'm sure—"

"That'll be all, Officer, thank you." Billy strode back to the Defense table. He sat and looked around the courtroom, then whispered to Jeremy, "Lucky Catherine's folks didn't come to this thing."

"The press would've had a field day," Jeremy said.

"Paper said they took off to the south of France," Billy cracked, "that's blue-blood parental loyalty, I guess. And, a helluva good corporate PR move."

"Wouldn't want it to affect his company's reputation," Jeremy whispered.

Edwin Butler stood at the Prosecution table. "State calls Mr. Roy Manis."

The gallery calmed. Then the doors opened and Roy, the doorman, in an uncomfortable civilian suit, marched in.

"Shit, Billy."

"Relax, Jeremy. I'll nail him." After the doorman sat, Butler questioned him until he had roughly established what time Jeremy had allegedly walked into the lobby of the 2650 building the day of the incident.

Billy rose.

"Mr. Manis?"

"Yes, sir." He fidgeted nervously.

Billy turned and shot the words at him fast. "You ever drink on the job, Mr. Manis?"

He flinched. "Never!" he said indignantly and looked at the jury, then the judge. "Never."

"Never?" Billy crossed his arms. "I mean, really. Never? Don't the folks in your building know you carry a chrome flask? Sure there's not orange juice in there!"

"Well, I guess when it's cold outside—"

"Were you drinking the night of February 13th?" Billy asked.

"Let's see." Manis fiddled with his jaw. "Well, how am I supposed to remember that?"

"It's possible, then?" Billy shrugged. "A shot here and a shot there?"

Manis' face turned red. "I guess it's possible."

"Thank you, Mr. Manis. That'll be all." Billy walked back to the defense table and sat.

Butler rose. "Redirect, Your Honor?"

"Go ahead."

Butler put his hands in his pockets, glanced at the floor for a second, then looked up. "So, did Mr. Lucas, the defendant, enter your building the night of February 13th?"

"I know I seen him, coulda been on the 13th," Manis frowned. Then his face lit up. "Yeah, the night of Ms. Dunne's accident. Yeah, he was there. First time he was there, I remember."

Butler said the next sentence routinely: "Your Honor? The State rests."

"But I see one more witness on your list, Mr. Butler."

"Mrs. Lucas has asserted her spousal privilege, Your Honor."

The people in the courtroom chattered.

"Mr. Stokes," His Honor cleared his throat and said loudly. "Are you prepared to start your case?"

Billy turned to Jeremy and whispered, holding his hand up, "That might-could be real good news if Rachel'll testify for us."

Jeremy chuckled. "Might-could?"

"Counsel?"

"Well, Your Honor," Billy said. "I'm not sure—"

At that moment, the rear doors swung open. The spectators in the gallery turned in unison. Lana Holub was swaying up the aisle wearing a silky pastel dress. Jeremy sighed, then gloated as he hit Billy in the shoulder. "Perfect timing, Billy."

Billy rose. "Actually, Your Honor, it so happens we're all set."

Minutes after Butler tried unsuccessfully to suppress Lana's testimony because he hadn't been able to interview her prior to trial, Jeremy watched Billy stroll back and forth in front of Lana like a bull deliberating his next charge. He snorted, as if she were a spectator at a bullfight, sitting there in the stands of some mystical auditorium. She nervously licked her lips as she watched Billy stare at the floor, as if his next question was buried in the mud divots that made up the imaginary stadium floor. Lana alternately stole glances at the jury, gallery, Jeremy, then Billy, then Bull.

Jeremy heard a giggle and turned. In the rear of the gallery, Daniel McNalley sat next to some young fellow with long red hair, an immature, bushy beard, and a University of Wisconsin sweatshirt. *God, he looks familiar,* Jeremy thought. *Hey, he looks like* Agers.

Jeremy was sure Lana could undo some of the damage wrought by McNalley, the cop, and the doorman—create some reasonable doubt.

"So, Miss Holub?" Billy asked.

"What, sir?" she said in a restrained monotone, her lips barely moving.

Billy's jaw muscles flexed spasmodically. "I guess the issue comes down to Jeremy Lucas' exact whereabouts the night of Catherine Dunne's death, that make sense?"

Lana nodded. "Yes, I guess. but I didn't hear the other testimony. They made me wait out there."

"Is that a 'yes' or an 'I don't know'?"

"A yes, but I didn't hear all the testimony."

"Well, anyway," Billy said. "Can you help us with Mr. Jeremy Lucas' whereabouts that night, February 13?" He crossed his arms and gloated.

Jeremy looked at Lana and couldn't hide the confident smirk on his face, opening his mouth as if he were about to mouth Lana's next words.

"Well . . . " Lana said.

Jeremy nodded at Lana encouragingly.

Billy looked straight at the jury and waited for Lana to answer. He crossed his arms. He turned his back to her and spoke into the air. "Well, go ahead, now, Miss Holub. We're all waiting."

"It's just that—" she said and stared at Jeremy.

"Was Jeremy Lucas with you that night or not, Miss Holub?" Billy asked.

She sighed and glanced at the jury, then up at the judge.

"Ms. Holub, answer the question, please," Judge Rogers said.

"No," she said. "He wasn't with me!"

Billy Stokes swirled back at her. "Say what?"

"I said *no*," Lana said firmly. "I went to a movie at the Coronet in downtown Cascade."

"But after that?" Billy asked.

"No, nothing," she whimpered. "Nothing, nothing, *nothing*! Not after three years of dating the man!"

Jeremy glared at Lana.

She held her hands to her mouth and looked away.

Just then, Jeremy heard commotion to his right and behind him. He looked back to see Margaret Martin stand and climb over two people on her way to the aisle. Handkerchief in hand, she wept as she rushed out of the courtroom. Harry Martin rose, and, after throwing a gruff expression Jeremy's way, rushed after his wife.

Jeremy hung his head and glanced at the jury with only his eyes. *Man-oh-man*, he thought. *Thanks, Bitch.*

11

Fon du Lac, Wisconsin

Later Monday afternoon, after court had recessed for the day, Rachel and her friend Julie sat across from each other at Rachel's kitchen table drinking coffee. Rachel sneezed and blew her nose. Julie reminded Rachel of a blonde pixie; her big, sparkling eyes were framed by feathery bangs and a small, always smiling mouth. Her sweet, piercing voice chattered like a kid. She would probably look thirty when she was sixty.

Julie sipped coffee. "Ooo, Rachel. When I told Gus about that charm thingy, he goes, 'Maybe she should bring it over to Madison.' There's a big archeology department there now, Rach. 'But, with all those big shots,' he goes, 'you should call ahead and make an appointment.' "

"Jeremy's got that charm now, anyway," Rachel said, "sort of good luck while he's in jail." She sneezed.

"Oh, Rachel," Julie said. "You poor thing."

"After that flying stuff I told you about," Rachel said, "Billy set up a special visitation for me this afternoon, so Jer and I could make peace—fat chance.

Mom and Dad told me all about Lana's testimony. Lord, my folks have even lost faith in him."

"Wait," Julie broke in. "You're going all the way back to Chicago? That's almost two hours!"

"I know." Rachel looked at her watch. "I better get going."

"Rachel, going back and forth like that is gonna kill you. Honey, there's only so much you can do."

Rachel sneezed. "Court's adjourned tomorrow and Thursday, at least." She wiped her nose.

"Thank God. You're catching a cold."

"Maybe I'll take it easy tomorrow," said Rachel. "I could head over to Madison and check out the charm right away, but Jeremy has it. Want more coffee?"

Julie shook her head. "Rachel! Honey. You need a break."

"No worries. I'm okay." Rachel looked at her watch. "Listen, I better git." She stood and wiped her nose. Julie pushed back her chair. They hugged lightly and patted each other's backs.

Chicago, Illinois

Later that afternoon, Larry Berger led Jeremy out of Cellblock A, past a row of heavy steel doors covered with shiny gray paint. Jeremy looked around as he walked. He hadn't realized there were so many cells. They looked so impenetrable. He had been recalling the testimony given by the cop, doorman, Daniel McNalley, and Lana, and he'd started imagining himself behind the bars of a more substantial facility for a long time.

The inmates began clanging on the bars as Jeremy and Berger passed. In seconds, chants and jeers echoed through the block. "Honky fucker!" one voice yelled.

"Piss-ass white collar sonofabitch!" another said.

Berger turned and yelled over the din to Jeremy. "Don't mind them, Lucas."

"Man. What's their deal?" Jeremy yelled back.

"Long-time residents. A little swearing breaks up their day."

"Sure."

"And you're white, of course," Berger said.

An arm lunged out from a cell. Jeremy dodged it. "What the hell's that have to do with it?" he asked.

"Don't you get it?" Berger counted on his fingers. "White, word's gotten around you're an executive, and walking through the block with a guard—it all smacks of privilege."

"But my handcuffs—" Jeremy dodged another flailing arm.

Berger laughed. "Listen, Lucas, you're what they hate the *most*. They think you're the reason they're in here."

Jeremy shook his head.

"Maybe that's why I like you," Berger said. He patted Jeremy on the shoulder. "It's nice to have a little higher class inmate around here."

Jeremy asked, "Say, Berger, how'd a guy like you end up being a guard?"

Berger shook his head. "My little brother was in for vehicular manslaughter. I was a beat cop, going for homicide detective. He convinced me I could raise the quality of detention officer and protect him in the process, so I took a job at the jail. Then, my brother got out early because of overcrowding, but I'm still here protccting other guys like him." He pointed around. "The heavies are intimidated by me because I talk in complete sentences."

Jeremy laughed.

"And, I don't get my kicks ripping off the stamps sent to inmates in their mothers' care packages." Berger shook his head. "Can you imagine: ripping off lousy stamps?"

"Man."

As they walked, the banging on the cell bars escalated, but Berger seemed unfazed. He just talked louder. "A little different than white middle class suburbia, huh?"

"Oh, yeah." Jeremy looked around warily. "I really do appreciate this, Berger."

"Well, I know you're not stupid enough to try whooping my ass or breaking my neck like they would," Berger said. "Besides, I heard things didn't go so great in court. You could stand a little one-on-one time with your wife to sort things out. Right?"

"No kidding," Jeremy said, "and my lawyer's coming at six."

"Maybe we shouldn't be talking," Berger said cautiously. "They could take this out on you later."

"Shit." Jeremy looked around. "Vito?"

"Or anybody."

Berger took out his keys and opened the door that led from the cellblock into a dark, narrow, muffled-sounding hallway. The door sucked shut, instantly leaving the inmates' hooting behind. Jeremy sighed.

"What happened in court?" Berger asked. "Didn't sound good."

Jeremy drew in a breath. "My ex-mistress, who's supposedly my loyal secretary, didn't give me an alibi. Now there may not be a way out of this."

"Sorry about that. Mistress, huh? Some of us aren't so privileged."

"Yeah, look where it got me," Jeremy said.

"Don't worry, you'll probably end up in one of those cozy minimum security joints, Lucas. Around here we call them country clubs."

They turned right at a corner. Berger opened two locks on a door that said *"VISITATION ROOM"* in chipped plastic letters.

"Here we are," Berger said. "You normally get thirty minutes for a special visit, I'll stretch it to forty-five because of the missus." He opened the visitor's room door and addressed a guard. "Hansen, Lucas here's got forty-five. Then, he sees his lawyer. After that, he comes back to Block A, my desk, okay?"

"Right." Hansen saluted and looked at his watch. He had a dumb monster look about him: pale skin; dark, piercing, little eyes; short-cropped, black hair on a forehead that sloped forward and ended at two barren eyebrows. He had a drooping lower lip and a muscular, bloated body, undoubtedly from steroid use. "Okay, Lucas, you got forty-five, then the phone goes dead." Hanson pushed a few buttons, then pointed down the secure side of the room.

Jeremy walked past the guard, looking away to avoid the man's piercing stare. Rachel sat on the opposite side of the second window. Jeremy took a seat, picked up the phone receiver, and looked at her eyes, teary and red.

"Rachel?"

"You bastard, you! You sonofabitch! Mum told me everything."

Hansen looked over.

"Say, I didn't come out here to fight," Jeremy said.

"Save it!"

Hansen looked over again.

Jeremy hung his head. "Cool it, okay. I'm not in the mood."

"Jeremy, do you know how I feel right now?" Rachel asked. "To learn about those . . . those women? Have my folks hear all of that?"

Jeremy couldn't muster a response. *Rachel doesn't often get this riled.*

"Mom said she called it flying?" She shook her head. "So, that's what you do when you're supposedly out with clients." Her tears started streaming down her face. "And, Lana—I was right all the time, and you were seeing her for three years?"

"Roughly," he said and hung his head. "I am so-o-o sorry."

"So, all the doubts I ever had were real." Rachel sniffled. "I shouldn't have lied for you at Madison. I just wanted you too bad. The up-and-comer you were—so slick, a great future. Mum and Daddy used to say you were the perfect catch—now they're not so sure. If I ditch you, they'll back me all the way, you bastard." She sniffled in her tears. "All I feel is hate toward you now, Jeremy. Pure hate."

"But, Rach, listen."

"Wait! You're listening, Jeremy," she said.

"All right. Go ahead."

"Do you realize I can never trust you again? This is it, Jeremy. Cheating on me like that. You're like a teenage boy." She set the receiver down, covered her eyes with her hands.

Jeremy didn't say anything. He just sat there, moaning. Of course, Rachel was right. For her to find out the way she had must have ripped her apart.

He knocked on the window. "Rach?"

She slowly picked up the phone and put the receiver to her ear.

"Rach, baby, you okay?" he said softly. He stroked the glass with his fingertips. "Come on, Baby, I love you. You're not just some old fling."

She looked up. "Oh, Jeremy. This whole thing is freaking me out."

"Man, did you see that kid in court?" he asked.

Rachel mumbled, "Who?"

"The teenager with red hair and almost-beard?"

"No, why?" She sniffled and wiped her nose.

"God, he looked like Timothy Agers, like my dreams: bright red hair and white skin—like a goddamn ghost. Except for the beard."

"Jeremy, you're seeing things," Rachel said. "Besides, Agers had dark hair."

"I don't know," Jeremy said warily. "This kid looked like the dreams, too, except that his hair's orangier, and he has that beard. Bright red hair skips a generation, doesn't it?"

"Who knows?" Rachel shrugged. "See, you're paranoid. It was probably a plain old student or reporter or somebody."

"I don't know," Jeremy said, shaking his head.

"Well, the papers have sure been covering this. It's page one news, on TV every night." She talked in a normal voice now. "Even CNN mentioned it last night. That could bring out the crazies. Maybe that red-haired guy. You never know who's out there."

"Man-oh-man," Jeremy breathed out hard. "That's all I need, the ghost of Agers. Or his real live son."

"Well, Jeremy, what do you expect? If you hadn't gone messing around, none of this would've happened."

"More scolding? Jesus, Rach, can't you just cool it."

Rachel sniffled. "Well . . . "

"Here," he said abruptly and grabbed at the black cord under his uniform. "Just take it."

"What?" she asked, surprised.

Jeremy pulled the metal charm from around his neck. "Guard?" he called. He knocked several times on the glass. "Hansen!"

The guard turned and grunted, "Yup?" He walked over to Jeremy.

"Jeremy, no, w-wait—I'm sor—" Rachel stuttered.

"Give this to her," Jeremy said to Hansen. "It's not good luck anymore." The guard selected a key and unlocked the little door. Jeremy gave the charm to Hansen, and he slid it through the pass way. Then, Hansen walked around the other side, unlocked Rachel's little door and pulled out the charm. “Some kind of love charm?” He handed Rachel the charm. “Here you are, ma’am. Better put it in this bag.” He handed her a used luncheon bag. “Declare it, but don’t put it through the detectors. They’ll take it.” He winked. “Tell ‘em I seen it and okayed it . . . Hansen, name is Kurt Hansen.”

“Thanks, Mr. Hansen,” Rachel said. She stuffed the charm in the bag. “Maybe I’ll bring it to Madison tomorrow after all.”

“What?” Jeremy asked.

“Nothing. Just nothing.”

“But show it to ‘em when you leave,” Hansen said. “They like givin’ their okay.”

She smiled. “Sure.”

“Hasn’t done me any good, that’s for sure,” Jeremy said, moping into the phone.

Hansen locked the door on Rachel’s side. Rachel raised the phone to her ear. “I heard that. Don’t you go feeling sorry for yourself, Jeremy Lucas!” She crossed her arms.

Hansen glanced back and shook his head.

“Rachel, please listen,” Jeremy said into the phone. “Please?”

"To what? More bullshit?" She squinted angrily at him for a second, then looked away.

"I've really blown it, I know that," he said, trying to sound calmer than he felt. "Rachel, you have to understand. Billy thinks Lana's testimony might be enough to convict me. We thought she would give me an alibi and save my ass."

"What? Convict? Alibi?"

Jeremy nodded. "Billy can still negotiate a reduced sentence for manslaughter if I make a deal with Butler," He shrugged. "But Carl's testimony gives me a clear motive."

"What does that mean?" Rachel asked. The concern slipped back into her voice.

"Five-to-eight years if we plea bargain the thing to manslaughter. Maybe a lot more if they convict me on the murder two, which is more likely now."

"Jeremy, this is too much." She put down the receiver and squeaked her chair away, gritting her teeth and shaking her head.

"Wait, Rach!" he shouted into the receiver. "Wait! Listen, I have another idea."

She stood. "I really have to go," she said. "This is just too much." Her voice whimpered faintly through the glass and her hands covered her face. "I'll see you in court—just whenever." She picked up the bag with the charm in it, stood, and ran to the door. Jeremy could hear her say to Hansen, "I have to go, Mr. Hansen. Please let me out." He unlocked the door, and she quickly ran out.

"Remember to declare it and tell 'em I okayed it," Hansen called to her. "Name is Kurt Hansen."

Jeremy remained in his chair, wondering if the worst would come true. Was it possible? He thought back to Ken—now freed. For a moment, he wished he had paid his dues for the Sterling Hall bombing years ago. Then, maybe none of this would have happened. Now, he'd probably pay for Catherine's death and his college crime for the next decade.

Fifteen minutes later, Billy Stokes barged his way into the visitor's room. Hansen held up his hand. "Who are you?"

Billy pointed to Jeremy. "His lawyer. Wanna see my pass?" He flashed it. "I had a six o'clock."

"Okay," Hansen said. "It's twenty after already. "Ten minutes is all I can give you."

"All right." Billy walked down the other side of the security wall, flicked the chair around that Rachel had sat in and picked up a phone. "Sorry I'm late," he said. His cowboy boots clunked on the old tile as he straddled the chair. "So, what the hell is up with all these el primo witnesses, Jer? They're killing my damn case."

"Sorry, Billy," said Jeremy. "This whole thing is falling apart."

"In school they never prepared me for this kinda bull—totally out of my hands. I'm gonna talk to Rachel; see if she'll be a Defense witness."

"Can she do that—switch sides?"

"Without discovery. If the judge okays it. We'll see. Let me work on it."

"Time's up, Lucas," Hansen butted in. "Let's go, sir. Lucas, I promised Berger I'd bring you back to your block after your six o'clock."

"All right." Jeremy stood and held out his hands.

The guard led Jeremy back down the cramped hallway, past the banging and yelling in Cellblock A, to Berger's station.

Just then, Berger appeared, cradling a fresh cup of coffee. "How'd it go, Lucas?"

"Not so great," Jeremy answered. "Say, Berger?"

"Yeah?"

"Before you put me in my cell, can I make a quick call? Please? It's really important."

"Fine, but make it quick—it's not regular call time. And Krause, here, will have to stand by." He motioned to a guard positioned a few feet away.

Krause stepped forward. From his well-starched shirt, perfect hair, and the way he fumbled nervously, Jeremy gathered that today was the young man's first day on the job, or close to it. He hadn't seen him on duty before.

Jeremy said, "Say, Berger? Borrow a couple of quarters?"

Berger reached in his pocket. "Jesus, some people have all the nerve." He flipped the change to Jeremy. "You guys are going to break me."

"Thanks, I really ap—"

"Never mind, Lucas, just hurry," Berger said, annoyed. "Krause, now you watch him real good. Okay?"

Krause saluted and patted his holster. "Yes, sir."

Jeremy walked over to the phone, awkwardly put a quarter in with cuffed hands, and dialed, then added the other quarter. As Krause leaned over to listen, Jeremy turned away and pulled the receiver closer to his mouth.

"Jeremy?" Lana answered in a shaky voice. "My God, Jeremy. Are you out?"

"No, listen, I only have a minute," he said.

"Wait, Jeremy," she said, "Time out. I hafta say this."

"Quick. What?" He looked around.

"I'm so incredibly sorry," Lana said. "It was like somebody else was talking up there this morning, I swear. I think it was unfair, the way he was twisting it. I can tell it must've been an accident with that Catherine. I was real mad, is all, and jealous."

"Jesus, Lana. It's a little late for apologies."

"Maybe—" she said.

"My lawyer said without an alibi, I'm cooked, and with your testimony—"

"Oh, shit," Lana said somberly. "Look what I did."

"Wait, Lana?"

"Jeremy, I didn't want this to happen."

"Sure."

"Shit. I'll never forgive myself," she said. "We'll never be together now."

"Oh great," Jeremy said sarcastically, shaking his head. "That's what I've been thinking about."

"But, wait," she said. "There's gotta be something."

"I doubt it."

"Wait. I got it, I'll testify again! I'll give you an alibi."

"No, Lana," Jeremy said slowly. "I don't think that'd play real well."

"But, there's gotta be something," she pleaded.

Jeremy nodded blankly at Krause's purposeful stare. "Wait, Lana." He held up his index finger. "Maybe there is."

12

Madison, Wisconsin

All around the campus of the University of Wisconsin were early signs of spring—birds, buds, and lovers.

Rachel drove slowly and scanned the area for the tall building that Julie had said housed the Center for South Asian Studies.

Then, she caught the words "Van Hise" on a wall. She pulled into an empty parking space on the street in front of the building. She entered and walked up the stairs to the third floor, then down the hall to Room #325. She knocked on the open door.

A short wisp of a man with dark, shiny skin and nickel glasses looked up from his tiny desk. "Yes?" The miniature room, about twice the size of a closet, was cluttered with wads of paper and crammed with dog-eared books, stuffed randomly on four shelves.

"Professor Lall?" Rachel asked, waving. "I called you earlier this morning."

"Yes," the professor grinned. "You must be Mrs. Lucas? Mrs. Lucas with the charm?"

She smiled, held up her paper bag. "That's me."

"Come, come. Please sit in what little space I have." He half-stood and pointed to a chair covered with papers.

"Just move those, lady. Here, put them on my desk." He quickly repositioned things.

Rachel wondered, *Could he really give me some background on the charm?* She glanced around at his books. "At the Fond du Lac campus, they said you might be able to help me." They shook hands.

"Yes, yes," Lall said impatiently. "May I see it?" He pointed to the bag.

"Some old relic I shined up." Rachel pulled out the charm, and the light immediately reflected its luster. "Is it important, professor?"

"Let us see." Lall held the relic under a dusty old table lamp with little glass prisms hanging around the shade. He looked at the back, turned it over, and inspected the front side. "Ah, the Goddess Prajnaparamita, goddess of translucent wisdom. She is our guide for cutting through the clouds that obscure our perceptions of life."

"You know what that carving means?"

"Oh, yes." He grinned. "My, oh my. Quite a fine likeness."

"Is it some kind of good luck charm?" she asked.

"In the literature, they've termed it the Charm from Delhi." Lall adjusted the charm in the light. "Actually, it has just started appearing around Wisconsin, every few months, over the last few years. Quite beautiful. Numerous papers speculating about its origin have been written, you know. You may be able to receive a nice finder's fee for this."

"Oh, really?" Rachel said, wide-eyed. "But, I don't think I want to part with it just yet."

"I am sorry to rush you," Lall said. "Over the last year or two, twenty-five different people have brought that very piece to various campuses around the state." He laughed. "My dear friend Van der Bosch at the Parkside campus in Racine told me I should be on the lookout for it. Really quite something." He chuckled again, holding his hand over his mouth.

"What's so funny?"

"Well, you see, more than one person has gone over to Professor Van der Bosch for a translation of this Sanskrit on the back. He hands them a Xerox copy, and they walk away."

"So?" Rachel said.

"Then, a couple of weeks pass," Lall went on, "and someone else calls, asking for the translation. When they bring the charm in, he gives them a copy of the translation, too. They then leave, and, having heard the translation, insist that *they* dispose of the charm."

"R-really?" Rachel stammered.

The professor shook his head slowly. "Stanley—that's Van der Bosch—told me the story one day. He's getting such a bang out of it. He says he should start charging for the translation—he'd make a fortune." He giggled squeakily.

"I bet," Rachel said. "How can I get the translation?"

"I can ask him to provide a copy for you."

Rachel smiled eagerly. "That would be very nice."

"I'd be delighted." The professor half-bowed. "You are from Fond du Lac?"

"Yes."

"The so-called Charm from Delhi is certainly making its way around the state and world, just as the monk and the boy intended!"

"Monk? Boy?"

"Oh, I'm sorry, the story of the charm."

"What can you tell me about it?" Rachel asked, intrigued.

"Oh, certainly, I can give you a bit of a preview and save you time doing the research yourself."

"Thank you, Professor. I'm real curious."

"Supposedly it was made many, many years ago, Mrs. Lucas; some say the twelfth or thirteenth century."

"*This* charm?" Rachel asked in disbelief.

"Oh, yes," Lall answered, "this very one. If the Indian government would start seriously supporting the recovery of antiquities—"

"Tell me more," she said.

"Certainly." The professor put his hands together. "According to legend, fairly well documented over the years, the piece was forged by a promising young craftsman from Kashmir named Senji—his name is here, on the charm. See? Since the artisans tended to come from the North, we assume that's where the charm was likely forged. He was probably a young man because, while the craftmanship is fine, it lacks some of the subtleties that appeared around that time."

"Cash-mere?" Rachel asked. "Like the sweater?"

Lall giggled. "No. K-a-s-h-m-i-r. Kashmir. The province in the north of

India. Back then India was called *Bharat*, you see. It's very beautiful in Kashmir: mountains, streams, meadows, orchards."

"I knew that . . . well, I guess I did," Rachel said, feeling herself blushing. Then, she focused her attention once again on the piece. "What is the language on the back of the charm?" she asked. "Sanskrit, I think you said."

"Yes, quite right," Lall replied. "It's the classic literary language of India. You see, research has shown that Senji had quite a problem."

"Problem?" She adjusted her chair.

"Well, you see, given the probable age of the charm, we can assume Senji wanted to preserve the teachings of his simple faith, actually more a practice than a faith."

"What is that?" she asked.

"It is likely that Buddhism inspired the charm," said the professor. "See the Buddha? It appears from the inscription that he was trying to summarize the concept of causality, what Westerners simplistically refer to as karma. It is likely that Senji took a trip to Delhi to have the charm blessed."

"This very charm?" Rachel inquired. "You're sure?"

"One never knows, but until we do dating, I cannot confirm anything."

Rachel stretched.

Lall said, "Oh, I'm so sorry, the chair is uncomfortable?"

"A little, but it's okay, really. What is this causality business? It sounds vaguely familiar."

"Oh, I term it the great chain of life: everything that happens leads to something else happening, and so forth. Like I said, you might refer to it as karma."

"Everybody's heard of karm—"

"But, it is a much more difficult concept than that. You see, whatever good or bad we do or say or think enters our *lifestream*—our chain of choices. That must be kept in balance."

So, everything we do—" Rachel began.

He cut in, "—and think, say, or ponder matters. All of it makes up our lifestream."

"Lifestream," she said.

"It goes on forever—our stream of choices. We each have a lifestream. Want to hear something most extraordinary?"

"Sure," she said.

"We are intricately connected by the interactions that make up the great chain of causality. Even you and I, after meeting today. That makes all of us one entity, don't you see? One!"

Rachel squinted. "Hmmm. That's really something."

"We all come from the same stock," Lall explained. "We all cry with the same tears. This is what I tell my daughter about this part. Just picture it, Mrs. Lucas." He waved the charm in the air. "It is a beautiful notion—Oneness. It is the most beautiful notion there is. In the universe, each of us has an essence that includes the bits of life from an infinite number of our own lifetimes—who we ever were or who we will ever become. The magnificent Oneness is comprised of that individual greatness of each and every soul that has existed. But, alas, that is the best I can do. Infinity is so great, I tire just thinking about it. Perhaps you will understand it someday."

"Hmmm, choices. Oh, my Jeremy—" She sniffled.

"Tell me," he said. "Who is this Jeremy?"

"My husband," Rachel replied. "They're trying him for murder."

"Has he actually killed anyone?" Lall asked, raising his eyebrows so his glasses jiggled on his nose.

"I guess so, twice probably."

"Oooh," Lall said, and exhaled a low whistle. "Did he have unwise sexual relations?"

She nodded. "But what does that have to do—"

"Does he engage in idle talk?"

"Idle—"

"Talk," he said. "Talking loosely about others. Criticizing, mocking; creating illusions that become people's thoughts and cause others pain."

"I guess so." Rachel laughed. "Doesn't everybody once in a while?"

"Oh, no," Lall said, shaking his head vehemently. "Is he malicious? Does he lie? Use harsh words? Carry wrong views?"

"Wait! You're going so fast."

"Oh, I am so sorry," the professor said. "You see, the Buddha taught that we should rid our lifestreams of all negative choices because they take happiness away for ourselves and others. It is important to understand that *our choices determine what will become of us.* That is what Senji inscribed on the charm—an abbreviation of the essence of causation. He also explained that throwing it away when we understand it, will allow its thoughts to touch many hearts, eventually *all* hearts. That's why the charm says, *'Discard this once you understand it.'* "

"Hmmm . . . Jeremy?" Rachel prodded.

"Oh, yes, your husband. There is not much I, or anyone except your husband, can do to remold such a corrupted lifestream as his seems to be. I am so sorry. This is not a positive time to be attached to him."

"He's in jail down in Chicago. The trial starts up again at the Civic Center day after tomorrow. They might put him away for years."

"The Civic Center in downtown Chicago by the Picasso statue? Yes, I know it." Professor Lall pulled on his chin and looked about as if searching for the answer to this poor woman's plight. "No, this does not sound good. Yes, I thought so—this is the case I've seen on the news. Hmmm. I do have a trip planned to the University of Chicago and the Art Institute week after next . . . Maybe I could stop by; it would be most interesting."

"That would be nice," said Rachel. "Is there a way this charm could help him?"

"No, hardly." He looked into her eyes. "It depends more on your husband, and the specific acts that make up his lifestream, than on any charm, no matter how inspired its creation."

“That sounds so hopeless,” she said.

“Not necessarily, but for your husband it does not look real good.”

Outside the building, Rachel walked past Sterling Hall. She could hardly recollect how it looked before it had been virtually destroyed fifteen years before, the smeared marks of mortar and newer-colored brick created a patchwork effect. Looking ahead and down steep Bascom Hill, she saw the students congregating in the State Street Mall across from the library, just as they'd done in the old days. She decided to take a walk down there.

When she reached the bottom, a woman about her age with black braided hair, wearing jogging clothes, walked across her path. She stopped, turned toward Rachel and stared at her inquisitively. “Rachel? Rachel *Martin*? Is that you?”

Rachel looked at the woman. She knew the face. Then, her name surfaced in her memory. “Nancy? Nancy Burke? Yes, it's you!” The two women hugged. “I thought I'd never see you again. I remember we always called you BB, for Baby Burke.”

“That's me!” Nancy beamed. “Remember, I said when I grew up, I'd end up a librarian here at UW. Here I am!" They held each other by the shoulders. "So, did you end up marrying Jeremy?" Nancy asked.

"Yeah. Right after school. Still married. Live in Fond du Lac."

"Oh, Rachel. How's it going? Any kids?"

"No, but everything's . . . fine. He's doing good. A little tough-going." Rachel looked down. "What about you?"

"I married Bill. One child, Jenn, then divorce. Jenn's a physical therapist."

"Nancy, I swear, you look exactly the same," Rachel said.

Nancy put her hand over her mouth, turned, and pointed across the mall. "Do you know who's right over there?"

Rachel looked left, then right, across from the library. "Who?"

"Ken Nordberg. I bet jail really affected him. Did you hear he got out early? The governor commuted his sentence."

Rachel nodded and said, "Which one is he?"

Nancy pointed. "That partially bald guy selling smoothies."

"Oh, my God, Nancy. He still has that little bald spot on top with long hair on both sides."

"Some things never change. Say, listen, Rach." Nancy looked at her watch.

"I really better scoot. I'm catching Emerson, Lake, and Palmer in Milwaukee tonight. Here, write down your number. I'll call you."

Rachel took a little pad and pencil from her friend. "Here you go. You're still the major rock fan, eh?"

"No kidding! Even have my own web site and everything."

"Just like your old radio show!"

"Keeps me young!" She waved, then turned and jogged up Bascom Hill.

Minutes later, Rachel strolled past her old apartment building on Mifflin Street, the first place she lived with Jeremy after he had saved her from the riots, snatching her from a mob seconds before the police moved in. She thought back to Ken Nordberg, who always possessed a heart of gold and now sold smoothies. He and his brother Harold had gotten out of prison early while Jeremy was now looking at doing some pretty serious time. She thought back to Professor Lall's discussion about an individual's lifestream—a stream of choices. Then, she thought about Paul and recollected how he had thought she was the smoothie type.

13

Fond du Lac, Wisconsin

The sky was dark when Rachel pulled into her driveway Wednesday evening, still pondering the significance of her visit to Professor Lall at Madison. Though she felt a little overwhelmed by the complexity of causality and the idea of a lifestream, she understood how her choices had sculpted her life. Jeremy had made choices, too.

After she parked and turned off the car, she patted the paper bag with the charm in it and thought, *Choice—that's really something*.

She looked across her front yard at the large spruce tree lit by the nearby streetlight and saw Paul walking toward her. She opened the car door.

"Hey, how'd it go, Rachel?" he asked keenly. "How's Jeremy?"

"Truth?" she asked.

He approached her. "Sure. What else?"

"That's all there is in your life, isn't there? Truth."

"The rest is illusion, they say. We create it to fool ourselves."

"Oh, Paul," Rachel cooed. "You sound like Professor Lall."

"Who?"

"A professor I saw at Madison today. You sound like him."

"Really?"

"I'll tell you about this charm some time—how you throw it away once you understand it, so its message will spread."

"That thing Jeremy found in the woods?" Paul sniffed. "Why throw it away?"

Rachel lifted the bag. "Sounds logical the way Professor Lall explained it. The inscription on the charm says to throw it away once you understand its message, so the message will spread."

"What's the message?"

"That our choices determine what will become of us."

"That sounds simple enough, actually obvious," said Paul, puffing his chest a bit. "So, I'm like the professor, huh? Never been accused of being deep."

Rachel laughed and said, "I meant it as a compliment."

"Thanks," he said.

She giggled, then shook her head. "Talk about truth. You know, my folks told me that in court it came out that Jer was cheating on me."

"Really?"

"Yeah, on the stand, his assistant said she'd been fooling around with him for the last three years."

"Incredible." Paul raised an index finger to his lips. "Are you surprised?"

She shook her head. "Not really. I've pushed my suspicions out of my mind, ignoring her lilac scent . . . for years. It's not just Lana though. I know there were others, too."

"I actually wanted to come clean on something myself," Paul said. "We all make lots of mistakes along the way, too, don't we?"

"I just don't think I have the will to love him anymore, Paul," Rachel said. Her head drooped. "At least my folks are telling me I shouldn't . . . Janell, my therapist, says that love is an act of will. I don't know if I can will it with him anymore. My folks are saying I should bail quick." She looked up and laughed. "I think it could be over. I really do."

"Wait, Rachel." Paul put up a hand. "You have to stick this out no matter *what* it feels like. You have to stick by your man, no matter what anybody says, even your folks. He's made terrible mistakes. Right now you're the one thing he's got." Then, he cleared his voice and looked straight at her. "And, if I can say this, you're about perfect."

Rachel looked up, surprised. "Why, Paul." She lightly touched his sleeve.

He looked up. "What'd I say?"

"I didn't know you felt—I mean, Paul Ersham—I think that's the nicest thing you ever said to me."

"Well, it's true," he said. "If you were my wife, I'd never go fooling around on you," he said. "And, I'd definitely never . . . whoops." He covered his mouth with his hand.

"What? Never what?" Rachel asked.

He looked away. "Forget it."

"Paul? Tell me."

"No, I can't." Then, he sniffled. "Dammit." He wiped his nose.

"Paul, what's the matter?" she asked. "You have a cold? Upset?"

"No. It's nothing. Really." He could barely speak, he was so choked up.

She squeezed his shoulder. He pulled away.

"Paul, come on," she urged. "It's something, I can tell. What is it?"

He took a deep breath and covered his mouth. "I hit her," he mumbled. Then, he fidgeted as he held back tears.

"Who?" she asked. "Claire?"

"Who else?" Paul turned his face away. "There, how's that for honest? You wanted honest. Now, you hate me."

"Paul, come here." Rachel grabbed his shoulders and turned him around so his body faced hers.

He looked down, hiding his eyes. "I never should've—" His trembling hand covered his mouth. "And, now she's gone, dammit . . . for good." He sniffed again and started to cry.

"Aw, Paul. Tell me," Rachel prodded. "Come on, you need to talk this out."

"I don't know," he cried. "I just don't know."

"Come on Paul, it's safe. It's just you and me and the snow."

"Oh, dammit."

"Please?" she said. "Please?"

"Well—" Paul said, hesitating. "One year we had a fight about where to plant the damn Begonias." He sniffed.

"So what."

"Well, she wanted them over by the front porch, but I already dug a bed, you know, in the back, along the garage, with more shade."

"Go ahead."

"Well," Paul said, "I was pointing and shouting back there, and lost it, you know? Can't explain how. It just hap—"

"What?" Rachel broke in.

"Her face was right there."

"Ooo." Rachel cringed.

"Where my hand was," he said.

"Oh, no."

"Yes." He slowed. "I hit her square on the side of the nose."

"Oh, my God. Paul."

"And, she bled." He sniffed. "She bled bright red. It was awful."

"Come here, Paul." Rachel pulled him to her, wrapping her arms around his broad shoulders.

"It was awful," he cried. "She was my angel. And now she's gone."

"Let it go, Paul," she said. She patted his back. "There, there."

"I knew I never should've swung around like that—getting all bent out of shape."

"That's right." She stroked his back, like family does at a wake. *How can Paul be this honest and vulnerable?*

"It was just the damn Begonias."

"Listen to me," Rachel said firmly.

"What?" he mumbled as he buried his head in her neck.

"She's not gone because of you."

He looked up. "What?"

"Really, Paul. All this time, you've carried this load?"

"I guess." He pulled out a handkerchief and blew his nose.

"All this time you've been so true to her memory . . . "

"Well—"

"It's time to let it go, Paul. It wasn't you who took her from us."

"Oh, Rachel." He sniffed. "I think about her all the time. I go around feeling miserable. Honest, I'm obsessed."

"I know, I know." She pulled him to her again. "It's time to give yourself a break, Paul. You don't have to feel like this anymore."

He breathed deeply a few times. "I guess I feel better now," he said. "Thanks."

They stood and embraced.

He whispered, "Rachel, maybe we shouldn't be hugging like this with Jeremy in jail."

She pulled away. "Oh, Paul. You're definitely one of those special guys." She leaned up and slowly kissed him on the cheek. She held her face against his and pressed close.

"Say, Rachel?" he whispered.

"What?"

"This may sound stupid."

"What?

"Can you call me Pauley? Just once?"

"Sure—Pauley," she spoke softly into his ear.

"Hmm, that takes me back," he said and pulled her tighter to him. "That feels good. I didn't think anybody would ever call me that again."

"Wait, Paul. You're right. We shouldn't—" Rachel pulled away.

"You're right," he said. "Now's the time you should be standing by your man, not hugging your neighbor, or your plumber, or whoever I am."

"Everybody's saying I should dump him." Rachel lowered her eyes.

Paul shook his head. "No, sir. Now's the time you should *forgive* him."

She tensed up and shook her head. "Like I said, Paul: You're just too good to believe."

"Well—" He smiled. "There is something else I've thought about for a long time."

"What's that?"

He pulled her closer. "It's the way I feel about you, Rachel. It's just that I think about it; then I think, no, I shouldn't say anything. I don't know. Then, I think about it again. Not saying anything is driving me nuts."

"Oh, Paul." She reached up and kissed him again on the cheek.

He closed his eyes and didn't move. Rachel felt his skin, rough and warm. But, it was skin you could feel—not like Jeremy's, so slick and smooth.

"Rachel?" he whispered.

"Yes, Paul?" she said.

"I was just going to say, right or wrong, this feels really good."

"I know," she whispered, a little breathless. "Lord, I feel so safe with you. I really trust you."

"Rachel?" he hummed in her ear. "There's something important I've been wanting to say to you."

"Oh, Paul," she said, then drew back. "Wait—better not."

She pulled away and ran to the front door.

Minutes later, after Rachel went inside, the phone rang.

She scampered to the phone on the little hall table and picked up the receiver. "Hello?"

"Rachel?" a female voice said.

"Yes, who is this?" Rachel looked at her watch.

"This is Lana," the voice said.

"Lana?" Rachel exclaimed. "The nerve, you calling me!"

"Wait, Rachel. Please."

"You bitch!" Rachel fumed. "Your testimony could have helped my husband. Now, he'll probably be going away for a long time! How dare you!" She slammed the receiver onto its cradle.

A minute later, the phone rang again.

Rachel let it ring two times, then picked it up. “Hello?”

“Please wait,” Lana said. “You gotta give me a minute.”

“Dammit, I shouldn’t give you a *second*.”

“Listen, Rachel, I called because I feel awful.”

Rachel laughed. “My, that’s big of you.”

“I called because I have this idea, see? Might even make up for what I said in court.”

“Go ahead,” Rachel said, and tapped her toe repeatedly.

“It hurts that he doesn’t have an alibi, right?” Lana said.

“No kidding?” Rachel said scornfully.

“Well, I can’t give him one.”

“Obviously.”

“Well, I was thinking, maybe *you* could.”

“*Me?*” Rachel stopped tapping her foot and slowly twirled the phone cord around her finger.

“Yeah, see, you haven’t testified yet,” Lana said. “Maybe you could testify for the Defense and give him an alibi for that night. You were alone, right?”

“Of course, I was usually alone on the nights he was out fooling around with his lady friends,” Rachel said, “like you.”

"You could give him an alibi, don't you see?"

"But, suddenly like this?" Rachel wondered. "That would sound sort of weird. I mean, he's the grand cheater and, out of nowhere, I come to his aid?"

"You could just say you were pissed at him, so you weren't coming forward."

"Billy did talk to me," Rachel said.

"See, maybe it'll work."

"Are you sure?" Rachel said and paused. "I don't know."

"Oh, please, talk to his lawyer."

Rachel was silent. She thought about what Paul had said—how she should be helping Jeremy, no matter what. "I don't know."

"I thought you cared for him," Lana said.

"I do, but—"

"And, I thought you were the big Katia fan."

"Lord, what's that have to do with anything?" Rachel shouted, and put her hand on her hip.

"You obviously haven't heard her song, 'He's All Yours.'"

"Of course I have," Rachel shot back, "I know the words to every—"

"Well, it's like it was written from me to you, right at this moment. You oughta listen to it again. Seriously."

"Wait. Have you been talking to Jer?" Rachel asked.

"I gotta go," Lana said suddenly. "See you in court."

"Right, I'll be sure to wave." Rachel slowly hung up. She walked over to the stereo cabinet, pulled out one of Katia's tapes and turned it on. She cued up the last song and closed her eyes, imagining that Lana was singing to her:

Hey, Rachel, take him back in your arms for good.
When he looks at me,
I know he's dreaming of you.
There is no denying it
He was never truly happy with me.

Take him back, Rachel, he's all yours.
Take him back, Rachel, he's all yours.

Ignore what others tell you.
Listen to the music in your soul.
Someone's told you it's just your pride talking,
But it's truly the best thing you've ever known, baby.
Do it against their will,
Do it against the tide.
You can't say it's not right.
Once and for all:
You have to take him back.

Words and Music — M. Litecki, K. Polankski © 1984 PLS Records

Rachel played the song five times. Then, she turned off the stereo, walked to the phone, thumbed through the Rolodex, and found Billy Stokes' home number. She fiddled with the card, flicking a worn corner.

She could be honest, as Paul had said. That would mean not racing to Jeremy's aid now, not like she'd done years before at Madison without a second thought. That could mean letting Jeremy go to jail.

Or, she could come to his aid. She could ignore everything Julie and her folks were telling her. She could lie for Jeremy to save him—yet again.

She flicked the card. *Honesty over loyalty, or loyalty over honesty?* She flicked the card again.

Billy answered.

"Hi, Billy. I think we need to talk."

14

Chicago, Illinois

On Friday, Jeremy looked up at Billy Stokes as he stood in court and cleared his throat. The gallery quieted. Billy shuffled toward the judge, papers in hand.

"Yes, Mr. Stokes?" Judge Rogers said.

"Request a sidebar, Your Honor," Stokes said.

"Fine. Mr. Butler?" Judge Rogers waved both attorneys to the bench.

Jeremy wondered what this was all about. *More legal gibberish, no doubt.* He turned around and scanned the packed courtroom. Today the trial had attracted more press, probably because of the dramatic testimony earlier in the week and the increasing press coverage.

Jeremy saw many strangers in the gallery, too—many of them college-aged, whispering and jotting notes. Some of these kids were probably law clerks scouting Judge Rogers for their firms' impending trials. An Indian-looking man sitting quietly in the last row of the gallery caught Jeremy's attention. He was a curious sight: worn, round spectacles; long, pointed nose; dark, shiny skin and sparse, salt-and-pepper hair, matted and curly.

"Hey, Billy," Jeremy whispered.

He looked over at him, then mouthed, "What?"

"Do you know that guy?" He pointed to the strange-looking foreign man. Several people looked as he pointed.

Billy shrugged. "Who?"

"That Indian guy over there."

Billy looked again. "Not really," he said in a whisper. Then, he gestured toward the bench.

"Order." Judge Rogers slapped the gavel lightly. "Ladies and gentlemen of the jury. Based on the little chat we just had up here, I wanted to inform you that Rachel Lucas, originally a Prosecution witness, will now be testifying for the Defense, which is her right. So, Madame Foreperson, please adjust your witness logs accordingly. Do you all understand that?"

Most of the jury nodded.

"Good." The judge tossed down his pen. "Now, Mr. Stokes, you may proceed to call your next witness."

Billy Stokes rose. "Thank you, Your Honor."

"You set, Billy?" Jeremy looked up and whispered. "Have you talked to her?"

"It's better y'all not know." Stokes patted Jeremy on the shoulder and whispered. "This'll work out just fine, Jer. Don't sweat it."

"B-but—" Jeremy stuttered.

"Jer, this is what you pay me for, right?" he said. "Now's the time you gotta let me do my thing."

Jeremy slumped back and mumbled. "Right."

Billy cleared his voice. "Your Honor, Defense calls Rachel Lucas."

"Order," Judge Rogers said, and pounded his gavel.

After all the preliminaries, Jeremy watched Rachel fidget in the witness box, wondering what she would say.

"So, Mrs. Lucas, y'all recall Thursday, February 13?" Billy asked.

"Yes, sir," Rachel replied softly.

"Tell us about that day—your appointments, your husband's, and so forth."

"Let's see. Jeremy had a luncheon in Chicago with Brad Coleman, one of Archer's district managers."

"Yes, that was substantiated by Mr. Coleman's testimony."

She nodded. "Well, I worked all day making dinner."

"For yourself?"

"Heavens, no. When I'm alone, I hardly ever cook; just pop in a TV dinner. Jeremy headed home late that afternoon."

The courtroom rumbled.

"Wait, wait, wait," Billy raised his hands and cocked his ear. "What time did your husband arrive home, Mrs. Lucas?"

Rachel shrugged. "Four-thirty, I guess."

A loud murmur rose in the courtroom. "Order!" The Judge shouted the din to silence, then gestured Billy to continue.

"Just to make sure we got that straight," Billy said, striding back and forth, "that was four-thirty p.m. on February 13, the day of Catherine Dunne's unfortunate death, right?"

"Oh, yes," said Rachel. "I remember, the accident was on the 10 o'clock news that night."

"So, when he got home late that afternoon, you two ate dinner?" Stokes asked, shuffling papers as he paced.

"Yes, about five thirty or six o'clock. I made ravioli with marinara, a salad, and strawberry sorbet with blackberries for dessert. Even made cappuccino after. We hardly ever use that machine."

"It sure sounds mighty dee-licious," Billy Stokes said slowly as he eyed the jury, smiling.

Rachel looked Jeremy's way. Then, she looked out over his head and squinted, like she had seen something. Her squint turned to a near-frown.

Jeremy scanned the gallery and saw nothing. But then, his eyes met a young man's—sitting in the back, wearing a University of Wisconsin sweatshirt. This was the same young man Jeremy had noticed before, the one resembling a teenaged version of Agers. After the two stared at each other for a moment, Jeremy looked away, back toward the witness stand.

Rachel cast Jeremy a worried glance. Now, Jeremy thought, she'd seen the teenager with the red hair, too. And, she must've realized who he was.

"Mrs. Lucas?" Billy asked. "What did Jeremy tell you about his day?"

"Objection." Butler stood. "Hearsay, Your Honor."

"Overruled," Judge Rogers pronounced. "Let's let this one pass, Mr. Butler. Aren't you a little curious what *she says* he said to her? Could affect the outcome, don't you think?"

"Yes, Your Honor, but—"

"Go ahead, Mrs. Lucas. You go ahead and answer," Judge Rogers said. "What did he say about his day?"

Rachel visibly swallowed hard. "Just that when he was eating lunch with Brad Coleman at the Chez Paul restaurant, a candidate—this woman he interviewed at Archer—Catherine Dunne—walked up and handed him a matchbook."

"A matchbook?" Stokes probed. "Then what?"

"Well, it had an invitation written on it. To come over to her place at five p.m. for a drink and dinner. Even had directions in little handwriting." Rachel shook her head at the jury. "The nerve of some of these aggressive businesswomen nowadays. She's from the University of Chicago, too. I hear they train 'em like that."

"And that's it?" Stokes asked and shrugged.

"No," Rachel replied. "He said he gave the matchbook back to her. Then she walked away."

Jeremy felt like bursting. Rachel's testimony was now supporting Billy's brilliant opening. Her story even explained the existence of Jeremy's thumbprint on the matchbook. Now, the older lady juror in the front row looked at him with maternal concern in her eyes, like he had been unjustly accused.

Wherever this outlandish story came from, Rachel's entire testimony sounded perfectly logical and supported the evidence. In fact, her colorful details even enhanced its credibility.

"Can we go back to dinner that night for a second?" Stokes asked.

"Sure." Rachel looked at Jeremy and smiled encouragingly, like a supportive mother. He smiled back.

"Do you remember Jeremy being upset about anything?"

"Not at all."

"Really? Well, then, did he go out that evening for more than half an hour?"

"Why, yes," Rachel said. "He did."

Billy Stokes spun around and looked at her, brow crunched. "For what? For what, Mrs. Lucas?"

Jeremy stiffened. *Is she about to blow it?* he thought nervously.

"To shovel the walk," Rachel said calmly and smiled. "See, little Clark had a sore throat and couldn't do it for two weeks. If you don't shovel it right away, it gets all packed down and turns to ice."

"Oh, I see," Stokes said. Jeremy sighed and smiled at Rachel's apparent decision to throw in facts about the snow shoveling, remembering they could be substantiated.

"Well. Guess that's all I need." Billy scratched his head. "Yep." He paraded over to Edwin Butler's table. "I believe it's yours, counselor." He turned to Judge Rogers. "I might still need some redirect, Your Honor."

Judge Rogers nodded. "Mr. Butler, cross?"

Edwin Butler rose and fidgeted with his pen. "Mrs. Lucas?"

"Yes?"

"How might you explain the dramatic difference between your testimony and Ms. Lana Holub's? You did catch her testimony, correct?"

"Actually not, but I heard about it, you know, generally."

"Well?" Butler asked.

"It is painful to admit, but I always had a feeling that Jeremy did have a relationship with that woman." Rachel looked at the jury. "But three years? My God!"

The gallery stirred.

"Oh . . . you *knew* about it, then?" Butler asked, staring her down.

"Let's put it this way: I got suspicious about the lilac scent he always had on his clothes after his Wednesday client dinners."

Jeremy looked up at his wife.

"After he dumped her, she called the house several times, but I just hung up on her. After I confronted him and we talked it out, things got better." She stared at Jeremy, who appeared dumbfounded at her words.

"Yes?" Butler said.

"Then, on the 13th, he calls and says he's coming home early."

"But, how did you have time to make that dinner?" he asked.

"It was only pasta," Rachel said. "That's real easy. We shared the garlic bread, and I went to the store to get his favorite marinara. The one with the fresh crushed tomatoes."

"What about Lana Holub?" Butler probed. "How did she sound whenever she called?"

Rachel said, "Bitter. Angry. I'm not surprised she's trying to get him blamed for this. Despite my problems with Jeremy over the years, I can't imagine letting him get unjustly accused like this." She looked at the jury and nodded.

"Unjustly accused?" Butler said. "Thank you. That's enou—"

Rachel butted in, "It's probably one of that Dunne woman's other lovers who let her go while they were doing that flying thing. That's not Jeremy's style. He's even afraid of heights, you know."

"I see," Butler said. "That's enough. Fine, fine." He nervously cleared his throat. "That'll be it, Mrs. Lucas." He hurried back to his table.

"Any redirect, Mr. Stokes?" Judge Rogers asked.

Stokes half-rose and grinned. "After Mr. Butler's illuminating cross, not necessary, Your Honor."

"Please step down, Mrs. Lucas," the judge said. "Thanks."

"In fact, Your Honor?" Billy Stokes remained standing and raised a hand. Rachel froze like a statue.

"Yes?"

"Defense rests," he said.

Judge Rogers dropped his pen and glared at the attorney.

Billy shrugged. "Really. That's it, Your Honor." He sat down and smiled broadly at the jury.

Jeremy leaned over. "That really it, Billy?" he whispered.

"Oh, yeah, that'll be plenty good."

"You sure?" Jeremy asked, his voice shaking.

"Jeremy, just ease up for once," Billy pleaded. "Pull the stick out, as they say."

After closing arguments that focused on the believability of Rachel's surprise testimony, compared to the compelling forsensic evidence, all circumstantial, the judge admonished the jury on the particulars of their deliberations and gave instructions as to how they should determine the proper verdict. His Honor pounded the gavel one last time.

"Good luck," he said to the jury.

Jeremy glanced back at the young man with long, red hair. Now, both Jeremy and Rachel had recognized him—the old newspaper clippings had come alive. Jeremy chilled as he flashed back to the moment just before the bombing, when he demanded that the frightened janitor at Sterling Hall be executed in the name of the growing anti-war cause. Jeremy shook as he recalled the hatred he'd felt that night, and how he had directed those feelings toward a man whose political position he knew nothing about, even as the man cried desperately about not being there for his young son, now a teen.

Jeremy's memories of the incident twenty-seven years before, which had visited him with recurring nightmares, kept tumbling back into his brain as the jury left the courtroom and headed for the deliberation room.

15

Chicago, Illinois

Rachel Lucas and Billy Stokes ate lunch together in the Civic Center cafeteria among lawyers, spectators, and students. She munched on vegetables. He gobbled a tough-looking steak.

"Billy, I think I was wrong about you," Rachel said suddenly.

"Wrong?" He looked up and stopped chewing.

"Well," Rachel said, "when we first talked about hiring an attorney, I tried to steer Jeremy away from you. I didn't trust your background—jail time, all that."

"Don't blame you much," said Billy, wiping his face with his arm. "Not real traditional."

"But that judge gave you a chance and you took it. I'm glad Jeremy picked you. He said you were naturally sly—a real master in the courtroom."

"Yep. That's me," Billy said and smiled.

"Now, I can see how good you are," Rachel said. "Especially when you cut the whole thing off at just the right moment."

"Might've worked a little earlier if Jer didn't insist on runnin' the show."

"He can be such a pain," she spurted, "the way he needs to control things. It's always been his way."

Just then, Professor Lall approached.

"Professor Lall," Rachel said happily. "I *thought* I saw you walking out of the courtroom. Thanks for stopping by."

"Well, of course," the professor replied. "This is an interesting case, and you see, I had those other appointments down here." He stood stoutly, his spare, curly, well-slicked hair gracing his dark face. "I became interested in the case from reading the newspapers. It is on the telly, too, you know, even in Madison."

Rachel gestured toward Billy. "This is Jeremy's lawyer, Billy Stokes."

Stokes stood. "Howdy." He and Lall shook hands. Stokes took his seat again.

"Most impressive job in there, sir," Lall said.

"Thanks." Billy nodded.

Turning his attention to Rachel again, Lall said, "Oh, Mrs. Lucas, I phoned Van der Bosch. Over at Parkside campus?"

"Yes," she said. "I remember."

"He would like to take an extended look at the charm," Lall said. "All this time, he's only seen it briefly. Van der Bosch says the Indian Consulate here in

Chicago is likely to contact you regarding a finder's fee, thanks to all the articles documenting its existence. May I have your address and phone?"

"Certainly," Rachel said. She pulled a scrap of paper from her purse and wrote the information on it.

Lall continued, "He would also like me to carbon date the piece at Madison to determine its exact age."

"Can that wait?" Rachel asked. "Sort of preoccupied now."

"After the trial—of course. He did give me the complete translation to pass along to you." Lall reached into his suit jacket pocket, then handed Rachel a folded piece of paper.

She unfolded the note and read its contents to herself. She looked up at Lall. "This causality business, determined by our choices, is it *that* powerful?"

"Oh yes," the professor said in a squeaky voice. "Ah, its power is greater than us all. It is as simple as minding the choices we make. That is everything there is, you see. Choices are what make up our lifestreams." He waved his hands. "If errant souls ignore their lifestreams and make bad choices indefinitely, the universe will deal with them in a most *terrifying* way."

Rachel shivered at the expressive way Lall had said the word "terrifying." "Yes, I think I see," she said. "Is that 'errant souls' part on the charm?"

Lall shook his head. "No, Mrs. Lucas, it is just the way it is."

Just then, Billy looked closely at Rachel. "You okay, Rach?"

"No worries. I'm fine."

Mr. Lall remained, but suddenly looked a bit discomfited. "Well, then. That is it," he said, holding his hands in a praying posture. He bowed. "See you in the courtroom, then. I think I have time to hear the verdict. Then I must go. And, good luck to you, Mr. Stokes," he said, nodding at Billy. "Mrs. Lucas, you will remember our earlier discussion?"

"Which one? About discarding the charm once I understand it?"

Lall nodded. "In order to keep its message circulating."

"Yes," she said quietly, "I remember."

"Oh, but, please," the professor said, "not before we get a chance to do that age testing to verify its validity. Maybe take some photographs, too." He bowed briskly and walked away.

"Wow," Billy said, "spooky dude. Spooky stuff."

"I think it's actually the simplest thing in the world, Billy," Rachel said, staring into space. "It's all about the real power of choice. But, that part about the universe dealing with errant souls in a terrifying way? That *was* pretty spooky. I wonder how the universe will deal with Jeremy."

"Rachel?" Billy waved his hand in front of her face. "You still there?"

"Oh, sure. It's nothing. Just nothing." She shook her head. "I was just thinking."

At that moment, Samuel Chen, Edwin Butler's clerk, burst through swiveling cafeteria doors and announced, "Attention, Lucas Case. Jury's about to come in!"

"Already?" Rachel said and looked at her watch, then Billy. "My God. This is *it*?"

Billy stood and pushed his chair back. "Some kinda record. Better git. This is either real good or real bad."

Up in the Division Ten courtroom, Rachel took a seat in the first row of the gallery, which buzzed with low-pitched voices as Judge Rogers pounded his gavel and called, "Order! Order!"

Billy huddled upfront with Jeremy, who nervously rubbed his hands together, looking back and forth between the empty jury box and the judge. Rachel had never seen Jeremy like this.

The door next to the jury box opened, and the jury filed in. Rachel studied each member as they entered: An elderly lady carried a hard, determined scowl. A restless young man with long hair hung his head. An Asian girl glanced about, fidgeting. The last one in—a tall, dark, distinguished lady with short hair and olive skin—studied papers as she walked.

"Be seated!" Judge Rogers said. The clerk took a page of paper from the dark-haired lady and handed it to Judge Rogers, who tapped his gavel once. "Will the defendant please rise?"

Jeremy and Billy stood. Rachel saw Jeremy curl his fingers so they barely touched the table, maybe to steady himself. He glanced up at the ceiling and sighed visibly, apparently ignoring the presence of everyone in the room. He looked bored, repeatedly drumming his knuckles on the table.

The dark lady stood and raised the papers she still had. She flapped them straight. Jeremy drew in a deep breath, then exhaled.

"Madame Foreperson, has the jury reached a verdict?" Judge Rogers asked as he read his copy.

The lady said, "We have, Your Honor."

Rachel watched the lady's black eyes for a clue, but the dignified-looking woman only glanced around the courtroom, then back to her papers.

"How say you, then?" Judge Rogers asked.

The lady inhaled and cleared her throat. The courtroom immediately quieted. Then, she read the verdict like a schoolgirl might have reported on summer vacation: "In State of Illinois Case #63097, the death of Catherine Susan Dunne"—she inhaled again, this time faster and harder—"a human being . . . the jury finds the defendant, Jeremy Wayne Lucas, in the above entitled action—" She stopped for a second. Then, she said, "Not guilty of murder in the second degree."

Rachel heard the young man with the bushy, red hair at the rear of the gallery rise and noisily scramble over four bodies on his way to the center aisle, cursing. "Fucking *bull*shit!"

Rumbling filled the gallery.

Judge Rogers hammered his gavel repeatedly. "I apologize, ladies and gentlemen, that you had to hear that outburst. Things obviously didn't turn out the way the young man hoped. Maybe next time they will."

The jury visibly eased their attentive posture. Edwin Butler and his prosecution team mumbled into each other's ears.

Jeremy flashed a tentative smile at the jury, as though he thought they might change their minds at any moment. Then, as if he'd suddenly remembered something, Jeremy turned to Billy, raised his arms, hesitated for a second, then threw them around his old buddy. "Oh, Billy."

"Hey, I always told ya it'd be okay, pardner," Billy bellowed, cutting through the din. Although the gallery's jabbering increased, Judge Rogers did not slam his gavel. He let reaction to the verdict circulate unimpeded throughout the courtroom. Law clerks scribbled, recording the details. Reporters mumbled into dictaphones, jotted notes, or scurried from the courtroom.

Rachel stood in her place alone, stunned at the verdict. She looked at Jeremy's bright eyes as he left Billy and ran to her. She raised her arms.

"Rach, I don't know what to say," Jeremy choked, tears threatening to run down his cheeks.

"Jeremy." She hugged him, but out of the corner of her eye, she saw Mr. Lall glance at them with a frown, before slipping past Donald and exiting the rear gallery door.

"Is it really over?" she asked. "Could it be over?"

"We're quite the team, aren't we?" Jeremy said.

"Order, now," Judge Rogers said halfheartedly. As he hit his gavel lightly, the noise in the courtroom waned. He stated, "I need to say this before we can all go home."

"All be seated," Donald called.

The crowd quieted. The judge cleared his voice. The jury members and spectators took their seats. "The jury is excused," he said. "Thank you for your diligence in this case; the defendant is free to go. All matters regarding criminal case #63097, State of Illinois vs. Jeremy Wayne Lucas, are complete." He struck his gavel once brightly and shook his head. "And, let me say, it's a shame that the perpetrator is still out there—somewhere." Then, he leveled a glare at Jeremy.

Rachel looked at Jeremy at the same moment. She watched him turn toward the rear of the courtroom and smile. She followed his gaze all the way back to the second-to-last row of the gallery. There, sitting behind the law clerks, huddling quietly, shoulders hunched, hands between her legs, was Lana. Rachel looked back and forth from Jeremy's eyes to Lana's, then Jeremy's, then Lana's again. She traced the connection between the two like a barely visible line.

Kettle Moraine National Forest, southern Wisconsin

As Jeremy and Rachel drove home from court, he said, "Boy, I remember the last time I was through here."

"The snowstorm?" Rachel asked.

"Yeah. It's hard to believe that a place so gentle and serene could be such a threat to life."

"No kidding." She stared into space gloomily. "I almost lost you."

"Hey, what's the matter, Rach? You look so down. Man, you should be happy now." He slapped her on the thigh.

"Something bothered me back in the courtroom," she said uneasily.

"What?"

"After they read the verdict, I saw you and Lana look at each other."

"Ah, Rach," Jeremy laughed. "She probably feels bittersweet about this whole thing. She's been mad at me, and probably wanted my ass kicked from here to Kingdom Come, but I'm sure she felt happy, too, because I got a not-guilty verdict."

"So I wasn't seeing love rekindling or something, like in some movie?"

"No, in the movies I would've been found guilty!" Jeremy laughed. "Don't worry, Hons." He patted her thigh again, then stroked her cheek with the back of his hand.

His hand feels cold, she thought.

"Watch the road, now," she teased. "Oh, Jeremy. I guess I forgive you." She felt good saying the words, but empty, too, for she realized that again—just like in college—her own false testimony had been the thing that set her husband free—not the truth. She felt this proved, more than ever, that her own submissiveness to him was too much like blind loyalty.

"You'd better forgive me," he said firmly. "Would I lie to you?" He cleared his throat.

She quickly looked back at him with squinted eyes. *Damn right you would,* she thought.

Light and shadow flickered on his face. "I've learned my lesson from all this. I really have. I'm a new guy."

"Honest?" she asked.

"God, I'd have to be a real fool not to get it after this nightmare. Jail, court—the whole deal."

"So, things'll really be different now. No Wednesday nights? No lilac fragrance?"

"You have a resurrected guy, Babe. Honest."

"No doubts?" Rachel thought back to Professor Lall's contention that choice is the only thing humanity really had. "Our choices determine what will become of us," she mumbled.

"What?"

"Oh, nothing. Just random thoughts." But, deep inside, Rachel wondered if Jeremy was making a choice now, just saying what he needed to say to bring her into the fold.

"No doubts, Hons," Jeremy said softly. "I unequivocally have learned that you're the woman for me, always. I was a dumb-ass to ever doubt that."

Rachel wanted to feel lulled by Jeremy's promises. *Maybe he's finally changed,* she thought. *Maybe it's taken jail and the trial to turn him around.* "Oh, Jeremy," she said. "I *want* to believe you. I really do."

He turned to her. "Well then, you'd better. I love you, Babe."

"Oh, I love you, too, Jer." She snuggled up to him. "Maybe we should celebrate tonight."

"How?"

"I could make you a special dinner, one of your favorites."

"That's *it*?" he said, slightly put out.

"Well, tonight let's celebrate alone, just us two, with this thing behind us. Okay?"

"Fair Dinkum!" He laughed.

"Oh, Jeremy." She snuggled close to him again. Maybe, just maybe, things would be all right.

As they cruised out of Kettle Moraine National Forest, Jeremy rolled down the window. The bright, warm sun shone on them again as he took Route 45 into Fond du Lac. He turned onto Melrose Avenue, their street.

"Hey. What's this?" Rachel reached over and touched his right hand, which was clutching the steering wheel.

"What?"

"This stain." She pointed to a faded blue stain on his right thumb.

"Oh, that. Just ink. Might've got it in jail."

"I didn't think they let you have pens in there," Rachel said. "Won't seem to go away, huh?"

He shrugged. "Must be indelible."

"Maybe try Lava soap?"

He turned into their driveway. "Nah, it'll fade over time."

"No," Rachel said. "If it's already lasted a long time, it'll take forever to go away without some kind of heavy-duty treatment."

16

Fond du Lac, Wisconsin

In the Lucas kitchen, Rachel alternately stirred two filled saucepans with separate wooden spoons. Next to them, a large pot of water bubbled. She pulled the pasta box from the pantry.

Jeremy sat at the kitchen table. “Rach, if it wasn’t for you coming to bat for me, I’d be dead meat.”

She nodded. “I guess. That how you see it?”

“You surprised me, Rach. You really did what you needed to do—all those juicy details in your testimony.”

“I am your wife, you know?” She resented owning up to that distinction, even as she cracked a bunch of dried angel-hair pasta in two.

“Right,” he said.

“Jeremy, when we got married it was for better or worse. And, I guess this was the worst.”

“No kidding.”

“Paul encouraged me to hang in there, too. So, I made a choice to do what I had to do.”

"Paul, eh? A little more plumberly advice, Rach?" he said. "Listen, I owe you, and I guess I owe Paul, too."

Rachel set the timer, reduced the heat under the pans, and turned to her husband. "When you think of it, Jer, you really sort of deserved everything you got. It's karma, whatever they call it. I mean, fooling around like that; a woman dying—the harm you've dealt other people . . . including me!"

"Honey!" he scowled. "That's the cruelest thing you could say to me right now."

"Well, it's true," she said. "And, you did get off pretty easily because of *my* testimony." She shook her head.

"Listen, Rachel. "No matter what you say, I've really learned my lesson." He raised his hand. "Honest Injun."

She turned and squinted at him. "Really, Jeremy? Promise me?"

"You keep saying that, like you don't trust me. Would I lie to you?"

"Well—"

"Scout's Oath," he said.

She snickered. "As I remember, you *were* kicked out of the Boy Scouts. You faked some merit badges, right?"

"Oh, *that*." He sniffed the air. "Boy, this meal's gonna be a whole lot better than that jail food. I can picture Albert right now. I hope he gets out of there soon. It's a class thing in jail, you know? If you have the bucks, you somehow get off. I think it's the great lawyer disparity."

"True," said Rachel. "You get off because you can afford a sly lawyer like Billy. The system at work."

"They'll probably roast Albert for stealing a damn truck. I wonder what he's eating tonight."

The phone rang once.

Rachel looked up. "That's weird. Must be more press. They've been calling here constantly, you know."

"Stay put. I'll be right back." Jeremy got up, left the room, and ran upstairs.

After a few minutes of hearing Jeremy mumble up in the bedroom, Rachel felt annoyed. She walked into the living room and called out, "Jeremy! Almost ready!"

"Right there," he yelled back.

"Sure," she said softly. "What now?" She reached for the phone receiver on the tiny table. *No, I have to trust him,* she thought. She took one step toward the kitchen, then stopped. Stepping back into the living room, she gently lifted the receiver, cupped her hand over the speaking end, and held the earpiece to her ear.

"Jeremy, when can I see you?" a familiar female voice on the phone was purring.

Rachel held her breath.

"Maybe tomorrow," she heard Jeremy whisper. "I can't get away tonight. It'd be too weird."

"It worked, didn't it?" the voice said triumphantly. "Wouldn't have if it wasn't for the hag. But, she bought the song bit, providing you with an alibi—all of it."

Rachel quivered. *Lana.* She clutched the phone hard to her ear. She slowly sniffed in tears. At that moment, she felt like just walking out of Jeremy's life, but, in the same breath, felt the insecurity and loneliness that would emerge. Why had she become so helplessly dependent on him?! She felt like a fool.

"I better go," Jeremy said. "She's making my favorite dinner."

"I better practice for when it's my turn, huh?" Lana chirped.

"Yeah, right," Jeremy said sarcastically. "You keep hoping."

Rachel clenched her teeth, turned her head, and, with her lips pursed, seethed in air slowly. She eased the phone back into its cradle.

Seconds later, Jeremy came bouncing down the stairs.

"Who was that?" Rachel asked flatly, stirring the sauce.

"Oh, just Billy," he said casually. "Final questions for the court record. Closing out the case."

"What kind of questions?"

"Legal gibberish," Jeremy said, casually waving a hand. "It'd bore you."

More lies. She bit her bottom lip and felt her head flush. *Never an end to this!*

She caught Jeremy's quizzical glance. "Say, Rach. You okay?"

"Oh sure—that time of month," she said through pursed lips. She laid the wooden spoon in the spoon holder and walked out of the kitchen. "Say, Jer, stir the sauces, will you? But, you can only taste the marinara. The other one's not for you, hear?"

"Right," he stated. "Where you going?"

"To the *loo*; freshen up. Remember, don't taste the sauce in back—that's only for me. Pasta's got two more minutes." *Serves you right if you taste it!*

She walked out of the kitchen and up the stairs.

"Got it," Jeremy said, on his way to the stove. The pasta sat in the gently boiling water in the large pot; the sauces simmered in two smaller pans, one in front of the other. He tasted the sauce from the front pot. Marinara—his favorite. "Mmm. That's good."

Then, he dipped his spoon into the beige-colored cream sauce in the back pan. That looked new. He sipped a bit, then a little more. "Man-oh-man," he said quietly, "she's been holding out on me. This is terrific. So *mild*!" *Vaguely familiar,* he thought. *Wonder what it's made of. Plenty of it, too.*

About a minute later, he took the pasta pot to the sink and emptied the boiling water. He went back to the table and spooned some steaming pasta onto his plate, then Rachel's. He returned to the stove and picked up the pot with the new sauce. *She won't mind.* He brought that pot over to the table, and spooned sauce on both piles of pasta, adding more to his. "God, I'm famished," he said.

He put the saucepan back onto the stove. "Why did she want this only for herself, anyway? There's still plenty." He lowered the heat. "Rachel! Come get it!"

"Soon!" she called back.

He walked back to the table and sat down. "Mmm, a lot better than jail chow, that's for sure." He looked toward the door. "Hey, Rach! You coming?" He opened a bottle of cabernet.

"I said give me a couple minutes," she called, sounding irritated.

As Jeremy began to gobble the pasta, he heard Rachel flush the toilet upstairs.

17

Fond du Lac, Wisconsin

A couple minutes later, Rachel skipped down the stairs and walked into the kitchen. "Jeremy!" she screamed.

"What?"

"What are you eating?"

"Mmm, this new sauce is super," he said, pointing to his plate full of pasta. "Where'd you get it? New recipe?"

"Jeremy, you're beet red!"

"What?"

"Where's your epinephrine?" Rachel asked.

"That Epipen? I got sick of carrying that stinking syringe around, like I was some kind of chronically ill patient or something."

"Seafood, Jeremy—it's in that sauce!"

"What!" He blanched from his plate. "But I feel fine."

"You look awful." Rachel bolted upstairs and, as she reached the second floor, she heard Jeremy cough a few times, then sputter. She ran into their bathroom, pulled open the vanity doors under the sink, and threw packages of soap and bottles of shampoo aside, searching frantically for the syringe.

"Ra—" She heard him gag.

Then she remembered: the syringe was in a yellow package with black print. She checked Jeremy's side of the vanity first, then hers.

Seconds passed like minutes, and Jeremy's gagging grew louder. "Ra—can't—"

More seconds, more gagging.

She threw stuff randomly around the bathroom and began to cry. "Jeremy, oh Jeremy." But she couldn't find the epipen.

Maybe he put it in his travel kit, she thought. He kept that separate, under his sink. She opened it. Unzipped it. *There it is!*

She stood up to run downstairs, and suddenly froze. *Why am I doing this?* she thought. Time after time she'd made choices that had saved Jeremy from himself. Now she could end this charade, just by taking her time. She felt despicable, but justified at the same time. She opened the package and slowly pulled out the Epipen. Downstairs, Jeremy's choking seemed to reverberate as if he were in a cavern—real, but not so real. Rachel walked slowly down the stairs, one careful step at a time. With each step, the chills crept up her spine. She listened as Jeremy's gagging increased.

Although she felt in a dream state of sorts, she knew she was now making a purposeful choice. This wasn't *her* normal self, maybe, but this choice was *for herself*. Her heart began pounding hard. She knew that quite possibly freedom and a new life waited for her at the bottom of the stairs. She felt justified, even natural, behaving this way, like she had experienced this over and over in a dream. When she reached the bottom of the stairs, she saw her husband, hunched over the kitchen table with his face in the pasta, slobbering and choking. The skin on his ears had turned bright red. The rest of his face was not visible.

Rachel walked to the phone and dialed 911. "Man with seafood allergy," she said calmly, twisting the cord so tautly that her knuckles turned white.

"Ma'am," said the emergency operator. "Now, what's the problem again?"

"I said that a man with a seafood allergy has had a reaction. He's gagging. 229 Melrose Avenue. Fond du Lac."

Rachel set the phone down, kneeled next to Jeremy, squirted about half of the epinephrine into the air, then jammed the needle through his pants and shot the rest into his thigh.

Five minutes later, the paramedics arrived in an ambulance. Seconds later, the doorbell rang. Rachel was waiting at the door to open it.

"I squirted some of the Epipen into him" was all she could muster.

"I'm sure you did the best you could," a paramedic assured her, as two more rushed past Rachel, following her pointing finger. She watched them lay Jeremy on the floor. One man opened Jeremy's mouth and removed some sauce. The second paramedic took Jeremy's blood pressure. The first readied a syringe of some kind of drug, while a third put a plastic tube down Jeremy's throat. Then, he attached an oxygen hose to the protrusion.

A fourth man ran into the house, pushing a gurney. "Excuse, ma'am." He rushed past Rachel to Jeremy.

Two paramedics lifted Jeremy onto the gurney, then wheeled him outside, across the bumpy snow on the sidewalk, to the rear of the ambulance.

Rachel grabbed a coat, closed the door, and ran out behind them.

She sat in the back of the ambulance as it raced toward Waupun Memorial Hospital. One of the paramedics—Jeff somebody—gave Jeremy another shot.

"I'm going to switch to Dexi," he mumbled. He reached inside a metal cabinet and pulled out an IV bottle. He hung it from a little hook, prepared the end, tapped it and inserted it into Jeremy's vein.

"What's that?" Rachel asked hoarsely.

"Deximethizone drip," the tech replied. "He obviously had a lot of seafood, his BP is way down. This'll get it back."

Jeremy lay there completely incoherent, flailing his arms, mumbling and scratching his limbs.

"Oh, Lord, Jeremy," Rachel said, pulling at her lower lip.

"It's normal to do all that." Jeff calmly placed Jeremy's arms at his sides. "I hope we were there in time."

Rachel felt faint. "The doctors said if this ever happened again, it could kill him."

"He's obviously hypersensitive," said Jeff. "With your help, ma'am, they might be able to save him. At this point, it's all up to the Man Upstairs."

18

Fond du Lac, Wisconsin

Hours later, a hospital social service car brought Rachel back home, after she'd confirmed that Jeremy, resting at the hospital in an intensive care staging area, was in stable condition. She knew that, despite her hesitation on the stairs, she had again done just enough to save Jeremy—so far. The doctor had said he wouldn't know for a few hours whether or not Jeremy would survive.

Once home, Rachel got out of the car and saw Paul marching across the front yard toward her, huffing steam. He was visibly a man on a mission; either that, or he'd been eagerly waiting for Rachel's return, so determined was his gait.

"Now, Rachel," he said as he approached her, swaying slightly from side to side.

"What's the matter, Paul?" she asked as the hospital car drove off.

He staggered to her side. "It's time, Rachel," he said. "It's time." Steam puffed from his mouth. "What was that car?"

"Hospital," she mumbled. "Jeremy ate some seafood. So far, he's doing okay."

"Oooh, that's good," Paul slurred. Then he said, "Listen, Rachel, I've been waiting too long." He belched. "I keep losing my nerve."

"Paul Ersham!" She could smell his alcohol breath. "You've been drinking! Do you know what I've just been through?" She pointed to the hospital transport, now rushing away.

"I'm sorry about that, I really am, but never you mind." Paul slurred. "You have to listen, Rachel, once and for all. You gotta stay quiet and let me say what I gotta say."

Rachel threw up her hands, exasperated. "Fine. What?"

"Well—" Paul tottered before her like a dancing bear.

"Well, go ahead," she said. "I'm waiting."

"Well, you see—I want to—I mean—"

"Paul, we should get inside unless you get right to the point. It's freezing out here."

"No, wait. It's im-*por*-tant."

Rachel folded her arms across her chest. "Go ahead, then. Say it."

"I love you," Paul stammered.

"What?!"

"You heard me. I think I love you. I think I've loved you for a long time."

She shook her head. “I don’t know what to say.”

“You don’t have to say anything.” He put his hands in his coat pockets.

They stood frozen, staring at one another.

“This is such a shock,” Rachel cried. “And, at this moment, after this day—” She started to sniffle.

“Oh, Baby, I’m so sorry. Paul looked down. “I’ve been trying to say it for such a long time.”

“You have?”

Paul’s eyes met hers. “Well, pretty long. If things ever don’t work out with you and Jeremy—”

“What?”

“I want you to think of me,” he said, sounding more sober now, and sure of himself. “You know, maybe down the road.”

Rachel couldn’t believe her ears. “Paul, I have to admit I’ve had special feelings for you, too. But, all along I’ve thought you were clinging to your past—to Claire.”

“Oh, yeah,” said Paul. “I finally worked that one out.”

She put her hands on her hips. “Oh? You have, have you?”

“That’s right,” Paul said with conviction. “I know now that Claire has to be . . . well, a memory. I know I have to move on. She'd want me to. *This* I know to be a fact."

"But, it's so sudden, Paul. I mean, you're catching me *way* off guard here. Jeremy's in the hospital from eating that clam sauce and you telling me that?"

"Oh, it was *my* sauce?" Paul looked horrified.

"I told him not to eat it, but he didn't listen."

"Well, Rachel, sauce or not, you told me once that love is an act of will, right? So, I'm *willing* it." He nodded.

"Well, Paul," Rachel said, "I've had special feelings for you, too, Paul. Honestly, I have. You've been a dear, dear friend."

"A friend?" he said. "That's it?"

"Well—maybe a little more than that," she said and sighed.

"And—"

"Well, I have been thinking about it and, after today, I don't think it would be too good." She shook her head. "Nope."

"Why?" Paul shrugged.

"Well, Jeremy said he'd start fresh with me—you know, no more hanky panky."

Paul waved wildly at the air. "I *knew* it! I *knew* you two'd get close again. Man finally comes to his senses . . . ” He shook his head slowly.

“Well, he might’ve, and then . . . ”

Paul looked at her with understanding in his eyes. “Rachel, you’re right. You did the right thing, helping him like that. I bet it made you two closer than ever. Now, I guess there’s no chance for me, ever.”

“Chance?” said Rachel. “Oh, Paul—I’m so sorry—I wish—”

“Yeah, I bet,” he said sarcastically. “All that hugging. Trying to *humor* me is all. More like feeling *sorry* for me!” He turned and marched back across the newly fallen snow to his house, huffing away like an angry polar bear.

Rachel entered her house, surprised that Paul had finally gotten up the nerve to say what had been so obvious. She recalled how they had come so close to saying those words on several occasions. During those times, she did feel something special for him, possibly a new found freedom, but one-by-one she had let each of those feelings flitter away. She had concluded that Paul’s feelings for Claire would always distract him. She hadn’t noticed the moment he actually let go of the obsession for those memories and replaced them with feelings for her.

She walked across the living room to the kitchen, stopping at the little phone table. She looked at herself in the mirror. *How do I* really *feel?* Besides being flattered that Paul had recognizable feelings for her, she was surprised and intrigued that he had actually expressed them.

Rachel laughed. Jeremy had never in sixteen years of marriage genuinely expressed feelings of love for her the way Paul just had. Jer had only said the words as a prelude to a lustful encounter.

She was totally confused. *I need to listen to my music,* she thought. So, she put away her coat, walked to the stereo, and put on one of Katia's tapes. As the first song began to play, Rachel closed her eyes and rocked back and forth. Then, she opened them and glanced at the photographs she'd framed and hung on the walls of the living room.

There was the one taken at Jeremy's last birthday barbecue, her cuddling him as the celebrants gathered around. In the background, Mary Coltrain, Bob Townsend's secretary, stared at them looking as if she had a question on her mind.

Damn. That tentative expression in Mary's eyes had always bugged Rachel—the way the tiny wrinkles shot up from the bridge of her nose and her squinting eyes formed crow's feet. *That's what that expression is: doubt. Mary must've sensed that being married to Jeremy is like being in some house of cards, waiting for the right breeze to blow it down.*

As Rachel rocked to Katia, she looked into Jeremy's eyes in the same picture and realized that they were staring into space. He was obviously less involved in the party or its celebrants or her—and more occupied by some distraction in his mind.

At that moment, Rachel realized something important: *Attention* was what had always been lacking in her relationship with Jeremy. For whatever reason—lovers, work, flying—Jeremy had never shown her the attention she'd craved. That's why she'd always felt so lonely.

Her thoughts turned to Paul. Even as her plumber, he'd always shown her a special kind of attention. First of all, he'd made a point of stopping by, even for little things. Second, she could tell he genuinely liked being with her. He would laugh or wonder or wish or share, like an old friend does. It was obvious Paul cared for her. It was that way every time they occupied the same room.

Just minutes earlier, Paul had expressed to Rachel his ultimate feelings. God knows that must've been hard for him, but, even though he was drunk, he'd made it clear that it was important for him to try. Even though their conversation had ended with the words from her that he might have expected, he had nonetheless spoken *his* words.

Her dad had once defined integrity for her: "Be honest and let the chips fall where they may." And, that was Paul, through and through—moments ago, in spades. Again, she realized what a gem she'd found in him, and what a gem she had regularly discarded out of hand.

A tear dripped down Rachel's cheek. Maybe she'd just turned her head because she'd always wished for that kind of love with Jeremy. She had always secretly envied Claire because she'd had a man who cared for her so deeply, in life and in death. Now, that same man had said special things to Rachel, expressing feelings for her from the deepest place in his heart.

"Have I blown it?" Rachel wiped a tear away. She had probably saved the life of a man who'd cheated on her, who would always cheat on her. His constant infidelity was evidence enough that she couldn't really satisfy him. She wondered if she should try harder, like in the old days when she was a naive student, and she'd done everything to capture his attention. All through the years, she concluded, it had only been her absolute submission to him that had kept him around. Now, it just didn't seem worth it.

Unlike Jeremy, Paul clearly appreciated Rachel for who she was *now*. He didn't need boyhood fantasies or obsessions or some sort of "master" status as the foundation for his relationship.

Am I stupid or just plain stubborn? I've always been so *immobile* in all this. It seemed so obvious that Paul was a man she could love for the rest of her life, and that he would love her back as long as he lived. He even had a child she could nurture, something she'd always lacked with Jeremy.

"What have I done with my life? My lifestream?" she muttered, shaking her head helplessly. "It's like all along I've been walking down the wrong path for the wrong reasons—making the wrong choices."

19

Fond du Lac, Wisconsin

Jeremy lay in the hospital bed, heart still beating rapidly from the drugs he'd been given. His attending nurse had said this was normal. Despite his fear of this anaphylactic shock, he'd panicked much more intensely when his throat had closed up; now he felt he was past the worst part. *On the way to recovery,* he hoped. One doctor'd said he could've died, *Charm or no charm,* he thought. *Indeed, I'm lucky I haven't died.*

He quickly scanned his room. *Wait! Where is it? Where* is *the charm? I thought Rachel brought it!* He had never realized how much he'd grown to depend on that thing, like a child would rely on a lucky rabbit's foot.

A nurse appeared at the door carrying a clipboard. "How are we feeling, Mr. Lucas?"

Jeremy thought that was the stupidest question he could imagine. He muttered, "Well, *I* feel like throwing a party and serving seafood, what do *you* think? Where's my damn charm?"

The nurse pouted. “You were very lucky, Mr. Lucas, and you should act like it. Don’t worry. Your charm must be around here somewhere.”

The nurse cleaned up around the room, but she said, “Didn’t find the charm, Mr. Lucas. Maybe Mrs. Lucas took it home.”

Jeremy scowled. “I doubt it.”

She looked at her watch. “Time for your vitals.” By the time the nurse had finished taking his vital signs, Jeremy had begun to feel funny. Again, he felt his face begin to flush all over. “I’m feeling heated up and itchy,” he muttered.

“You’re BP’s down,” the nurse said.

Jeremy felt panicky as his throat began closing a little. He cleared it repeatedly and pushed himself up on his elbows, trying in vain to get more air into his lungs.

The nurse felt his forehead. “Hmmm. A little hot, but not enough to be a fever.” She leaned across him, her girth nearly knocking him off his elbows, and turned on the overhead light. “Hmmm. You *are* looking a little flushed; your hives are coming back and you’re getting more of that red color in your face. I better get a doctor.”

“Oh, shit.” This didn’t sound good. Jeremy cleared his throat more and felt increasingly afraid. He sat up more erect and looked at the nurse, who was now dashing toward the nurses' station. She saw her skid to a stop, pick up the phone, then jabber. He heard the urgency in her voice.

Jeremy gagged a little. His throat was getting worse. He cleared it repeatedly, but he couldn't keep up with the swelling, the feeling that it was closing up on him, and it was his windpipe and not his esophagus. He knew this because he reached over to the table beside his bed, took a sip of water from the little pitcher and glass, and had only a minor problem swallowing. His swollen windpipe seemed to be encroaching on his esophagus, or vice versa. *That* was scary . . . like he had a massive lump in his throat.

The nurse, now at his door, announced, "The doctor's coming." Minutes passed like hours, as Jeremy watched the clock, his gut churning with anxiety. He felt hotter and hotter and itchier and itchier.

Jeremy gagged again. He couldn't talk and frantically pointed at his throat.

"Oh, my," the nurse said.

A young doctor, probably an intern Jeremy thought, appeared behind the nurse, dragging an I.V. stand.

Jeremy gagged again and pointed to his throat. He pushed air out and croaked in a barely audible whisper, "I can't swal—"

"Nurse, get me a trach tube—now!" the intern ordered.

"What size, doctor?"

"The same size as we were going to use before!" The intern looked confused and a little panicky. *First-week jitters?* Jeremy wondered.

The nurse dashed away, across the hall, and threw open the door to a supply room. Less than a minute later, she returned. "I think this one's okay," she said. "It's a little large but it's the good kind."

Jeremy was becoming more afraid by the second, now, not just because of his swollen windpipe, but because he wasn't sure he was receiving the best care. He felt a little light-headed, like he wasn't getting enough air, but he knew even this intern probably knew that—or maybe he didn't. Or maybe his blood pressure was dropping again. He felt like he had once when he'd held his breath too long, or when he'd once had a panic attack, like he was fruitlessly gulping for precious air and he was going to die.

Maybe the doctor had read his mind. He said, "Nurse Potter, get me an oxygen tank and hose. *Move it*!" The nurse made a hasty exit as Jeremy began to sputter at the back of his throat. Excess skin seemed to have suddenly grown back there, obstructing his windpipe. He could tell that his condition was worsening. He felt itchy all over now, and he could see a checkerboard of fuzzy black spots.

"Not . . . enough . . . oxy—," he gasped, but wasn't sure if the words were even coming out, or if anyone could even hear them.

"Hurry, nurse!" the doctor yelled. He stuck two of his fingers as far back into Jeremy's throat as he could go, but they wouldn't go completely in. "Damn!" the doctor roared.

Now, Jeremy felt his eyes pulse with pressure. Scenes from his past began flashing before him like a slide show: dropping a dud bomb with the gang at U. of W. ; Tim Agers' white face that night at Sterling; Lana the night she told him she was pregnant with his child; Catherine the night she fell to her death.

Why have I lived such a fucked up life? he thought. *Did I have any other real options? Could I have been anything but . . . me?*

"Here it is!" the nurse shouted, sprinting into the room. Jeremy couldn't see her; all he could see were images from his past, clouded by large, soft splotches of black.

"Give it here!" the Doctor shouted excitedly.

Jeremy felt something forced into his windpipe. *Lousy fit,* he thought. Then the doctor firmly wiggled the intrusion, and Jeremy felt liquid—thick liquid seep into his throat. Then the doctor pulled the thing out, and Jeremy tasted blood.

"Nurse, this one's too large," the doctor snapped. "Get me a thinner one!"

"I didn't see any . . . "

"Well, check the second floor!" the doctor shouted. "Move!"

The nurse dashed away and Jeremy shivered. Was all this as serious as it was sounding? He thought again about his life: Had he done nothing but evil things with no conscience? Was he some kind of sociopath? Couldn't he grasp right from wrong or good from bad? Had it all come down to this? *Nah, that's preposterous*, he thought. A sense of urgency overtook him.

Other voices broke into the room. "What's the problem, Mark?"

"He's back in shock, but the trach tube won't fit! He needs air."

"Did you hit him with some more Dexi?"

"Not yet. Would you do that? I'll work on the air."

Jeremy felt his arms flail. God, they itched badly, and he only found relief by slapping them on the bed. Then, to make things worse, he itched all over at the same time he struggled harder to breathe. *Incomprehensible.*

"Just hold still now, Mr. Lucas," a female voice said.

But, Jeremy's breathing became fainter and fainter, and soon the blackout sensation took over and he felt extremely lightheaded. Then, all he saw was black.

Voices mumbled all around him. Jeremy felt himself convulsing, but he felt no pain, for somehow he had floated *away from himself.*

Suddenly, Jeremy felt relieved—even at peace. More voices echoed throughout the room. Jeremy lay still, wonderfully removed from the commotion that surrounded him. He felt trangely held him in a safe caress . . .

20

the afterlife

Jeremy feels himself grow lighter and lighter. Soon nothing is holding him down and he feels himelf rising. But, wait! He feels pressure on his chest, then a shock rattling his chest walls. Then another shock, but it's all getting farther away, like a distant whisper. Jeremy opens his eyes wide, and realizes he has risen off his bed. *How can this be?* In fact, he sees that he is levitating; he has nearly reached the ceiling. He looks down and sees an image of himself, lying on that cursed, white steel bed, and, while the commotion continues, he can't make out what *they're* doing—only that they're working frantically. Then, after another minute, *they* mumble to each other, and their heads shake in unison.

"Call it, Jim," he hears one doctor say to another, as if in an echo chamber.

My God! Jeremy realizes, *I'm dead! They've given up! This can't* be*!* The feeling he's always had—cleverly avoiding the sting of reality; getting away with things, even killing—does not visit him now. Instead, only a sort of deadly finality is taking him over—a pit in his gut that is unimaginably deep and complete. He feels as if he should be scrambling for life now, but he remains eerily calm, yet very empty. There's nothing he can do. He knows it's too late.

My God, help me, Jeremy thinks. He feels himself rise higher, leaving the fear behind, and now the panic he felt seconds earlier seems like a distant memory. He rises faster and, as he looks down, the slideshow of his past has totally fallen away. He glances up and sees only more darkness, then a sudden flash of white light on a horizon above him. He doesn't fear the radiance. The light extends brightly from left to right in the distance, waiting, waiting, *waiting* for him as he floats toward it. In a second, he adjusts himself and grows comfortable with the sensation of floating. He looks down at himself and notices that he is translucent now, sort of a translucent bubble. He touches himself and feels only a springiness beneath his fingers, like a balloon.

He turns his head upward again and finds himself floating through darkness; the source of the bright, white light now clear. He approaches the edge of a fifty-foot-wide hallway of light extending hundreds of yards before him. Shiny, perfectly white tiles stretch from side-to-side across the floor, and similar tiles appear on the ceiling and walls. Other than this strange hallway, only white surrounds him and a powdery light is shooting everywhere, especially from far down the hall.

He now sees that his arms have become transparent; his whole body has become transparent. He is himself as he had known him, but he is less dense now. He reaches for his own arm and can no longer feel it! He listens intently, but can hear nothing—the same "nothing" he heard the night he was trapped in the woods in the snowstorm.

Now he spies a graceful silhouette gliding toward him, still quite a distance away, but floating inches above the floor of the hallway. He studies the willowy form and, as it draws nearer, he thinks he recognizes it. *A swishy, little red dress?*

"Catherine?" She's now about fifty feet away from him, and as she walks, her hair bobs in space. Jeremy can see that she is licking her lips, as usual.

This has to be . . . heaven! he thinks. *How else can this be happening?* He floats there, in space, in a sitting position, as Catherine saunters toward to him.

"Nice seeing you, Jer," she says dreamily, her beautiful voice especially striking in absolute silence. "Looks like a great ride."

"Ha-ha," Jeremy snickers. "Man-oh-man, this is unbelievable. See, losing that dumb charm didn't mean a damn thing. I can do just fine, all on my own. Just like always."

She laughs haughtily. Besides the sound of her voice, only silence prevails. "Still with the 'man-oh-man'?"

"Yeah. Hey, what's so funny about that?"

"Oh, Jer, you never learn, do you?" Catherine laughs again, and this time her voice seems to echo through the silence.

"What do you mean?" he asks. "I'm here in heaven, and you're here, too. It's perfect; it's just *too* perfect!"

She laughs again. "Hey, Jeremy, I have a question for you. Just one." She produces a joint from the air, lights it and takes a gigantic drag.

"So what's your question?" Jeremy asks. He watches her turn away, smoke ensnaring her head. As she turns back to him, she growls in a deep, echoing voice that frightens him. Her silhouette scrunches up, and expands before him into an ugly hunchback form. Then, her beautiful mouth transfigures itself before his eyes into a large, hideous orifice, with long pointed teeth, dripping with blood and saliva.

Jeremy screams into the silence: “*No-o-o-o!*”

“Jeremy,” the deep voice laughs, and it says, “Here’s your question: Did you ever learn to *fly*?!”

Then, in a split second, Catherine vanishes. All of the light flickers off—darkness returns. Jeremy feels himself begin to tumble, head over heels down what was the hallway. He gains speed, and tries futilely to grip the void around him. Spinning out of control, he realizes this must be how Catherine felt the night of her death. His stomach flip-flops as he falls. He feels the same “gulpy” feeling he’d experienced when he stared at Catherine in the restaurant. Vomit races up his esophagus. He chokes on it and remembers his anaphylactic shock experience—the sensation of suffocating. Soon his tumbling ceases, and he rights himself, floating again in sitting position surrounded only by the dark.

In front of him, he can make out a small speck, darting around in the blackness like a honeybee on a hot summer day. Something urges him to move closer to this speck, to study it. He senses that being close to the speck will steady him, stop him from feeling the vertigo. He attempts to swim through space toward this dot, but he finds no resistance to propel him. He notices then that he doesn't need to propel himself at all; he's actually floating nearer and nearer to the speck, as if he's meant to go there. As he approaches it, the speck grows in dimension and stops darting about. He can now make the vision out as a shiny orb, the size of a large basketball.

I'm okay, he thinks. *I'm always okay. Things always work out for me, and they will especially in heaven. I knew it.*

21

the universe

Jeremy reaches the orb, which is about four feet in diameter. He can see that it's a shiny, gelatinous bubble floating in the blackness. He touches it with his left hand. As he presses on it, he feels little resistance. In fact, he finds that, despite the fact that he remains semi-transparent, he can reach *through* its surface—*into* it. More of him, then all of him, works its way into the orb. He observes that the orb's *inner* dimensions are larger than its *external* dimensions. *How is that possible?*

In fact, as he rights himself inside the orb, Jeremy views an infinitely large world before him and around him, darkness peppered with cosmic specks in the distance, drifting slowly from left to right. Before him, he observes a series of vertical sheets containing rows of clear caviar eggs, tinted red and blue, lined up in parallel. At least as tall as a football field, or even taller, the sheets extend for hundreds—no, thousands!—of yards into the cosmic nighttime.

This is incredible! He studies the compilation of sheets up and down, then side-to-side. On further inspection, he finds that on each vertical sheet, in each gelatinous egg, is a fuzzy seed of some sort at its center. The entire group of sheets is so massive that now, as Jeremy scans it from side to side, he can barely make out an ending—each sheet extends to his left . . . forever! The sheets seem to continue vertically forever . . . to infinity. He realizes this must be heaven. This must be *the compilation of all souls for all human beings to be born in the future!* He floats near the closest vertical sheet of eggs, which for some reason feels warm and safe and familiar. The sheet pulses increasingly with a yellow glow as Jeremy nears. As he studies the countless eggs stacked on this sheet, he feels overwhelmingly that this sheet of eggs must, in fact, be the sum of *his* essence, of who he is or was or will be—multiple souls forever—a whole world of Jeremy possibilities. All of this he knows—he can sense it somehow—and the realization amazes him. Something is transmitting this information directly to his brain.

On the other sheets lie an infinite number of seeds, each of which is undoubtedly the essence of another soul. This entity, made up of discreet parts, is so great and so infinite, Jeremy can only reason that it must be a manifestation of

. . . God—the sum of all souls, over all time! He shivers with fear and overwhelming joy as he comes to this realization without a doubt.

He studies the entirety of the massive collection of sheets and its features—the shapes and sizes of the eggs, the red and blue tint on each egg, the clarity with which he can now make out the seeds in the eggs, like they are each the intricate nuclei of a cell.

Curious, he takes a closer look at the first sheet—the one that must be *his* sheet—and feels safe as he floats toward it, still in sitting position. He figures this sheet must be his for, in his mind, undoubtedly eminating from the sheet, thoughts of his life now flash before him again.

From the events he witnesses, he recognizes how he has managed to move through his life, much like Teflon, never being rigidly stuck to the outcomes of his actions, like he was always entitled or uninvolved in some way. Not because of his inheritance, but just because he was a special being. It occurs to him, almost magically, that the lack of attachment to the consequences of his actions was in some way a form of . . . godliness. He has always been above the consequences: even when he was a youth and denied culpability for contributing to his father's death. Jeremy had gone for a joyride and enraged his father so much it may have precipitated his stroke. The minister insisted it wasn't Jeremy's fault, and Jeremy readily agreed without an inkling of guilt.

He understands his nature as he merely looks at the first sheet of the group—its information magically enters his mind and shares these concepts. The culmination of guilt begins to overwhelm him now. He feels so powerful, being in this magical place, but as he understands his very essence, he feels miserably guilty, too.

Then, the edges of his sheet seem to wrinkle, to cringe, almost defensively. Jeremy looks up at his sheet, one hundred feet to the left, and sees a large, clear bubble, one of the cellular eggs, detach from the sheet. This shocks him, and he wonders what will happen next as he watches it drift away into the void. In a second, the bubble pops, completely vaporizing. An instant later, a second bubble from his sheet splits away, pops, and disappears.

His sheet of eggs seems to dim as each bubble escapes; likewise, his own clear bodily form becomes more transparent and dim.

As this occurs, Jeremy feels that at his very core, his godlike being is becoming *less* than it was just a moment ago. Anxiety fills him, then fear, then, after he's clearly noticed the dimming effect, stark terror. He can't explain this intense, *absolute* fear. *Who he is or was or will be* is rapidly disappearing from existence.

Closer on the first sheet, he catches sight of another gelatinous bubble—a manifestation of his essence—as it splits from the sheet, floats into the black nothingness for a second or two, then silently pops and disappears. It seems to have imploded on itself and become some sort of mini-black hole. This event is so final, so complete, that his feelings change from fear to wonder to fear again. *What could be happening to me*? he wonders. He shivers, then involuntarily screams. Still, he hears nothing.

Just a short time ago, this whole experience seemed like Jeremy's entry into heaven, complete with Catherine. Now, it has become far more terrifying. He realizes that his transparent body holds slightly less density and brightness than it had a minute ago.

He floats along the first sheet of eggs. His fear grows as he realizes that more and more of the gelatinous bubbles comprising it are separating from his sheet, floating into the morass, popping, and vaporizing. Immediately after each inaudible pop, he looks down and can see that his transparent body has reacted, becoming more and more clear and dim. He understands fully that the disappearing bubbles are directly related to the lessening density of his body.

As the process continues, Jeremy comprehends the totality of what's happening around him. He looks at the infinity of the first sheet, and realizes that if these are his essences, past and future and present, and they are slowly popping into non-existence, he will likely *not* be reborn into another earthly existence—far from it.

Instead, he thinks*, the very essence of who I am, this gelatinous sheet, a part of the godly form, is slowly and inescapably disappearing from existence!*

My God! Jeremy realizes that the being he is, the cosmic nature of it, while it had made him feel so comfortable moments ago, and maybe even hopeful that he would somehow experience another earthly future, is becoming *nothing*. He knows that he has not witnessed a grand self-perpetuating mass that exists in some primordial world. His part of heaven is becoming nothing—*he* is becoming nothing. Jeremy panics and shudders with fear. He looks about helplessly.

Soon he realizes that his efforts are futile. He spies one, and then many—hundreds—of young boys, lined up in rows, floating toward him along the edge of the form, gracefully wobbling in unison, their little legs and arms like pudgy little cupid wings. As the boys approach, Jeremy can see that all of them look the same—about six or seven years old, wearing little shorts and a sweatshirt. Jeremy shivers when he notices that written on the sweatshirts is, "University of Wisconsin BADGERS". As the mass of little boys drifts just fifty feet away from him, Jeremy can see that they're all crying. He cannot hear them, but can see the expressions of great sadness on their faces. *I get it! They are essences of little Mark Agers, upset that his daddy won't ever be coming home from work, and that he will never have any younger brothers or sisters because a bad man made him die.*

When Jeremy realizes that this is a scene *he* created by his own actions the night of the bombing, he screams again, as he's done in so many dreams. "*No-o-o-o-o!*" His insides pull at him, like the pain of a million deaths. But, Jeremy hears nothing, and the silence makes this vision even more terrifying.

The line of boys drifts toward Jeremy's sheet of eggs, and enters a space behind it. Then, the first row begins to pulse. Suddenly, and with great force, Jeremy's own sheet is expelled from the whole of the form. His sheet glows bright yellow as it pulses. More and more eggs leave it, floating away, and popping, until—

Suddenly, Jeremy's sheet of gelatinous eggs, now a hundred feet away from the form, silently but violently explodes! *The little boys have caused it to explode!* he thinks. He cringes as his own eggs fly past him and through him. A great pain rushes through his own dead and transparent body. He watches as the flying eggs are sucked toward a swirl of a hole in space made by one of the disappearing eggs. The black hole is only one hundred feet away and is sucking in all matter that approaches it, including him!

He paws helplessly at the nothingness, pulled closer and closer to the swirling abyss. "Help!" he screams, but he hears no sound . . . feels no feeling . . . smells no odor. The hole seems to be swallowing everything around it. Suddenly, the horrible rift begins to suck Jeremy's form into itself, and he looks back and realizes that he will never ever see the great group of sheets again . . . ever. At the same moment, he is sucked over the edge and into the black hole. More of his eggs fly through him and rip through his transparent self, shredding it into countless bits. So, now the compilation of sheets is gone from sight, his sheet obliterated, and all the sheets of existence have disappearred from his view. His transparent body has been ripped apart. All that remains is his miniscule, fading consciousness, which will fade slowly for an eternity . . . and, along with it, unfathomable cold.

22

Fond du Lac, Wisconsin, Lucas residence

The phone on the little hall table rang suddenly and startled Rachel. She picked it up. "Yes?"

"Hello, Mrs. Lucas?" an unfamiliar voice said.

"Yes?" Rachel replied.

"This is Nurse Potter. Waupun Memorial. We need you to come down here right away."

"Why? What's the matter?" Rachel asked.

"Hurry, please."

Rachel raised her voice. "Is it my Jeremy? Is he all right? What's wrong?"

"I-I'm sorry, ma'am," the nurse said. "It's best I not talk about it over the phone. Hurry, please."

Rachel slammed the phone down, got her coat and buttoned it as she ran out to the car.

Rachel rushed into the hospital and up to Jeremy's floor.

Three men stood alongside the emergency staging area talking in low voices. One of them wore a state police uniform. As Rachel approached the men, she could hear one of them say, "Here she comes now."

A familiar-looking man, the one in uniform, stepped forward and tipped his hat. "Mrs. Lucas. Hello. Officer James A. Rainero, here. State Police."

"Oh, I remember you," Rachel said. "You're the officer who picked Jeremy up."

"I was in the area tonight. They called me in on this since I'd already met you folks at the beginning."

"Sure," Rachel said. "What is this about? What's wrong?"

The officer looked solemn. "The Cook County D.A. called us. He asked that we collect Mr. Lucas and bring him down there again."

Rachel immediately tensed. "He's in no shape—"

"Ma'am," Rainero cut in, "this fellow Butler was pretty steamed at the verdict, so he made a fuss. He convinced the judge to let them extract any remnant evidence from Jeremy, perhaps a fresh hair sample that might clearly tie him to the moment of Miss Dunne's death. Assuming he can come up with convincing evidence, the D.A. would attempt to retry."

"My word," Rachel whispered.

"Butler's really got the judge on his side, too. Friend of Mr. Dunne's."

"I thought they couldn't try someone twice." Rachel trembled inside.

"Usually they can't," said Shultz, "but with overwhelming evidence that never was presented at the original trial, they sure can—happening more and more. Especially, with advanced forensic techniques. In San Diego, they're developing this new technique where the DNA from one piece of evidence can be compared to another. I heard that'll be the perfect test—million to one odds. That'll change everything, but won't be perfected for another five years or so. We'll be able to figure out the truth long after the evidence has been gathered."

Rachel shook her head. "Will this ever be over? My Jeremy has been through so much . . . "

"Better come here, Mrs. Lucas," the nurse called.

"Jeremy?" Rachel asked.

"Hurry." She led Rachel into the emergency staging area. He lay completely still under bright lights, a sheet haphazardly thrown across his head, only bare, pale-blue shoulders exposed. A team of medical people hunched around him.

"Jeremy!" Rachel screamed.

"I'm afraid we've lost him, Mrs. Lucas," a doctor stepped forward and said as he shook his head. "We couldn't get the trach properly inserted, so we couldn't get him enough oxygen. He went into convulsions and expired. I'm so sorry."

Rachel wept, looking back at the other nurses and Officer Rainero.

"His windpipe was totally cut off," the doctor pleaded. "No matter what we did."

Rachel fell into Rainero's arms.

"Mrs. Lucas, I'm so sorry," he said.

She cried against his shoulder.

Rainero held her. "There, there. I remember the first day I met him. He was a sharp one, all right. A real sharp fella, ma'am. I remember."

She shook as she cried.

"Had a ton of things thrown at him recently, didn't he?" Rainero said. "I read about it in the papers. Even saw it on TV."

"Oh, dear God," Rachel moaned. "What am I going to do?"

Rainero seemed unfazed. "Like his whole life came up and bit him in the—well, you know."

She sniffled. "His damn lifestream."

"His what?"

"Oh, nothing." She stared numbly into space. "His lifestream, his choices."

"Oh, I guess this is yours, Mrs. Lucas," said a nurse, handing Rachel the charm. "I found it on his little shelf, under a towel. We didn't want it to get lost. We'll pack it up with his other things."

Rachel could barely speak through her tears. "Sure, thanks. And, I brought it here for good luck."

Officer Rainero handed her a handkerchief. "It's a horrible shock, I know."

"We were working things out," she cried and blew into the hankerchief. "Things were almost the way they were meant to be."

23

Fond du Lac, Wisconsin July, 1985 (three months later)

Rachel stood at Jeremy's grave one clear summer morning. *It seems so long ago that things were normal.* She had finally summoned the strength to visit his grave. After being investigated for possible links to his death, she was finally exonerated. The DA had stopped the witch-hunt, thanks to Paul's interview and his unquestioned community stature. Rachel saw no one else around the old cemetery grounds except a distant car driving toward her down a long, gravel path.

She shook her head and cast a bunch of flowers randomly across the mound. "You were my hero at first, Jer, but I know I was never your real choice. You always owned me; you never really loved me."

She stood, rocking back and forth for a few minutes, fiddling with a paper bag, thinking about how they had necked at the movie theater near school, laughed joyfully on their wedding day, and barbecued countless ribs with the family—better times. She wondered where Jeremy's heavenly spirit was now.

She thought about Professor Lall and wondered how the universe had dealt with her Jer. She pictured its wonder and surmised that Jeremy's eternal soul had undoubtedly been forgiven for its corrupted lifestream. *He's in heaven, no doubt.*

The car honked, interrupting her daydreams. Paul was back.

She turned her head, smiled, and held up her index finger. She turned back to the grave. "This is good-bye, Jeremy," she said. "Probably forever." She read the inscription on the gravestone, part of the translation of the charm that Professor Lall had given her:

JEREMY LUCAS
(1950-1985)

Our choices determine
what will become of us.

SENJI OF KASHMIR A.D. 1220

She walked over to Paul's car, pulled open the door, and climbed in.

Paul's son was behind the wheel. "Tommy!" Rachel exclaimed. "Er, Tom. It's you."

"Surprised, Mrs. Lucas?" Tom said. "Home for a visit."

"How's school?" Rachel asked. "And, by the way, you can call me Rachel."

"School's pretty good so far, Rachel," he replied. "Say, I'm real sorry about Mr. Lucas . . . Jeremy."

"Thanks." She rolled down her window and let the soft, warm summer morning breeze flutter in. "So, where's your dad?" she asked.

"He told me to pick you up. He has a surprise."

"He does, does he?"

"Yeah," Tom said. "Did you bring the charm? He told me about it."

"Actually, it's right here." Rachel patted the paper bag in her lap.

"Off we go, then." Tom stepped on the gas.

Rachel reached into her purse. "Look at this." She pulled out a cassette and held it up. "Ever heard of Katia?"

"Sure." Tom smiled. "She's great."

"I brought it along to cheer me up a notch. Your dad likes her, too." She popped the tape into the stereo and clicked "PLAY":

I could not see the world like it really was,
Then, I thought you were everything to me,
How wrong, baby!
Now my heart opens up to a brand new world.

Words and Music — M. Litecki, K. Polankski © 1984 PLS Records

"I sure do love that song," she sighed, "so full of hope."

Tom nodded, turned right at the stop sign, and cruised away.

Less than a half hour later, the light flickered through the treetops as Tom and Rachel slowly rounded turn after turn through the north end of Kettle Moraine National Forest. Rachel clicked off the tape and rolled her window down all the way.

"Listen, Tom," she said, leaning her head out the window. "It sounds so pretty."

"Yeah, all the birds."

"And the kids, too. Here 'em echo through the woods?"

"Yeah."

"I remember when I was first up here from Down Under," Rachel said. "I used to hike through there and play Capture the Flag. It reminded me of New Zealand summer vacations."

"It's so green." Tom made another turn and pulled across a wandering, two-lane, blacktop road. He stopped and they got out.

"So, where are we, Tom?" she asked and looked around. "This doesn't look familiar."

"Dad said you should take that path." He pointed to a tiny trailhead that led into wavy, freshly trimmed brush. "And, bring the charm thing." Then, he climbed back into the car.

"I'll play along," Rachel said. She took her bag and walked down the path, pushing aside summer brush. After a minute, she approached a clearing. Paul stood there among the foliage.

"So, here you are," she said sweetly.

"Yeah," said Paul. "Beautiful out here, isn't it? Sorry about the mystery."

"It's a bluff!" She pointed past him. "I never knew this was here. It's beautiful here in July."

Paul jangled the keys and change in his right pocket. "So'd, you bring the charm?"

"I should've left it back at the cemetery, damn thing," Rachel said. "But, it‘s time to pass it on. Boy, this view is really something." She gazed out at the expanse of bushy treetops spreading to what seemed like infinity before them, starting one hundred feet below the cliff's edge. She sniffed in deeply. "How'd I ever miss this?"

"Think they must've just trimmed it or something," Paul said. "It popped out of nowhere. But, it was here all the time."

"Incredible." Rachel twirled like she was dancing.

"You be careful, Rachel," Paul said. "You don't want to fall."

"I've already fallen, Paul. For *you*. Things are so much clearer for me now. Five months ago I couldn't have said that."

He smiled. "Oh, yeah. Amazing how we get fouled up. Like we forget what we want out of life, because we so easily defer to others . . . or even the memories of others. I've always known what I wanted, but haven't faced up to it . . . until recently. Now I realize that my dreams didn't die with Claire."

"Yeah. Professor Lall said that our lifestream can easily get fouled up; it's just our set of choices in life."

"I finally get that."

"And our choices determine what will become of us," Rachel said with a wink. "That's what it says on the charm." She pulled it out of the bag.

Paul nodded. "That sounds so simple, but it's so difficult to do," he said. "Give it here."

Rachel's eyes glazed over. "Now I'm seeing things like that goddess—what's her name—the Goddess of translucent wisdom—said to see things. Cutting through the fog we live in and making the right choices, not feeling like a victim of our circumstances."

"Well, I think it's time to make some pretty important choices, right here and now." Paul took the charm from her hand and walked over by the bluff, turned around so his back faced the expanse of trees, and tossed it backwards over his shoulder—like salt.

"Someday," she said, "somebody else will find it—and maybe discover that the power of choice will help them.

"Not like it helped poor Jeremy."

"Well. his choices were always so wrong. How *could* they help him?" she asked.

A horn honked nearby. "I think we have a young man waiting back in the car," Paul said.

"I almost forgot—Tom!" Rachel smiled.

Paul touched her shoulder lightly and stared into her eyes. "So then, Rachel, are you saying you could put up with both

Tom and me?" he asked. "Sometimes we can be quite the pair."

"I want to try." She hugged his arm and cuddled close. Her eyes filled with happy tears.

"Well, good then. It's a plan." Paul leaned over and kissed her cheek. They strolled back down the trail, hand-in-hand.

Other titles by Jack Eadon, only from Eloquence Press

Got To Make It!

ISBN 0-975-33006-3

The collectors' edition of this highly touted 60s coming of age memoir, revolving around a suburban teenager's association with a rock band that helps steady his ride through turbulent life experiences. With retrospective CD and photo gallery.

A Consequence Of Greed

ISBN 0-975-33003-9

A novel of mystical revenge. X-Files meets Shakespeare meets corporate America. Ten years after a murder, an idealistic young man becomes possessed by the spirit of the victim and, with the guidance of a "heavenly" traveler, avenges the crime.

Latent Image

ISBN 0-975-33004-7

A short novel about conflict, loss, and love. A "virtual" lover guides a broken man to recovery. The sequel to GREED.

The Armstrong Solution

ISBN 0-975-5-33001-2

Kathy Armstrong is foisted into the role of a marketing savior at Pepe's Cafe, Inc. while her boss directs a scheme to deliver his financial commitments. Meanwhile, a coworker discovers the scheme and is detained in Mexico. The story builds to a crescendo as Kathy seeks to foil the plot and save her friend.

"Gigolo" on the Row

ISBN 0-975-33000-4

A twisted neighborhood drama slowly unfolds after a young woman is killed by a hit-and-run driver, supposedly by accident.

Lacey's Day

ISBN 0-975-33005-5

An intense cross-cultural Internet love story. It drips with realism!

Also see . . .

http://www.eadonbooks.com